LAST DAY

RICHARD LA PLANTE

Last Day

First digital editions 2013 Escargot Books and Music.

ISBN 978-1-908191-77-9

Cover Design: RL Designs

Author Photo: Betina La Plante

 Escargot Books and Music
Ojai, California

SPECIAL THANKS TO:

Joe V., The Man

Doctor Steve, The Source

Doctor Rothman, The Brain

Murray, The Reader

Jack And Tomás, The Distractions

Big Bett, The Fan

Nat, The Agent

Melissa, The Editor

Tom, The Publisher

Escargot, The Backbone

LAST DAY

~ 1 ~

CHARLIE WOLF WAKES UP ALONE on the last day of his life. While other men live in uncertainty as to the exact hour of their demise, Charlie Wolf knows. He has known for a long time. It's not a question of when, because when is three o'clock this afternoon, on the third day of July; the question is how, and it's eating him alive.

I know this because I am Charlie Wolf, at least for a while.

A long way from here my wife and daughter are awakening to the smell of the sea, listening to waves crashing against the shore as the breeze rustles the heavy cotton curtains of their windows.

They are waking up in a different world.

My daughter's name is Jade. I remember the day she was born, at six o'clock in the morning, on a humid Fourth of July. She arrived after twelve hours of labor, headfirst, face up, with two black eyes and a mop of red hair. Swollen and pink with full, fat lips and the most perfect hands I had ever seen. She was tiny, less than six pounds, and when I touched her, as she lay naked beneath the heat lamp, I could hardly see through the tears in my eyes. Nothing I had ever known had prepared me for that feeling. She was my flesh and blood, a part of me forever.

She'll be three years old tomorrow, and I'm not even sure what she looks like. I haven't seen her in eighteen months, not even a photograph. The last time I had a conversation with Carolyn, my wife, she told me that Jade's hair, which had turned from red to blond, was now nearly white, and that her eyes were green. Green? But they were deep blue last time I saw her. All babies have blue eyes, my wife explained; a child's eyes can change color till the child is three years old. Jade's little girl now, not a baby anymore. That really hit hard, connecting with a part of me that I had tried to shut down, leaving me open and vulnerable, desperate for more contact. Demanding it. Jade was growing up, away from me. I needed answers, like does she still remember who her daddy is? But my supply of quarters had run out. The next time I called was three weeks later, at two o'clock in the morning. I started asking the same questions, demanding the same answers, getting frustrated and angry. That's when Carolyn broke down and sobbed. It was the first time it had happened. She's a strong person, and very practical, but it finally got to her, just what I was doing and the effect it was having on our lives, and on our child. After that, which was two months ago, I decided not to call anymore, not till it was over.

Wait till Charlie Wolf was dead.

Then it really got tough. Night after night, lying awake, staring at the ceiling, thinking of Carolyn, as if by thinking hard enough I could make her materialize from the cracked yellow plaster. Trying to create the details of her face, imagining her eyes, soft and blue, her mouth smiling, her right front tooth chipped, making her look like a naughty kid, her dark hair hanging loose and stringy, as if she'd just come out of the sea. Then her body, long-legged and full-hipped, the soft skin of her neck, her perfume smelling like lemon grass, like summer.

What if she really couldn't take any more? There were plenty of men on the island who would offer consolation. What if she was sleeping with one of them? I imagined her in bed with someone else, doing the things we used to do, whispering and sighing. I couldn't turn off the thoughts.

I was losing everything that mattered.

That's when I got up and took my gun out from underneath the mattress and sat on the edge of the bed, staring down the black hole into the barrel. Ordering my mind to stop making me crazy. Threatening to shoot, like my body was one person, my mind another. Stop it, I ordered. Stop it. But it wouldn't stop, and I couldn't shoot. Because if I did, I'd never see them again, my wife and my daughter, the two things I had to live for.

Last night was another rough one. I never got out of my clothes, a sweat-stained white T-shirt and a pair of torn jeans, size thirty-three, the same size I've been wearing since I was twenty-six years old, ten years ago, except now, when I tighten my belt, the denim bunches at the sides and in the front. I haven't been eating too well in the past three months, mostly fast food and Chinese takeout, and a lot of coffee, but that's not the reason for the weight loss. The reason is the methamphetamine. The drug started as a matter of business, and trust, but after a few weeks snorting it, I began to add a line or two to my morning coffee, like a vitamin. At first, it made me feel sharp and clear, taking away all the insecurity and uncertainties. It made me feel like I could handle what was going down. Like I could handle anything. I was totally aware, completely alive.

Now, at night, I lie on these clammy sheets, with my teeth grinding and my mind racing out of control, thinking about Carolyn and Jade, thinking about who I am and what I'm doing. Thinking about calling it all off, about blowing the whistle or blowing my brains out.

I'm locked inside a lie.

Get up. Hands shaking, fear all around me, walk barefoot to the window. Stare out through the dirty glass and rusted iron bars that keep me safe at night. My view, directly across, is a concrete wall. Up, I can see the edge of the sidewalk, but nobody's moving. It's too early for any of the residents in this ten-room shack to be up. I'm lucky. For eighty bucks a week I get the basement to myself. My own private hell.

Next is a trip to the bathroom, which is a converted closet equipped with a porcelain sink, one of those antiques with twin taps, one hot, one cold, guaranteed to give you third-degree burns if you're trying to shave, that is if you can get any hot water. The toilet is squashed in next to the sink, and the shower stall, divided from the rest of the room by a dirty plastic curtain, isn't big enough to raise your arms above your head, but this morning I need the toilet. Fear is a strong purge.

The small mirror above the sink lures me as I squeeze by. Inside, I see a reflection of a man I hardly know, his upper body so thin that I can see the muscles and striations that hold it together, like the victim of a concentration camp. Checking it out with a morbid, almost detached curiosity, I tell myself that it's not really me staring from those sunken blue eyes. That can't be my face, almost skeletal, hiding behind that reddish blond beard. No, that's not me, that's the face of Charlie Wolf, a dying man.

I use the toilet, then retreat. Back across the tired beige carpet, marked by the stains of spilled red wine and cigarette burns, to the card table in the corner with a few books stacked on top of it. Books that were my mainstay for years, carried through the many changes in my life. Pirsig's *Zen and the Art of Motorcycle Maintenance*, Hemingway's *Death in the Afternoon*, and Musashi's *Book of Five Rings*.

There was a time, when confined to this squalid, depressing room and three-minute calls to Carolyn, I held tight to the wisdom inside my portable library. When I thought I was involved in something worthwhile, that I was the personification of Pirsig's man of simple values, finding my way across an American landscape ruined by the worship of status, celebrity, and symbols, or Hemingway's matador, challenging death with dignity, or Musashi's Samurai, forced to acquire a state of permanent awareness through the discipline of mortal combat. They were the times before my area of employment turned from red, white, and blue to a murky gray, before the bad guys and the good guys merged to form one guy.

I don't open the books anymore. They look like castoffs from a former life, something I may have read when I was a student. I have used their covers, though, when I've needed a hard, clean surface to chop a line of meth.

I pull off my T-shirt and toss it to the floor beside the cot bed. My armpits stink, which makes me want a shower, but I'll let that pleasure wait like a reward, a symbolic shedding of this skin.

Coat myself with another layer of Old Spice. The smell of sweat masked by the deodorant reminds me of the boxing gym in the Bronx. I trained there for a few months, over a year ago, but even that was a charade, another way to gain the trust of the man I was setting up.

My father used to tell me that the ring was the measure of the man. It showed how much pain he could take, how much courage he had, how much heart, and how he reacted to pressure.

I know one thing, boxing is a pure physical truth, and the best lies are always based on truth. Even so, mine was difficult, and sometimes I wonder how I managed to get this close to a man who has built an empire on guts and instinct.

In a perverse way, Ray Sasso is as near to Musashi's warrior as I've ever encountered. Aware and intuitive, attentive to details, street wise and decisive, economical with both his words and his actions, Ray believes in justice.

~ 2 ~

HIS OLDEST TATTOO IS HIGH up on his right shoulder. It's a faded green snake coiled round a dagger. Beneath it, the words, "Death Before Dishonor," have been inscribed, the motto for the U.S. Infantry.

I know, from my records, that Raymond Elliot Sasso finished advanced training at Fort Bragg before his seventeenth birthday. He was too young for the armed services, but despite the fact he'd lied about his date of birth, he was discharged honorably.

The second tattoo is a black death's-head with a fiery red halo. About three inches in diameter, it sits on top of the ropy blue veins on the inside of his left forearm. Beneath the death's head, the initials S.F.F.S. have been branded with a hot iron, so that the flesh is thick and congealed to form the letters. The letters stand for Sons Forever, Forever Sons, and the death's-head is the symbol for the Sons of Fire Motorcycle Club.

Ray Sasso is president of the Nomad Chapter.

In looks he's almost beautiful, a cross between his Native American mother and his Sicilian father. His nose, although broken and reset, is neat and flat to his face, like a young Marlon Brando's nose, and his hair is shoulder-length, thick and black, with a widow's peak that cuts down through the swarthy bronze skin of his forehead, adding a touch of menace to his features. His cheekbones are high and

prominent, while his dark brown eyes are set wide apart.
Strange eyes, they seem sleepy one moment, with the lids
almost drooping, and intense the next.

At five-ten and 173 pounds, Ray Sasso is not physically
imposing, but he carries himself well, as if he's comfortable
with his body, and his movements are fluid: most natural, and
the rest developed through twenty years in boxing contests
and gymnasiums. Never a slugger, he is a true boxer, defense
comes first. It is almost possible to watch him thinking in the
ring, then witness his thoughts translate into physical
movement, rapid foot shifts and quick hand combinations.

He thinks the same way outside the ring, defensively.

One of the most memorable Ray stories, which were all
part of my preparation for this job, concerned an incident
that took place eighteen years ago, when Ray was still new to
club life. At that time he had very little money and most of
what he did have was invested in a Harley FX 74. The FX
wasn't just any bike. Ray had bought it as a basket case,
rebuilt it, bobbed it, which means he took off anything that
wasn't necessary for function, and then spent another month
getting the red-and-black paintwork as close to perfect as he
could. The bike was Ray. It was his work of rolling art.

The first day he parked it on the street it was stolen, and
three days after that he found it in a chop shop, reduced again
to a bare frame. Everything else was gone. After a bit of
persuasion, he learned that the theft had been committed by
two members of an upstart Chicano bike club. He went after
them alone, found them in a bar, beat the hell out of both of
them, and hauled them off to a deserted warehouse. There,
he tied them down and skinned them. Not all of their skin,
just their club tattoos, which included a section of back and
half a biceps. According to legend, those tats still decorate a
wall in the SOFMC clubhouse.

Ray always evens the score.

There's also a certain Robin Hood quality to him, Robin
Hood mixed with the Godfather. He's a hero in his
neighborhood, keeping both drugs and punks off the streets.
If people have a problem, they come to Ray. I was with him
once, sitting at a traffic light in the front seat of his Range
Rover, when a young gang of wanna-be hoods decided to

shake down the owner of the local butcher shop. We watched them go inside, four of them, the largest carrying a baseball bat. The next thing that happened was the sign on the front window was turned from OPEN to CLOSED. "Wait here," Ray said. He left the Range Rover in the middle of the road, got out, and walked unarmed into the shop. A couple minutes later he was back outside, carrying the bat, with the boys walking like obedient schoolchildren behind him, the biggest of them bent forward, nursing a bleeding nose.

"Sometimes you've got to spank these kids," were his first words as he got back into the car. "Don't want mine growing up like that, without a sense of values."

These days, Sons of Fire isn't what it used to be, which was a bunch of misfits and rebels on bikes, drinking and whoring, involved in petty crime. Today it is an international organization, with its own website, selling T-shirts, bike accessories, and bumper stickers. Behind the open-to-the-public façade, the club is all business, from strip clubs and massage parlors, to the manufacture of illegal silencers for firearms, but their main business is the manufacture and distribution of methamphetamine.

It's a drug that fools the brain, tricking it into releasing vast quantities of a neurotransmitter called dopamine, which creates intense feelings of euphoria, razor-sharp alertness, and a sense of omnipotence to rival Superman's.

That's the high side of the meth; the low is the crash, when the chemical wears off and the brain's natural production of dopamine stops. It feels like death. The antidote to this is more meth, which begins a deadly cycle.

Methamphetamine is a hard, dangerous drug, and that's the paradox of Ray Sasso. Although he does not condone it, it has become the major part of club business in the past five years, spreading outward from the heavier, more criminally oriented SOFMC chapters in the Midwest. In this respect, Ray does what is expected of him, which is to enforce club policy and generate club business. The consequences of refusing to do this would be his life.

"I don't sell product to minors, and never in my own backyard," he claims. I think he believes this because, inside, he needs to believe it.

Meth is serious business, and Ray's chapter of the
SOFMC controls the tri-state area with connections that
stretch all the way down the East Coast.

About two years ago, when the Mount Vernon Speed
Dream Custom Motorcycle Shop opened, Ray was
advertising for mechanics. I answered the ad, just like any
other guy who needed a job.

From the beginning, we got on well. We had a rapport.
I'm good with my hands and fast with my mouth, quick at
seeing the humor in even the darkest situation, which is sort
of a requirement in this job. I could always make Ray laugh,
which meant a lot since he was often hung up with petty
interclub rivalries along with the heavier side of his
businesses. Plus I could hold my own in a boxing ring, and
boxing is a passion with Ray. Not that he didn't check me
out. He did, but my police records, provided by one of the
local cops on his payroll, came back clean.

So when I introduced him to Jimmy Sipriani, a narcotics
dealer, formerly from Yonkers and recently relocated to
South Beach, Miami, it all made sense. Club business,
particularly in the meth trade, is not a secret, and I wasn't
asking for anything in return. On the other hand, Sipriani
asked for a lot. Two kilos of crystal. Ninety thousand dollars'
worth of rock in a single buy. He could step on it twice and
turn it into a quarter of a million dollars.

The negotiations took three months, long enough for
Ray to investigate Sipriani and find out that he had, just as I'd
told him, been a dealer, handling light weights of cocaine and
a little smack. It looked like Jimmy S. was trying to take a step
up on his new turf.

Still, Ray wanted to be sure. That meant trusting the
people close to him. That meant me.

After a year and three months under, it was my first
moment of truth.

~ 3 ~

WE WERE IN THE CLUBHOUSE, sitting in front of Ray's old wood desk, with the SOFMC flag unfurled and hanging like the warning on a bottle of poison behind him on the wall. Ralph Menzies, the club's sergeant-at-arms, was there standing to his right and Willy Davis, an enforcer, was in the room, too.

It was my first time inside Ray's office, and I remember looking around, up at the wall, my eyes searching for the Chicano tattoos.

I had been prepped for situations like this. Warned never to comply. Compliance means committing a felony, punishable by prison. There are no exceptions and no excuses. But I was there, caught and scared, both for myself and my badge. Left with nothing to do but to do it. Either that or blow the takedown, maybe get a bullet in the head and wind up in the trunk of the club's black Lincoln, fitted with cement shoes and bound for a wet grave in the Hudson River. I thought of Carolyn and Jade then. I shouldn't have, but I did. More than anything else in the world, I wanted to see my wife and kid again.

After that it was all slow motion, watching Ray chop a piece off the rock, which looked like a lump of dull quartz, using the blade of his knife, smiling as he worked it into powder. The light from his desk lamp reflected off the blood red ruby in the heavy gold ring he wore on his index finger. The gold was rough and porous, as if the metal was old and beaten, and the stone seemed to dance in its rough setting, as he sculpted a short gray line of powder on the mirror.

"For you," he said, extending it across the desk, knowing that if I was a narc, I'd do anything to avoid committing a felony. Watching me, studying my eyes.

"Go ahead.

It was the first time I had really noticed his teeth. The front two had been knocked out and replaced with badly matched caps. They looked like pieces of yellowed ivory, particularly in the glow from his desk lamp, and his incisors seemed abnormally long. I focused on them. Sharp and pointed, they looked like fangs.

"Go ahead," he repeated.

A moment later, I crossed the line between cop and criminal. The stuff hit my septum like a blast of battery acid. A moment later the taste reached my tongue; it was bitter and metallic. My mouth went dry. After that came the first rush, as my central nervous system kicked in. I remember thinking that it was no wonder doctors used meth to treat narcolepsy. I was waking up for the second time that day. Visually, everything in the room became very clear and defined, as if my eyes had been suddenly washed clean. I looked across the desk and found Ray waiting, studying me, his eyes penetrating mine, opening me up.

He knows I'm a cop, I thought. He knows.

Finally, he spoke, saying, "I want you there when this Sipriani thing goes down." There was a friendly edge to his tone, which meant two things. The first was a show of trust, which is what I had been working toward. The second was a darker truth. If anything went wrong, I'd be the first to take a bullet. That was a certainty.

I nodded, struggling to keep my paranoia from stampeding. Not confident enough to speak, it felt like my nervous system had been hot-wired to my brain.

Ray ordered Menzies to retrieve a bottle of Jack Daniels' from the liquor cabinet and poured a glass.

"This'll smooth it out," he said, pushing it toward me.

I downed the whiskey in a single gulp.

The alcohol bit my throat, then tasted sweet and settled easily in my belly. Suddenly I got all warm inside. Another double shot and everything began to level out.

After that I was back in control. It was like a warm flood of honey had been released in my brain. I suppose it was the dopamines, the pleasure transmitters, discharged by the neurons in response to the chemical, filling the synapses in my brain and sugarcoating everything, but it was the most euphoric feeling I had ever known. I felt completely safe and secure.

Ray almost whispered his next words, "know the ways of all professions." It was straight from Musashi's *Book of Five Rings*, one of the governing principles of a warrior's strategy.

I remember smiling. How the hell did Ray know about Miyamoto Musashi, the Japanese sword saint? But under the circumstances it seemed relevant.

"Do not think dishonestly," Ray said, repeating another principle. Adding, "Hey, bro, you think you're the only one who reads?"

That's when I caught the glint in his eyes. Then he started to laugh. It was a spontaneous laugh, one that rolled me in. After that, Ray dismissed the other two guys. I felt like I'd made the cut. I was on the team.

"You feel like a ride?" he asked.

It was April. The roads were dry and the night was cool and clear. Hanging on to the ape hanger bars of my Shovelhead, the stroker running smooth and sweet, following Ray's red-and-black Softail at eighty miles an hour, I felt like I could reach up and pull the stars down from the sky.

We rode out to Jones Beach. By the time we'd parked and started to walk, I was talking. I couldn't seem to stop myself. I wanted to talk, about my dead brother Robert, my mother who died in a psychiatric hospital, my time working as a rock 'n' roll roadie on the West Coast. About the sword saint, Musashi. I talked about everything but Carolyn and Jade. I kept them safe. Everything but who I really was. I came close, but never close enough to give myself away.

At first Ray was reserved, the listener. Taking it all in, weighing my words, offering comments, but later on he spoke. He told me that he'd grown up in Lynbrook, New

York, in a white Protestant neighborhood. His father was
long gone by the time he was ten and the local boys
nicknamed him Guinea Ray. Beating him up was a favorite
pastime. That's what turned him to boxing. He'd gone on to
be a Golden Gloves champion while his mother dragged him
to church on Sundays and prayed for him at night. He was
sixteen when she died of a stroke. After that he'd faked his
birth certificate and joined the Army. He'd learned to handle
weapons at Fort Bragg, but more important he'd learned that
a single-minded group of trained individuals could
accomplish anything. It was that understanding that, twenty
years ago, drew him to the Sons of Fire Motorcycle Club.

Lately, things had changed. Maybe it was inside the club
or maybe the change was inside him, Ray wasn't sure, but he
was having doubts. He had begun to question his
commitment, and in his business, commitment was
everything. He had a wife now, and a seven-year-old son. For
six of those seven years, he had been trafficking in drugs.

"What goes around, comes around," he said. It was a
phrase I had heard my late brother use many times.

"I don't want my kid ever touching meth."

Family came first in his life, and, for any member of an
outlaw organization, that was a dangerous thing.

By the time the sun came up, like a ball of red fire against
the slate gray sea, I felt close to Ray Sasso in a way I'd once
felt close to my brother. It was a strange feeling, very
personal, almost like we were the same person. I could have
been Ray, given different circumstances, but from somewhere
I wondered if he could have ever been me. It was that feeling
that started to get to me, like a slow erosion, starting with my
confidence, then burrowing into my conscience.

We rode back to Mount Vernon, where Ray lived in a
two-story house off Gramatan Avenue. He took me inside, in
time to meet his wife Maureen and his son William before the
little boy left for kindergarten. I had a hard time with
breakfast. The meth had worn off and so had my armor. I felt
naked, as if my feelings were raw and exposed. The lie was
beginning to beat me. I talked to his son about school. Asked
if he had a girlfriend. That made him laugh, and his laugh,
free and innocent, made me lonely for Jade. I broke another

rule that morning. I accepted a gift. It was a toy soldier, made of wood, painted blue and in full dress uniform, playing a drum. William gave it to me. The soldier made me realize why the acceptance of gifts is forbidden in my business. They create debt, and mine had become personal.

***

Trouble came that evening. There were members of the club who resented me. Didn't trust me, worming my way in with their president. I wasn't a brother. I was a hanger-on. Not even a prospect. They must have wondered what I was playing at.

The incident took place on the street, behind B.J.'s, a club-owned bar. I had just kicked over the engine to my bike when Ralph Menzies and Jim Walker walked from the back door and onto the sidewalk.

I had never sensed anything but hostility from Menzies, and Walker was somewhere on the wrong side of neutral. I knew that both of them were dangerous. Menzies had done seven years on a second-degree manslaughter conviction, and Walker had been inside twice for aggravated assault, but it was the way they looked at me that told the story. With a dead concentration, like hunters close to their prey.

I sensed what was about to happen, and I knew it would be bad. I'd been up all night and worked all day, my body felt weak in a way that I'd never felt weak before, drained and shaking. My stomach was scared hollow.

Nobody spoke, there was just the deep thump, thump, thumping sound of the Shovel's exhaust ricocheting off the curb.

Menzies was a step away. His eyes were like big dark pools of water. I could see my fear reflected in them. Freezing me like an animal caught in the glare of the headlights. That's when he made his move. It was a looping left hook, backed by his solid 240 pounds. The kind of punch that I should have stepped away from, or gone inside to counter, but my timing was gone. I'd barely got my hands up when his fist caught the back side of my head. It felt like a bag of wet cement, landing flush, sending me sprawling on all fours beside my bike. That's when the stomping began. Big, steel-tipped engineer boots, sinking deep into my ribs and abdomen, over and over again. I could hear myself grunt as my body was lifted and the air was forced from my lungs, then everything went numb. Everything but my brain. My thoughts were like abstract splashes of color in red and black. Death. This was it. Right there, in the gutter. I must have rolled onto my back, because up above, I could see my bike begin to topple. Four hundred pounds of steel and hot pipes coming down in my face, coming down to crush my skull. *Thump, thump, thump,* it was still running.

Faces flashed through my mind. Robert. Carolyn. Jade. And all the time, the thump, thump, thump, was getting louder, closer.

Until the voice of God cut through the noise and the pain. "Back off him, motherfuckers. Now!"

The bike stopped in midair. The engine died.

"Back off!"

There was silence.

I was groggy, and my vision was blurred, but I still recognized Ray's face, inches from my own, looking into my eyes. I could smell his breath, pretzels from the bar, a whiff of whiskey. Feel his hands, his strong fingers, climbing up my body, see the ruby in his ring.

Then his gruff voice. "Nothing's broke, Wolfie, you'll live. Get up."

But something had been broken. Ray had broken an outlaw code. He had gone against his own for me, an outsider.

It was at that point that I decided to save him.

Maybe it was my dead brother I really wanted to save.

I felt like I owed one of them, maybe both, and that's when the real confusion began.

~ 4 ~

I WALK TO THE FORMICA COUNTERTOP next to the sink. There's an electric kettle there. I push the button in, turning it on. It takes about two minutes to boil. In that time I remove an old jam jar, which sits next to William Sasso's wooden soldier on the shelf, pop the lid, and dump its contents onto the countertop. The small rock is the color of quartz and I use a serrated-edge knife to scrape a piece of it into a coffee mug. It looks benign, lying like rough sugar in the bottom of the mug. So benign that I think I might need a bit more, so I double the original amount. Two teaspoons of instant coffee on top, and I pour the water. My hand is trembling, something that I've noticed in the past few weeks. It's all to do with the meth overloading my central nervous system. It doesn't matter now, I can't function without it. Or more accurately, I don't trust myself without it. I'm too tired and too slow. Haven't had more than four hours' sleep at one time in over a month.

It's okay, I tell myself, it won't be long. I'll clean up. I'll get myself back together. I can handle this.

Today I need to be sharp, on my toes.

Today I need to do the right thing, to tell the truth.

"Ray, we need to talk." I say this out loud before pulling off my jeans and boxer shorts, standing there naked, smelling of fear. My stomach is jumpy. Maybe a slice of bread, anything to take away the feeling that I'm raw on the inside. I need lining, cushioning. A glass of milk? I open the old

Frigidaire and pull out a half-gallon carton of low-fat, pop the lip, and gulp a mouthful. The taste hits me like rotted cheese, so I spit the curdled mess into the sink. Then I retch. I'm talking to myself all the time. I can't turn it off. It's my mind. It won't stop. The kettle pops, and I pour the boiling water into the mug, using a teaspoon for the mix. I sip the coffee. It tastes sharp and metallic as I suck it through my teeth to cool it down. Another mouthful, and I can feel my balls start to retract, my scrotum tightening against the insides of my thighs. Finally, my hands steady, enough to turn on the cold water and top up the mug. After that, I chug the remains, desperate to get it all inside me.

Rummaging through my gym bag, past the white towel, the gray sweats and Asics training shoes, past the plastic box that contains my mouthpiece, until I find a jockstrap. I only keep the thing for one reason, and that has nothing to do with physical training. Pulling it free from the tangle of dirty clothing, I pull it on, up over my thighs, then put the jeans back on and sit on the side of the bed to get into my boots, an old pair of Tony Lama snakeskins, my lucky boots. I've owned these through five resoles, and they fit like gloves, giving me a vague sense of security as I walk back into the bathroom and bend down beside the sink to retrieve the Kel from its hiding place in the pipes beneath the bowl. The cigarette-pack-sized transmitter fits perfectly inside the pouch of the jockstrap, in the place where my pre-meth balls used to go. I run the wire up so that the tiny mic just peeks out over the waistband of my Levi's, holding it tight with my leather belt.

After that, it's back to the bed. The Smith & Wesson is waiting beneath the mattress. I slide it out, check to see that the magazine's full, click the safety off, and slip it down the back side of my jeans. The wood grip fits snug and familiar into the small of my back, and the slide feels cold against my spine.

I pull my T-shirt back on, letting it hang loose, over my belt, hiding both the S&W and the wire.

Still, I've got the guilt, riding me hard. It won't quit. Thinking I shouldn't do this, but I'm halfway round the bend, moving too fast to stop.

My voice sounds like a prayer in an empty church. "Ray, we
need to straighten something out."

Going to do it, to clear it up, to pay up, then I'm going
to walk away from this ugliness. Back to Carolyn and Jade.
I'm finished with lies. There's no more justification. It's a
bent game. Everything is politics and power. No more, it's
over. I feel ruptured inside, burned out. I don't believe in
Charlie Wolf, and belief is crucial. You've got to believe in
who you are. That's what my brother Robert said before
ending up in an alley with his throat cut, dying in front of a
crowd of spectators.

"Ray, don't do this today. It's a bad idea. You're going to
get hurt." My prayer continues, but I sense the church is
empty. God is not listening. "I owe you, Ray."

I need to get back to my family before I forget who they
are. Before they forget who I am. Memories of Jade, holding
her, naked and warm against my bare chest, smelling the
newness in her hair, on her skin, feeling a sense of love and
obligation that I'd never felt before, and scared that I'd let her
down. Making silent promises that I'd stay safe and healthy,
that I'd live a long time. Long enough to protect her and
teach her, and love her. Green eyes, blond hair? I don't even
know what she looks like.

"Ray, this is crazy."

But will Ray Sasso let it go as crazy? Can he? To him,
betrayal is a mortal sin.

I've got to get it together one last time. Stop doubting.
Stop thinking. Discipline my mind. Pay attention. Think like a
professional.

A long time ago, when I was a boy in Montauk, when my
dad was trying to teach me to be a man, we'd do this thing
called scratch fighting. The idea was to stand on a line
scratched into the dirt, throwing punches till one of us was
knocked down.

I remember him eyeing me before the first punch was
thrown, ordering me not to move. I used to feel so small,
knowing that I was about to be hurt, and asking myself why I
had to do this thing, why I had to be a tough guy when,
inside, I knew I wasn't. It was then that I'd practice a mental

exercise. I'd close my eyes for a few seconds and take a few slow breaths, letting the air fill my lungs, imagining that I was a lion, hungry and fast, locked inside the body of a boy. Nothing could hurt the lion, no punch could make him cry or bleed. Sometimes it worked. I could block my father's punches and hit him back. Mostly it didn't work, and I'd be beaten to the ground. Over and over again, until the lesson was done.

I try it now, closing my eyes and breathing inward. The air is heavy with mildew and sweat. Another few breaths and I begin to get there, to that place beyond the terror, to that place where the lion lives.

At 8:05 I walk out of the basement, up the steps and into the humid gray morning. The Shovelhead sits on the sidewalk, double-chained to the iron railing. I open the saddlebag on the left side and slip in a full, extra mag of 9 mm shells for the S&W, intending to retrieve it before the takedown.

The Kel is secure, my gun is clean and loaded, I'm going through all the motions. I can do this. I know I can. It will all be over in eight hours. I'll be on the other side of this nightmare. Eight hours? I think again. I'll need help if I'm going to keep my head straight for eight hours. I'll need more glue to hold the lid down tight.

Back down the nine stone steps and in through the open door to a place I never want to see again.

Straight to the Formica countertop. The rock is much smaller than when I bought it two weeks ago. It looks like milky ice, about the size of a frozen pea. Still, that much in one dose would incapacitate me, so holding the rock firmly between my thumb and index finger I grind away with the knife until I have turned half of it to powder. The other half, still solid, I brush into the sink, then dig down inside the cupboard and come up with a piece of tinfoil. I use this as a wrap, scraping the powder into it before squaring and folding the edges, then slip it into the watch pocket at the front of my jeans. My last act is to lick the residue off the countertop.

All I taste is bitter as I walk out the door.

~ 5 ~

MACQUESTEN PARKWAY, WHERE THE Speed Dream shop and warehouse are located, is in the industrial section of town and the roadwork outside the warehouse has been going on for two weeks. A jackhammer, a couple of men digging and tamping, a small Cat with an operator, a service van. There's nothing unusual about roadwork, it happens all the time.

I ride into the shop, jump the curb, and park the bike on the sidewalk in front of the open garage doors. Careful not to look in the direction of the bare-chested man working the jack, less than a hundred yards away from me. I know that it's not the same man or the same crew that worked there yesterday, and the last thing I want is eye contact.

I also know that Morgan James, my contact, is inside that van wearing a set of headphones. The Kel is not a particularly sensitive instrument, sacrificing sound for size and concealment, so he'll be listening very carefully. With no visual surveillance, the entire operation is going to depend on my voice, speaking four words, a prearranged code. "Looks good to me." It's as simple as that. Then the doors crash inward and this part of my life is over.

I know I'm going through with it from the moment I step into the shop. It's like stepping onto a stage. I'm an actor, and the script is written. Maybe there has never been a question of following through. I feel this certainty as a sickness in my gut, but my mind is at least beginning to focus

on the task. I don't like it, but it's my job. No, more than a
job, my purpose. Raymond Sasso is a criminal. He
manufactures and sells narcotics. The same narcotic that is
currently flooding my veins, driving my nerves, and altering
my ability to think straight. As quickly as this surety hits, the
façade of professionalism and duty fall away, leaving me,
once again, naked and vulnerable. I am a coward, and a liar,
about to destroy another man, a man with a wife and child, a
man with heart and guts, a man who has crossed the line to
save my life. Let somebody else take Ray Sasso down; I don't
want the job. I don't feel right. Ray Sasso is the only real
friend that Charlie Wolf has ever known. He's a man trapped
by circumstance, the same as I am. My inner voices are at
war, one telling me one thing, the other contradicting it. No
way to enter a critical situation, I've got to get myself straight,
think this through. I need time, but time's up.

The shop is small, about twice the size of a two-car
garage, and it smells of gasoline, coffee, and oil. Rock music
blares from the boom box on the wall, and there are three
chassis up on hydraulic lifts. They look like steel skeletons,
with their engines in pieces on the floor beside them. One of
them is an old Triumph Bonneville, the other two are
Harleys. All but the Bonneville are here for speed work,
which usually means porting and polishing the stock engine
heads, a change of camshafts, a high-performance carburetor,
a single-spark ignition, and a set of tuned-length front and
rear pipes.

I was always a natural with my hands, and my brother
Robert taught me how to work on the Shovelhead, twenty
years ago, in Montauk. That and a twelve-week mechanic's
course before this assignment, and I'm up to speed with the
new American technology, which in the case of the V-Twin
engine hasn't changed much since the 1940s.

"Hey, Wolfie, how are ya'?" Axle Barfoot says, as I walk
up to the bike I've been working on for the past couple of
days.

Barfoot is the new boy in the shop, the general
dogsbody, sweeping up or making coffee, maybe doing some
basic mechanics.

"Hangin' in," I answer, looking at him with a feeling of contempt. He's young, and he's green, and I feel that he's out to prove himself. I also feel he's had his eyes on me all week, waiting for me to fuck up. I can't figure how they got him in, so close. Ray does not employ club members in any of his straight businesses, but it still strikes me as too much of a coincidence that Barfoot and I are working the same gig.

There's one more guy in the shop, a Londoner by the name of Ian Smith. He comes in when we've got something foreign on the lifts, which is rare, and I know him just about well enough to say hello to him.

I nod a greeting as I walk to my station.

An hour later, while I'm torquing the cam cover on a silver Fatboy, Ray walks in.

Ray always seems to be thinking, which troubles me on this particular day, especially when he looks in my direction, nods quickly, and smiles.

"How you feeling?"

"Good," I lie.

Mick Jagger is belting out an oldie from the speakers as Ray stops and takes me in with the sharp eye of a drill sergeant inspecting a soldier.

"You wired?" he asks, his voice low enough so that Barfoot and Smith are out of earshot.

His question hits me hard. I think of the Kel, stuffed inside my pants, and suffer a rush of paranoia, then cover for my thoughts by lowering my eyes.

Recovering, I answer, "A little," then look up so that he can see the dilation of my pupils.

He hesitates, considering. Finally, he says, "That's not good."

"I can handle it," I reply, keeping my eyes on him.

Ray smiles again, cocky, as if he's accepting a challenge. "Don't be a fool," Ray says softly, then touches my shoulder with his right hand, squeezing gently, before he walks toward his office at the rear of the shop.

After that, I have a lapse in nerve. Followed by an urge to trail Ray into the back room and tell him everything.

Ray, we've got to straighten this out before it gets crazy. I can hear my own voice like the whine of a frightened child.

Instead I go back to the business of nuts and bolts with a single-minded intensity, trying to harness my fear through sheer concentration.

Two more hours go by before Ray reappears.

"Your buddy called. Time's been changed to two-thirty."

Buddy? I don't like the sound of the word "buddy."

"Why?" I ask.

Ray looks at me and smiles like he knows something I don't, then walks away, out the front door, where his white Range Rover is parked by the curb.

I watch him get into the driver's seat and start the vehicle. He glances in my direction and our eyes meet for a second before he drives off.

After that I pick up a wrench and go back to the Fatboy, but my hand is trembling too much to connect with the bike.

I don't eat lunch. Not solid food anyway. At 2:19, with my mouth dry and my nerves raw, I grab one of the chipped porcelain mugs that live at the bottom of the stainless-steel sink on the far side of the shop and walk to the coffee machine. Smith has gone to test-ride the Bonneville, and Barfoot is buried in a Subway hoagie and a Starbucks' Frappuccino, stealing glances at me when he thinks I'm not looking, but I sense him.

I ram my fingers into my watch pocket and retrieve the squared foil wrap, keeping my back to Barfoot as I open it. Dumping the contents into the black coffee, I use the communal spoon to dredge the bottom of the mug, crushing the grainy lump and mixing it.

Barfoot's got to be nervous, probably shitting himself, and he makes no attempt at conversation, which suits me fine as I sit on the workbench facing the doors and sip from the stained mug. Halfway through I feel a rush of panic. Like running straight through the open doors and out into the street. All the way. All the way to where? It's too late. There is nowhere to go, so I hold on tight, absorbing the soak of caffeine, meth, and adrenaline as it seethes through my body, opening up cavities of doubt everywhere. Doubt is worse than fear. I can handle fear. I've had plenty of it. There is always fear before a takedown. Hoping that everything works, that everybody is on their mark, ready to go when the signal

comes. That the team is together, fast and smooth. That there
are no casualties. Then there's the personal fear, performance
anxiety, but I've learned to turn that into a positive.
Channeling and directing it, using the adrenaline charge to
heighten my senses and guide my awareness. This feels
different. This feels like a downhill ride with no brakes,
hanging on trying not to crash.

I finish my coffee and wait for the meth to do its job,
expecting it to turn my jitters into brass. Enough to get me
through the actual event, but it isn't happening. I'm high,
then I'm low. The stuff is roller-coastering my insides. I steal
a look at Barfoot, sipping his bottled coffee through a straw,
with his pudgy face and short blond hair. He's trying to grow
a mustache, but it isn't working. That, a few pimples, and
twenty pounds of puppy fat give him the look of an
adolescent aspiring to be a man. Who the fuck in his right
mind would ever bring him in on something like this?

He looks over at me and raises his eyebrows. His lips are
turned upward in an inquisitive smile, but his voice sounds
tentative, "You okay?"

He looks nervous as I slide down from the bench. Why
should he be nervous? This is my show, not his. He's not
even invited to the main event.

I feel the S&W, like a pole against my backbone. The
meth is sharpening my thoughts till they're spiked.

I stare at Barfoot. Who is this guy anyway? What's he
doing here? How the hell did he get in so easily?

Ray's smart all right. It would be just like him to have a
man on the other side, in his pocket. Somebody I'd never
suss. Barfoot looks all wrong, sitting there, staring up through
wide blue eyes, his meaty hand looking clumsy around the
neck of the small bottle. Frappuccino? Who the hell drinks
Frappuccino?

Sensing danger, he places his coffee on the floor and
holds up both hands like he's surrendering.

His voice is tight with nerves as he stands up slowly.
"You don't look too good. What's the matter?"

We are eye to eye as an electric slide guitar screams from
the boom box, filling the space between us, adding a trippy
rhythm to the dance and Jimi Hendrix begins to sing.

I walk to the far right of the Fatboy, my hand inching toward the small of my back, where the S&W is concealed, lining Barfoot up for a clear shot to the head.

~ 6 ~

I COULD TAKE YOU OUT right now. One shot and
your head will be decorating the back wall. I'm thinking it
so hard that my thoughts feel like a solid bridge between
us. Barfoot is staring at me, and his head is shaking side to
side, more like a tremble than an actual shake, like he's
begging me to let him live.

Then comes a revelation. I'm not going to shoot
Barfoot. What the hell am I doing thinking about shooting
him? Why Barfoot? It makes no sense. In fact the absurdity
of the thought causes me to laugh out loud; it's like a burst of
crazy energy expelled from my gut. This total about-face
seems to stun him, which makes me laugh even harder. His
mouth drops open, then he half smiles, like he doesn't want
to trust a full smile.

I laugh some more and he laughs along with me, forced
at first, then really getting into it. Ha, ha, ha. Ha, ha, ha ...
What the hell is he laughing about? What's so fucking funny
that he's laughing? I stop abruptly. So does he. I'm about to
question him when I hear the sound of a car's engine and
look out the front doors to see the white Range Rover pulling
in to the curb. Ray's at the wheel and there's another guy
beside him, but he's cast in shadow and I can't make out who
it is.

It's 2:26 in the afternoon. Half an hour early. I wonder if
Morgan is ready, prepared for the change in plans.

At that moment, Jimmy Sipriani's blue Mercedes sedan rolls in behind the Range Rover. He's alone in his vehicle.

Jimmy S. worked a patch in Yonkers before Morgan took him down. That was four years ago, and the bust was kept quiet. Now Jimmy S. works for the DA's Office, at least till this is over. Then he gets a new identity, a new state to live in, and a job selling vacuum cleaners, all provided by the federal government and set up by Ms. Jane Carroll, my boss. His alternative is fifteen to life upstate.

I watch as he gets out of the Merc, carrying a leather satchel containing ninety thousand dollars in old bills. With his Fifth Avenue haircut, fawn suede jacket, Gucci loafers, and new jeans, he looks like a New York City advertising executive. He's even making a cheroot. Sipriani is a natural, if his nerves hold.

Beyond the cars, the road crew is hammering away, silent and dripping with sweat, knowing that it's only matter of minutes and seconds till Showtime.

Hendrix has stopped wailing and Jim Morrison's taken over with "Back Door Man."

I hear a clank: and turn to see that Barfoot has gone back to work, wrenching away on the front forks of a Softail.

By the time I look out the doors again, Jimmy S. and the second man in Ray's car have disappeared from view, and Ray is headed my way. He stops at my bike, looks it over, then looks in through the doors at me. I turn away quickly and go back to the Fatboy, trying to stay calm, trying to keep my head together.

It's going down now, like it or not, there's no turning back.

***

I hear the heels of Ray's boots against the concrete before I hear his voice.

"Charlie, let's go."

Charlie? Ray never calls me Charlie. I've always been Wolf, or Wolfie. Warning bells are ringing as I get to my feet while Barfoot continues to work as if nothing is happening.

I feel it again as we walk the short distance between the buildings. Something is wrong. My gut is telling me to stop, but the meth won't listen. Everything is moving forward in a series of teeth-grinding progressions. In the midst of this feeling, I feel like I've lost something, or forgotten something. What is it? What the hell is it? Hold on. Stop. "If you don't feel a hundred percent right, don't do it." That's what Morgan James would say. "A hundred percent, not ninety-nine. A hundred." The sensation intensifies as we walk past my motorcycle. I glance at it quickly. Then on, not chancing a look toward the street, at the workmen or the van. Morgan is inside that van. My anchor, listening to me breathe, watching my back. "Looks good to me." That's all I've got to say to make it stop. "Looks good to me." After that it will be a question of staying alert. If I'm sharp enough, and Morgan's team is fast enough, we can get through this without blood. Nice and smooth. At least I'm thinking like a cop again. Circumstance is forcing me back into the mold, defining me.

Ray stops in front of the side door to the warehouse and turns in my direction, smiling. But there is a slyness in his smile.

Then he bangs on the door with the back of his fist.

The metal base scrapes against the sidewalk as it opens, revealing the second man in Ray's car.

Ralph Menzies stares down at me. It's the first time since the stomping that our paths have crossed, and I feel a chill run upward along the length of my spine. I don't like the fact that Menzies is here. It scares me. Then it's across the threshold and into the shadows of the warehouse.

Inside the place is filled with boxes and cartons, many marked with the brand names of after-market parts manufacturers. I figure that a few contain silencers, manufactured after hours on the lathes in the machine shop. There's money in silencers, but a limited demand, so the meth, made from ephedrine and refined with benzene and cleaning fluids, stuff that is available at the local hardware store, is the heart of club business.

Behind the boxes are rows of steel shelving, all numbered and filled with motorcycle accessories: fenders and headlamps, handlebars and air cleaners, spark plugs, even chopped frames.

The place has a funny smell, like wet cardboard mixed with pine-scented air freshener.

The ceiling is high, and Jimmy Sipriani looks small and thin, his face gaunt and his skin drawn and sallow beneath the bare bulb that hangs directly above him. He also looks very frightened.

"Stay close to me," Ray orders, as we walk toward the money, stopping a few feet in front of Jimmy S.

Ray eyes him up for a few seconds, then asks, "You ready?"

Jimmy S. holds the satchel forward. His voice sounds like he's inhaled a balloon full of helium. "Ninety in used bills."

This is the part of the deal that really bothered Morgan. Usually the money is kept separate from the product. The extra trip to the trunk of the car to retrieve it, or the telephone call to bring it in, provides either time or the signal for the team to move, but Ray was too sharp for any of that. He set this up inside, on his territory, with the money where he could count it.

Menzies extends his hand and takes hold of the satchel, but Jimmy S. snatches it back. It's all so fast and awkward that it would be funny as hell if it weren't life-and-death serious.

"I want to see what I'm buying first," Jimmy S. blurts out. He was a lot cooler during rehearsals.

I glance at Ray.

He looks alert but relaxed, standing with his hands to his sides and his feet slightly spread. He looks set for a round of sparring.

"Yeah, sure, just one thing," he says, turning to me. "Charlie, I didn't know you owned a gun."

His words catch me cold.

"You carrying it now?" he continues, that sly smile returning to his face.

I stand there, aware that my right hand has begun to tremble. I can't stop it. Then my lips begin to quiver. *Looks good to me.* The code sounds in my head but I keep my mouth shut, jaw clenched and teeth grinding. How close to the line can I play it? I see my own fear mirrored in Jimmy S.'s eyes.

Finally, I answer, "No."

"No ... ? No you don't own a gun, or no you're not carrying one now?"

Everybody knows that only cops and bad guys carry guns. Maybe Ray is playing my bluff, testing me one last time.

"Ray," I answer, pulling the last of my balls up from my boots, trying to infuse my voice with the same ease that Ray is showing. We're sparring again. Concentration is everything, and I feel the meth is giving me the advantage. I smile a dry-lipped smile and reply, "I've never fired a fucking gun in my life."

With that Ray turns and starts walking toward the door with Jimmy S. frozen in place, the satchel stuffed under his arm, stuck to his side.

Another step and Ray turns back to me. He has removed something from his pocket and is holding it out. It's small and dark. What the fuck—

"Wrong answer, Charlie."

My thoughts stop as he tosses it at me.

Clack! It hits the floor and slides.

Dark and metallic, the extra mag for the S&W, the one I left in my saddlebags, stops at my feet.

Ray's got a strange look in his eyes, like he's just seen me for the first time and can't quite believe who I really am. Our eyes hold as the first blow from the heavy sledge hits the door of the warehouse.

After that there is nothing but violent shouting and movement as six men, clad in Kevlar vests and cargo pants, rush inside, their voices bellowing. "Down on the floor! Get down! Now! Now!!"

One of the them points a Heckler & Koch semi-automatic rifle at Ray's head. One burst of the 9 mm shells would decapitate him.

I should back away from the action, but I can't. It's that look on Ray's face. That look of utter betrayal.

Then someone grabs a handful of my T-shirt and hauls me backwards, off my feet, using me for cover, dragging me

into the aisles at the rear of the warehouse. The barrel of a
gun digs deep beneath my right ear, into the nerve, numbing
my jaw as my boots slide against the floor. I catch a last
glimpse of Ray, on his knees, with three Kevlar-clad banshees
screaming above him while Ralph Menzies' shouts inside my
skull "Fucking cop, I'll kill you!"

Then, in front of me, coming down the aisle, I see Axle
Barfoot, with a gun in his left hand. The barrel is nickel-
plated, and the weapon looks small, like a toy. It's a Seacamp,
a backup piece. It shoots silver bullets.

He raises his arms, steadying the gun with both hands.
He looks like a rookie, in his modified Weaver combat stance,
his legs spread, left foot slightly forward. Young and scared,
his belly wobbling as he moves forward, knees bent, his face a
tense mask. I still don't know whose side he's on. He's not
saying anything, not telling me he's a cop. What's he doing?
Coming for me?

He's one of Ray's. That's my final thought as I turn
inside Menzies' grasp and grip his gun with both hands,
locking his finger in the trigger guard, levering it downward. I
can feel his finger snap and break as I spin with the gun in my
hands. Dropping to the floor, fumbling as I try to aim it
upward at Barfoot. He opens his mouth to shout something
that never comes. There is panic in his eyes as he squeezes
the trigger.

Boom. Boom. Boom.

~ 7 ~

FOR WHAT FEELS LIKE ETERNITY there is nothing but pain, hot and searing, like a flaming poker through the socket of my eye, twisting into my right temple, melting my flesh and bones, obliterating all sound and vision. Ending in pure calm.

It is as if I've entered the eye of a storm and found it to be clear and blue. Light blue to be precise, almost white, with several cracks in its surface. With that observation my perspective shifts. There's a light coming from directly over my shoulder. I turn to see a bare bulb, hanging from a wire. Really see it. Satco, 100W, 130V, is written on its underside, and I can see the filament, glowing white, through the thin clear glass. What's happening to me? This is crazy. I look up at the ceiling. It's three inches from my eyes, cracked and light blue. Where am I? What's going on?

Roll over, as if I'm in a soft bed. Look down. Jesus Christ, I'm flying. I can't do this, it's impossible. The jolt of this reality makes me drop, almost on top of a bearded man, sprawled on his back, eyes wide-open, staring up at me. I know this guy, really know him, just can't quite remember from where. There's a wound, neat, like a puncture in his forehead, with just the kiss of blood, like the red stain of lipstick surrounding it.

He's got a broad face with high cheekbones. His eyes are blue, glassed-over, and his mouth is half-open. He looks like an actor, playing dead. Hold on, look at his right foot. That cowboy boot, it's twisting to the side, like it's falling off, making his foot look clubbed or broken.

A black man rushes forward, shouting, "You stupid fucking asshole. Identify yourself! Why didn't you identify yourself?"

The man he is yelling at, a pudgy man with a scraggly mustache, is barely supporting himself against the steel frame that forms the aisle. His nickel-plated gun is hanging limp in his hand. His face is a dark, shadowed grimace.

The puppy-dog face, the blond hair, the mustache, I know him, too. His name is Axle. I know all of these people, it's all coming back.

Axle sputters, "All happened so quick. I was about to—" The black man smacks him in the face with the back of his open hand, bloodying his nose, before pushing by him as he steps over the body of a big man wearing a cut-off denim jacket with the insignia of a death's-head on the back.

Although I am aware of everything that is going on, it is the man lying on the floor beneath me who captures my attention. I keep staring down at him, until I realize that I am staring at my own body.

In the background I hear a voice, harsh and clear, "You have the right to remain silent. You have the right to an attorney ... "

Then, in the periphery of my vision, I see Jimmy Sipriani. He's standing in the far corner of the room, away from the action, looking around, as if to make sure that no one is watching him. He misses me because I am up above and invisible. I watch him squat down on the floor. Why is he doing that? It seems out of context with the other things going on below me. He's moving quickly, doing something inside the briefcase, taking out a plastic-wrapped package, laying it down, glancing from side to side, like a magician performing a sleight of hand.

"Jack!"

Jack? I haven't heard that name in months and it takes a few moments to register. It's my name, my real name, Jack Edward Lamb.

I watch as Morgan James kneels beside my body, looking into my eyes, repeating, "No, this isn't going to happen. Not today, not today." Bending over and touching my lips with his own. Inhaling then blowing, over and over again. Another breath and he stops, then with both hands joined, begins pumping down against my sternum.

"Breathe, Jack, breathe!" he repeats as he continues to pump. In the background there is the sound of police radios, tinny and crackling, the continued call of 10-13, officer down, and far away, the lone, plaintive wail of an ambulance siren.

It's the boot that does it. The Tony Lama snakeskin cowboy boot, turned sideways on my foot, like it's about to fall off. I know those boots. They were bought in Corpus Christi, Texas, en route to the border at Brownsville, with Carolyn sitting beside me in my old Mustang convertible. The road trip to Mexico was my idea. The cowboy boots were hers, a gift.

Now, as I stare at the boot, while the paramedics bring in the stretcher, my chief concern is that it's not lost. The boot means something to me, something solid and real. To me, Jack Lamb, the man lying on the floor, and suddenly I am desperate for normality, to be in one place, mind and body, but I can't get there. Can't wake up from this nightmare.

~ 8 ~

ANOTHER THUMP TO THE sternum. It feels like a mule kicking me and, for a moment, I'm lying in the street, in front of B.J.'s, with Menzies and Walker stomping down on me with their great steel-tipped toes. *Where are you, Ray? I need you right now.*

"You're not going to die," Morgan James continues. "Not going to die." It's like an oath.

Sorry man, but—

Then I'm back, looking up into his moss green eyes.

"He's breathing," Morgan says. "Jack, Jack, can you hear me?"

I am confused and disoriented. My head feels like it's been cleaved, half is alive and throbbing, the other numb. What happened to me?

"You took a bullet, but you're going to make it," Morgan says, answering my thought.

The paramedics begin to lift me on to a stretcher.

"My boot," I mumble.

"What was that?" Morgan asks, getting his face close to mine, too close. "Talk to me, Jack."

I want to tell him to back away, that I can hear him just fine, that he doesn't need to spit at me, that the sound of his voice hurts inside my head, but I'm traveling again.

I hear a voice shout, "We're losing him!" and there's another thump.

They are hammering again, really hammering, and my body is jerking. The boot falls from my foot. My white sock has a hole in the heel and looks dirty gray. There are sweat stains, like half-moons, beneath the armpits of my T-shirt. My fingernails are long and filthy and my hair is matted and appears dark in places. I remember it as much lighter. And my face, is that what I really look like? My features are hard and rigid, and I look older than I remember. I don't like this at all, this ugly wasted shell. My desire is to get clear of it, to step around and leave it to rot, like something foul and stinking that has washed up on the beach after a storm.

Another man, in overalls and a cap, takes over from the black man really bearing down, using all his mass to smash his joined hands into my sternum.

If he bears down any harder I'll crack open. The thought is mercifully detached from my reality. I'm floating, above the pain.

The paramedic's voice sounds urgent, "No good. He's not responding! "

Then the box arrives. In size and shape it looks like an ice cooler, with wires and twin paddles attached. A stocky man carries it, placing it beside my body.

I watch as my grimy T-shirt is lifted and the paddles are placed on the bare skin above my ribcage. I look undernourished.

The men stand back as the power is turned on.

My body jumps and convulses. Saliva drips from my mouth. Someone gives the command for "clear," and they jolt me with another charge.

"Got him!"

I feel a click, like the shutter of a camera closing inside my head, and everything goes black. When my vision returns I am staring at a ceiling as it moves above me. Strapped down, being carried. I panic and struggle, but the restraints hold me tight.

"We're going to get you to a hospital," Morgan James assures, as I'm lifted up and into the ambulance with the technicians.

Morgan pulls down a jump seat and sits beside me, looking into my face.

I'm not certain if I can talk, but I try, sensing the sensation of movement in my lips.

"What happening?"

Morgan leans closer.

"What's happening to me?" My words are a parched whisper.

In the background I can hear a man's voice, urgent and precise, talking about a single .32-caliber bullet wound to the right side of the head with no visible exit site, requesting an OR and a neurosurgeon. Then a sharp bleep as the radio stops transmitting and another voice cuts in, saying, "I copy that."

"You took a bullet," he replies. "Somebody made a mistake and you got hit. But you're going to be okay. We're getting you to a hospital—"

He not answering my question. Not the question that I asked. I want to know where I keep going. Why I keep leaving, then coming back. Tuning in, then tuning out. But James is in another place, on another frequency. He rambles on about stray bullets and hospitals and doctors who will make me well.

Then his voice trails off into the distance, until finally there is nothing but vibration, like a low steady hum. I try to tune back in, but can't. Desperate and scared, I know it is about to happen again. I can feel the numbness, creeping up from my toes. I am going to that peaceful place above the pain, but I'm scared because it's a place I don't understand, a solitary place. Morgan James won't be there to explain things. I'm all alone in that place. The numbness is in my groin now, like a slow-crawling anesthetic, robbing me of physical sensation, taking me piece by piece.

"Talk to me, Jack," Morgan pleads, watching anxiously as one of the medics stares at the heart monitor.

"Got a flatline here!" the medic calls out. "I need adrenaline!"

There is a cracking sound as I separate from my shell again.

Then I'm in that place, above my body, looking down, watching dispassionately as one of the medics rams a long needle through my chest.

I watch the fluid drain from the barrel, feeling nothing.

"He's not responding," the man calls out.

"Come on, Jack, come on!" Morgan shouts.

"He can't hear you," the man answers him.

Morgan shrugs him off, continuing. "Come on, Jack, stay with us. You can do it, don't quit, for Chrissakes don't—" his voice breaks and fades. "Don't fucking die on me."

"He's gone," the man states.

~ 9 ~

MY BROTHER'S HAIR HANGS WAY past his shoulders; it's gold, streaked with white, bleached by the sun and salt. His eyes are nearly turquoise, clear and shining, and he's smiling, that great white-toothed smile that lets me know everything is going to work out just fine. His skin is tanned, a reddish brown, and his body is lean with long, well-defined muscles, developed from hours of paddling his long board out into the surf, his broad shoulders and back tapering to a small, flat waist. He's wearing his baggies with their swirls of blue against the white-canvas fabric, standing knee deep in the water, the waves building, breaking to the left, a stone's throw behind him.

"I've been waiting for you," he says, as I look down from the boardwalk that leads to the beach. Behind me, the Atlantic Terrace Motel stretches long, flat, and mustard yellow. Ahead, the beach is vacant.

Should be people here, I think, but there is no one, just my brother Robert.

There is maybe five hundred feet between me and the water, and to my left I see the cliffs and the small houses perched on top of them, their windows lit like jack-o'-lanterns by the reflected sunshine. To my right I see more beach, acres and acres of silver sand.

Everything is perfect. Too perfect.

On a day like this, with a west swell and the wind offshore, holding the waves up like billowing sails, there should be a dozen boards leaning against the railings of the walk. There should be a crowd in the water, all the usual faces. Where are they?

"You coming?" Robert asks, extending his hand.

I look at the huge swells and hollow yellow-green tubes of water. Robert's the surfer, not me.

"Looks like a hurricane," I say. "On its way up from Florida. Too heavy for me."

"You're not going to drown," Robert promises. "I'm not going to let you go under."

I believe him. I always believe Robert.

Barefoot, I walk down into the sand, a few steps closer before I stop again.

"Where's your board?"

"Don't need a board today," Robert answers.

A few more steps. Funny, I can see the waves breaking, and they're big, at least six feet from the base, and I can hear a roar, but the roar is steady, like a drone.

Something doesn't feel right, and I can't put a finger on it.

"Where's Danny and Peter?" I ask. Daniel Mack and Peter Rose are part of the regular crew. Always at the Terrace before a hurricane, forming the hierarchy of surfers, always in position, just out beyond the break. But today, there is no one else in the water.

"They're coming later," Robert replies.

I continue forward. I'm not sure what's happening. No boards, a big surf, but I trust him.

Above, the sun is mounted like a diamond in the blue, yet there is no glare. I can stare straight into its light and not blink my eyes, and its warmth penetrates deep inside me, giving me a sense of comfort and tranquility.

"You coming?"

When I look back at Robert, the drone has given way to what sounds like distant wind chimes, and the sea is calm, shimmering, its water reflecting the light above. There are sparkles and splashes of light, like tiny dancers, pirouetting against the glassy surface, each coming to life for an instant, shining and spinning before slipping back beneath the surface.

Robert puts out his hand.

I'm coming, Robert, I'm coming.

One foot in the water; it's not cold, it's not warm, it's like a nothingness. Watching as my body merges with it, my flesh dissolving without physical sensation. I can't see anything of myself below the water. It's as if the sea is a cutoff point between being and not being. I step in with the other foot and watch it disappear, while the upper half of my body is mirrored against the still surface.

A voice comes from behind me. "Jack!"

It takes a moment to remember who Jack is, like he may be someone I used to know, a friend who has slipped from my mind.

"Jack!" The voice is desperate, as opposed to this infinite peace that I am experiencing.

I turn to see the rise of sand, the end of the boardwalk, and the sky beyond.

"Please don't go!"

Then I realize the voice is coming from inside my mind, an echo from the world I am leaving.

"Jack ... "

I know that voice.

"Come back, please, come back."

But I'm almost there, all the way in, my body and mind dissolving, giving birth to something more pure and refined. Not without consciousness, but without the awareness of consciousness.

It takes a tremendous effort to turn and look once more. This time I see her, standing on the crest of the beach, where the earth meets the sky. She is carrying a child in her arms, a beautiful white-haired child wearing a yellow-cotton dress and white sneakers. The woman is tall, dressed in loose beige pants and a blue-knit shirt that clings tight to her body. She is wearing leather sandals with high, squared heels. Her hair is dark and long and appears to be blowing in a wind that does not exist where I am. Her eyes are light blue and very sad, reaching out to me.

It is Carolyn and Jade, my wife and my daughter.

"You won't see them again, not like before," Robert says. Now it is his voice which seems to come from inside my mind. I'm running away from it, up the beach, to the other side. Running as fast as I can.

~ 10 ~

TO ANOTHER TIME. ANOTHER VOICE. This one is neither high nor low, more a tenor, and very clear in its pronunciation. Is it coming from inside or outside my head? It is hard to tell.

"Officer Lamb? Officer Lamb?"

I smell coffee on the breath, covered by a thin layer of peppermint, but it's basically coffee.

"My name is Howard Metzler. I am a neurosurgeon, and I am going to try to explain your situation to you. Can you hear me?"

The small gray eyes are concentrated behind the thick lenses of a pair of wire-rimmed glasses, the mouth is pink and thin and there is the hint of dark shadow surrounding it where hair, a shade darker than the auburn hair on his head, is trying to break through the skin.

"Officer Lamb?"

I try to answer "yes," but my lips and tongue feel thick and numb. Then I try to nod my head and nothing happens. I'm paralyzed. The realization causes a rush of fear and I gasp for air.

The man continues as if I have just responded in the affirmative. "You are the victim of a shooting. The bullet entered through your forehead, passed through your frontal lobe and is still lodged in the right temporal lobe region of your brain."

My panic has no form of expression other than my eyes, which are locked onto the ones behind the round glass lenses, begging for some kind of mercy. Maybe I'm still dreaming. Maybe this whole thing is just one bad dream.

He seems to sense my desperation.

"What you are experiencing is a traumatic stress reaction caused by the shock of the injury to your nervous system, along with the high level of amphetamine in your blood. You were badly dehydrated, and undernourished, which didn't help. But there is no damage to your spinal cord." He stops speaking and studies me. His eyes seem forgiving. "Your paralysis is temporary."

Temporary? He did say, "temporary," didn't he? Please let it be temporary.

"You should come through this just fine."

I know that I'm crying with relief because it seems like I'm looking up at him from below the surface of a pool of water. He looks shiny and out of focus.

"Provided you take better care of yourself," he cautions.

My tears spill over as I stare past his face and up at the pale green ceiling, then move my eyes to the right. I can see a battery of monitors and a clear solution, suspended above me in a plastic bag, with tubes running down toward my body.

The softness drains from his voice, replaced by a professional detachment.

"What I did was clean your wound and repair the dura, which is the layer of tissue protecting your brain, so the most important thing right now is that you rest and let your body heal."

Up and into his eyes again. They're changing color, from gray to green, green to black. They seem to glow.

"You're in a safe place," he assures.

Safe from what? Is someone after me? I'm defenseless, not only unable to move, but hollow and empty, as if every drop of life has been squeezed from me, leaving a parched skin with nothing inside. My mind does a quick jump, from fear to need. Where are my jeans? Did I use the last of the meth? I'm crashing. That's what's wrong. I need the meth. I catch myself on the edge of the precipice.

He must sense my anxiety because the next thing he says
is, "Now I'm going to give you something to help you rest."

He lifts his hand and I see a syringe, its needle flashing in
the overhead lights, its barrel half-full of some clear solution.
He injects the solution into the IV tube as it continues to drip
into my arm. At first I feel nothing, then gradually the
confusion, fear and desire fade as I float with the tide, into a
warm gentle sea.

~ 11 ~

BACK TO THE BEACH, WITH the strange white sun that casts the light without glare, where Carolyn and Jade are still waiting at the top of the rise.

I hear my own voice saying, "I thought you'd never get here," as I run the last few feet to meet them. My voice sounds weak and far away.

"What did you say, Jack, what did you say?"

"I thought you'd never get here," I repeat, struggling to get the words to clear my throat.

"Oh my God!" A flood of emotion flows from Carolyn's voice. "Jack ... "

She is wearing the blue-knit shirt and linen beige pants, holding Jade in the crook of her right arm, while, with her free hand she is gently stroking my forehead. I can feel her warm skin against mine. I can smell her perfume, adding the fresh scent of lemon grass to the air. My daughter's hair is nearly white, and her skin looks soft and tanned against the cotton of her yellow dress. She's wearing the gold chain and St. Christopher's medal that I mailed to her for her second birthday. I've never seen her wear it. I haven't seen my little girl in a long, long time.

I reach up to touch Carolyn's hand, realizing as I do that I can move. I can feel my fingers and toes.

"We came as soon as we heard," she says, crying now. "They said you were paralyzed. That you couldn't speak."

Her statement silences my internal revelry.

"Who said?" I ask.

"The doctor," she answers, reading the confusion in my eyes.

"Where are we?"

She looks at me as if I'm fragile, about to break.

Answering slowly. "We're in New Rochelle, at the medical center."

"What day is it?"

"The third of July," Carolyn answers softly.

Suddenly the entire room comes into focus, the green walls, the yellow overhead lights, the high railings on my bed, the plastic bag, dripping its clear liquid into my arm.

"How did we get here from the beach?"

Her voice softens. "Jack, you've had a severe head injury."

"Last time I saw you we were on the beach, all of us—"

Jade buries her face in her mother's shoulder as she pulls back from me.

"Mama, is that my daddy?" Jade whispers.

Carolyn holds her closer, whispering, "Shhh, it's okay Jade. Yes, that's your daddy."

"Why does he look different than the picture by my bed?" Jade asks.

"Daddy's been sick."

"Oh," Jade replies, as if she understands. "Because of that boo-boo on his head?"

"Yes," Carolyn answers.

"Will it go away?"

"Yes," Carolyn repeats.

Jade smiles and looks at me. She looks shy but determined.

"Are you coming home for my birthday?" she asks.

"I'd like to," I reply.

"It's tomorrow," she says, staring at my bandages. "Will your boo-boo be better by then?"

"When Daddy's all better he'll come home," Carolyn answers on my behalf as she puts Jades down on the floor. Then, looking at me, she says, "You nearly died." It is as if it's the first time that this truth has really hit her. Her voice crumbles. "We almost lost you. Oh God. We almost lost you." Bending forward, she kisses me on the lips. Her mouth feels warm, soft, and reassuring.

I return her kiss, then reach out to touch my child. The effort required to extend my arm is enormous, but so is my need for contact. Finding her hand, stroking it, I say, "You are so beautiful, and your hair is so blond, it's white, almost pure white. Have you been at the beach, in the sun?" I'm not letting go of my certainty that I last saw Carolyn and Jade at the beach.

Jade turns her head slowly and looks down at me curiously, without answering.

Carolyn fills the silence. "We were at the beach this afternoon."

"At the Terrace?" I ask.

"Yes," Carolyn answers, then looking at me more intently, changes the subject. "You're so thin, just skin and bones."

I lower my eyes. My memory is returning in dark, bruised patches, the meth, the bungled takedown. I'm ashamed.

I reply, "Yes, I lost some weight." Reaching up, I touch the layers of bandages that wrap like a turban round my head.

At that moment the door to the room opens and a thin redheaded woman in a white nurse's uniform enters, the rubber soles of her shoes padding with a quiet suction against the linoleum floor.

She looks surprised. "Officer Lamb, you re awake. That's good. That's very good." Then she proceeds to walk to the bed and check my monitors while changing the plastic bag on my drip. She seems oblivious to Carolyn and Jade as she goes about her work.

"How are you feeling?"

"Happy to see my wife and daughter," I answer, mildly annoyed by her interruption.

"I'll bet you are," she answers. "The doctor wants to see you again, and there are a couple of other people out there who seem very anxious to talk to you, but so far"—she turns, finally acknowledging Carolyn and Jade—"no one but immediate family has been allowed past the police guard."

"Police guard?" I ask.

She nods. "Two of them, right outside your door, and another two at the elevator." She looks impressed. "You must be a very important man."

My irritation with her evaporates, replaced by a fresh sense of anxiety. A barrage of questions fills my head. I wonder why I need a police guard. Have there been threats?

Meanwhile, the nurse, whose nametag reads Maude Haines, hovers above me, looking down into my face. Her eyes, brimming with curiosity, linger on mine.

Finally, she asks, "Are you really a police officer?" Her tone is innocent.

I force a smile, and the simple act makes the bandages feel tighter, as if my head is being constricted by a steel band. I think I can feel the bullet, lodged like a pulsating mass above my right ear. It's a disquieting sensation.

My smile ebbs as I answer, "I'm an investigator."

She stares a moment longer, as if she is wondering if there is a difference between a police officer and an investigator, then the spark in her eyes clicks off, and she exits the room.

I look at Jade until she meets my eyes. Her voice is meek as she asks, "Did that boo-boo bleed a lot?"

"No, not a lot," I answer, thinking how beautiful she is, a mixture of both Carolyn and me, as if she's managed to inherit the best features from each of us. Then my mind turns again to the police guard outside the door, and I feel a sickness in my stomach. If this mess is over, why the guard?

"Did it hurt?" Jade continues, forcing Carolyn to step in again.

"Jade, that's enough, your daddy's tired."

Jade never takes her eyes from mine. I can feel her making a crucial decision.

Finally, she says, "I don't care if you have the biggest boo-boo in the whole world, and I don't care if your face is skinny like Marley's ghost. You're my daddy, and I love you."

Her words send a rush of emotion through me.

"I love you, too," I reply, reaching out again to touch her neck, above her shoulder. As my hand makes contact with her flesh, a pain, like the stab of a knife, tears through the

flesh above my right ear. I wince and shut my eyes but Jade is
still there. I see her clearly, but we are in a different place; it is
as if a trap door has opened and we have fallen from this
reality into another. We're outside, at a children's playground,
with green-plastic swings, a red merry-go-round, and a blue
sliding board. Jade is on top of the slide, ready to go down.
I'm holding her by the shoulder, ready to let her go, but there
is something wrong. There is nothing below us. Nothing but
a dark hole, as if the ground has opened in a dark chasm.
There is no bottom.

My eyes snap open, but I'm still there, in the playground,
gripping Jade's shoulder. Holding on tight. There is danger in
what I see, great danger.

"Daddy, you're hurting me!"

Carolyn's voice is sharp. "Jack!" Severing my connection
with this other place.

"I'm sorry," I say, relaxing my grip. "I didn't mean to
hurt you." But the fear lingers. It is absolute, like a certain
doom. What's happening to me? Is it the residue of the meth,
causing hallucinations?

"Shall I find the doctor?" Carolyn asks.

I am confused and suddenly exhausted. I don't want to
be fussed over or examined. I don't want to talk, not until I
understand, inside myself, what's going on.

"No," I reply. "I'm just very tired."

Carolyn takes Jade by the hand.

"We're going to be spending the night at Morgan's
apartment," she says.

"I'll phone you later. I'll feel better then, I promise ...
" My voice trails off.

Carolyn's lips are warm against my cheek, and I hear
Jade's voice say, "Bye, bye, Daddy," as I slip away.

~ 12 ~

IN MY DREAM RAYMOND SASSO is on his knees looking up at me, past the three men who stand above him. Two are shouting obscenities, threatening to kill him, while the third is striking down at his face with the butt of his rifle. He is beaten, almost beyond recognition, his nose spouting blood and snot, bent so far to the right that it appears stuck to his cheekbone. His eyes are swollen, almost shut, but still he can see me through the slits.

I can feel him reaching out, like a man drowning.

You know I can't help you, I think. I want to, I owe you, but I can't.

Still, Raymond Sasso clings on.

How is it that he can see me? No one else can. I am invisible to everyone else, like a ghost or a vapor, floating above them, but Ray knows exactly where I am.

I wake to the sound of the door opening and footsteps walking toward me. Protected only by a blanket and a sheet, I feel naked, frightened that I may have been tracked like a wounded animal to its lair.

"Officer Lamb?"

Relief. I recognize the soft, slightly nasal voice. "Did you have a good sleep?"

The curtains are drawn, it's dark in the room and Dr. Metzler's face is a silhouette against the wall.

"What time is it?" I ask.

"It's ten o'clock," he answers.

"Night or morning?" I feel strangely disoriented, like I've lost the structure of day and night, but I also feel slightly stronger, and my mind has cleared. I remember almost everything that has happened to me.

"Morning," he confirms, as he turns on the bedside light. "You've slept for twelve hours. That's good."

"I had some bad dreams," I say, my tone contradicting his, which is light and a little too breezy for me.

"Sorry about that," he answers, still without much concern.

"Is it because of the bullet?" I ask, thinking as much about my out-of-body trip in the warehouse and my experience with Jade as of my dream of Ray Sasso.

He shakes his head as if he doesn't understand.

"The dream? Could the bullet affect my dreams?"

He smiles, continuing toward me. "No, I don't believe the bullet could influence your dreams."

Pressing a button on the side of my bed, Metzler brings me to a sitting position before he goes to work, his soft, sure hands comforting as they unravel the long bandage. "Let me see how we're doing here," he says, pressing almost imperceptibly against the swelling above my ear. The slight pressure feels good, like it is releasing some form of toxin from my brain, restoring a stability to me. Finally, my fear is subsiding.

"When are you going to take it out?" I ask. Surgery makes me uneasy, but the idea of having a bullet lodged inside my skull is worse. Besides, I don't buy his dismissive attitude toward what it's doing to my mind. "When are you going to take the bullet out?" I repeat.

He begins to rewrap my turban while answering in a very noncommittal tone, "Don't know yet. It may not be advisable to remove the bullet at all."

"Why?"

"The scan shows it to be very close to a main cerebral artery," he answers.

"You said it's in my right temporal lobe?"

"That's correct," he replies, tightening the bandage. "Is that comfortable?"

"Yes, fine, so what does that mean?"

He continues to work without answering.

I persist. "What does the right temporal lobe do?"

"It processes memory and emotion, and may have some bearing on our spatial orientation. Why, have you been having problems?"

"A few experiences," I answer defensively.

He stops fidgeting with the bandage and pays a little more attention to what I'm saying.

"What type of experiences?"

"For one, I watched the paramedics resuscitate me," I reply, needing to get this out, to hear some type of explanation. "I was out of my body but still conscious. I watched the whole thing from the ceiling of the room. I was floating above everything, completely disconnected from what was going on. I met my brother—" I hesitate, studying Metzler's face. "He's been dead for nearly twenty years." Waiting for his reaction, expecting him to be surprised, even shocked, by my disclosure.

Instead, he smiles. Metzler appears relatively youthful, maybe thirty-five or forty, and the smile doesn't suit him. It makes him look smug, not wise.

"Sounds like you had an NDE," he says.

Now it's me who is surprised. Surprised that he has just taken the most incredible thing that has ever happened to me and treated it like another bloody nose.

"What's an NDE?" I ask.

"NDE stands for Near Death Experience," he explains. "I ran into a lot of them when I was interning, working the emergency units. Enough to get my interest aroused for a while. The bottom line is you had a form of hallucination."

I feel belittled, as if I have just been trivialized.

"My heart had stopped, I wasn't breathing," I counter.

"There was a lack of blood flow to your brain. That can trigger a delusionary state. It's a common thing. People see their entire lives flash in front of them in a matter of seconds. A lot of people have had an NDE."

"There was more to it than that," I insist.

"I understand how you feel," he continues, filling the vacuum with a contrite authority. "You've been through a lot in a very short time."

If what he is saying is true, about it being an hallucination, how come I am able to recall so many details, like the missing cowboy boot, or watching my own body jump when they put the paddles on my chest, or seeing Morgan slap Barfoot in the nose. Did those things happen or not?

He looks at me as if he's assessing my mental condition, then out of the blue he asks, "How do you feel about having some visitors?

Visitors? I assume he means Carolyn and Jade.

"You mean my wife and daughter?" I ask.

"They've been in already, while you were sleeping. I think they're down in the cafeteria now, I believe your daughter was hungry," he answers. "It's Mr. James and Ms. Carroll who are outside, and the lady, in particular, is very insistent about speaking to you."

I'll bet she is. Can't wait to put me on the grill and turn up the heat. I knew it was coming, I just wasn't sure when. Why put off the inevitable?

"Do you feel strong enough to see them?" he asks.

"Yes," I answer. "I feel strong enough."

I don't even notice as Metzler walks away from my bed. His footsteps seem silent, probably because my mind is so loud. He seems no more than a shadow on the wall, growing smaller. The door opens, then closes behind him.

Less than a minute later it opens again.

~ 13 ~

A REDHEADED WOMAN ENTERS. Her footsteps are not silent; in fact, her heels sound like they are piercing the floor as she walks. Clack clack. Clack clack. Like someone driving nails.

She is wearing a silver-gray suit with a pleated jacket and high-heeled shoes, but even with the heels she can't be more than five foot three or four.

Her name is Jane Carroll, and she is the district attorney for Westchester County, which makes her my boss. I've often wondered if she's had a face-lift since the skin across her forehead, cheekbones, and beneath her eyes seems a size too small for her head which seems a size too large for her body. Lift or not, she looks older than her forty-six years. There's a hardness to her features—nothing feminine or giving about Jane Carroll—she's all take, and even though I know she's done a lot of charity work during her career and that she's been given awards by Women Against Domestic Violence and the Blythedale Children's Hospital, the truth is I've never liked her. She seems, to me, ambitious in the extreme. She wants to be a star, and her professional life is an ulterior motive.

Morgan James is right behind her. His foot must be hurting because he's limping. It's an old and famous injury, at least around the Richard A. Daronco Courthouse Building in White Plains, which is where he works when he's not in the field. His foot was broken by a Cadillac hearse, or more specifically, by the front tire of the vehicle running over it. Morgan nailed the driver, but the guy he wanted, an aspiring rap artist by the name of China White with a sideline dealing crack cocaine, jumped out of the back and ran. Morgan, busted foot and all, attempted a pursuit and nearly wound up a cripple. The rapper got away.

About a year later, he heard China White's first song on the radio. "Busted by the heat, took to the street, fast on my feet, no time for retreat—"

It was a hit.

Morgan looks like an African king. He's six-foot-four, which means Jane Carroll's head just about reaches the armpit of his white-cotton shirt, and his features are strong: full lips, a wide, flattish nose, big white teeth, and dark green eyes. Today, his skin looks ebony. It gets lighter in the winter, but in the sun he goes this color. I never knew that black people got tanned before I met Morgan, but then I've never had a close friend who was African-American before him. The friendship wasn't instant. It took a few months working together for me to see that he was a stand-up guy, no bullshit about him, and loyal to the end.

It was Morgan James who first suspected that I was using. It was about two months ago, during one of our prearranged meetings. He asked me, straight out. "Jack, you're fucked up, aren't you?"

I denied it, but when you're doing speed the eyes don't lie.

"I'm pulling you out of this," he vowed. He was concerned, like any good friend would have been. He put my health, and my ability to function properly, above the bust.

It was Jane Carroll who kept me in. Raymond Sasso had become her personal obsession. A dirty little hoodlum, that's what she called him. He'd wiped the floor with her predecessor, walking away clean from two previous trials. To Ms. Carroll, I was expendable. "We'll get a state guy in there to cover him," she said, and along came Barfoot.

Now as I look at them, it is as if all my senses have been heightened. I can smell her scent, sweet and heavy, and I can see what looks like a halo growing from the top of her head.

That's the thing that really grabs my attention. This mushrooming flower of thick yellow and red, mostly red.

Morgan has a halo, too, but his is primarily orange. I want to say something about it to them, but I control myself. There's no need to let them in on what's happening to me. It must be another hallucination.

"Hey, man." That's all Morgan manages. He looks worried, and his eyes are riveted on my turban. He clears his throat. "Glad you made it."

"Yeah, well, that was thanks to you," I say. I want to tell him that I watched while he banged away on my chest, saw him cry when I died. I want to tell him these things, but I'll save them for later, when the time is right and fire head isn't around.

Jane Carroll switches on the overhead lights, then says, "I hope you don't mind," after I'm suitably bathed in their fluorescent glow. It ends the halo effect. Now I see everything in sickly yellow.

"Jack, we need to talk," she announces. Leaving out any formalities, like how are you feeling, or isn't it amazing that you were brought in here a DOA and here you are, with a bullet in your brain, talking shop.

"Very seriously," she adds, as if I might be trifling with the importance of her visit.

I hear what sounds like a groan come from Morgan, which is stifled midway by a stony glance from Ms. Carroll.

She continues, arms folded across the front of her silk-pleated chest, like she needs to protect something. "Your doctor has explained that we have to be brief, but we really do need to talk. Look, bottom line, it's important that we're perfectly clear about a few things before anybody else comes in here to interview you or before you make any kind of a statement, to anyone."

I look up at Morgan. He shrugs his shoulders, and says, "Sorry, bro."

I'm about to lose my job. That's my first thought. My second thought is that I don't care. It's over for me, anyway. I blew it. I'm guilty. I was weak, and it nearly cost me my life. I deserve to be fired. That knowledge gives me a hidden strength. Jane Carroll isn't going to cause me any more pain than I have already caused myself. She's guilty, too, of greed and ambition. In fact she looks silly right now, the shoulders of her jacket slightly padded and too squared, with her jaw set as if she's about to be cast in plaster. She looks all puffed up, like a blowfish, trying to intimidate me with her importance. The problem, for her, is that my priorities have gone through a drastic shift since I was shot. Carolyn and Jade are what matter to me. Jane Caroll is no longer high on my list, so let her do what she's got to do. I'm ready.

She begins. "Because of you, Jack, our team pulled off a first-rate takedown. We all owe you a great debt of thanks." She hesitates, studying my reaction, while cracking her lips in a well-tutored smile. She holds it as if waiting for the flash of a camera.

"You are a courageous and dedicated man," she adds, speaking through clenched teeth.

First-rate? Courageous? What's she talking about? Thanks to me, the takedown was a fucking disaster. I blew it. My stomach contracts as I perform a semi-sit-up, rising just enough against my pillow to meet her eyes. Waiting for the punch line.

Her smile fades, her eyes home in on mine. Here it comes. "With the hard evidence that we've got—"

What hard evidence? There was no hard evidence, unless she's talking about the spare mag for my S&W that Ray threw at me before he began to walk.

Now that she's got my full attention, she continues, "Two kilo weights of methamphetamine should be adequate to keep Mr. Sasso inside for the next fifteen years."

Morgan looks at me and shakes his head. It's a subtle movement, sort of a warning, a keep-your-mouth-shut kind of warning.

"Mr. Sipriani is prepared to corroborate your testimony that an exchange took place, so we should have a fairly open-and-shut case," she adds.

So far I haven't said a word. I'm too shocked to open my mouth, actually questioning myself as to what did happen. One thing that did not happen was two kilos of meth. Still, Jane Carroll is an A-type citizen, full of the public good and charitable donations. She can't be meaning what I think she's meaning.

Finally, I say, "There was no exchange." I feel weak as I say it, too weak to fight.

She contradicts me. "Yes, there was." I see the flames flicker in her eyes.

I look at Morgan James for support. In the time I've known him I've never seen him bend the law, let alone break it.

He doesn't meet my eyes, saying, "The department has two kilos of product in the evidence room." His tone is noncommittal.

I know, and he knows, that he's just told me that we're setting Ray up.

I look at him and shake my head, not quite believing this is happening.

"Morgan, what are you asking me to do?"

Jane Carroll tightens her arms against her chest, really flexing. Her nostrils flare as she inhales the situation, looking at me as if she can't believe that I could be voicing such a question.

"We're asking you to finish your job," she says.

I think of Ray, on his knees, getting the shit beat out of him. Then I remember myself in the same position and Ray stepping in to save me.

"There was no exchange and, to the best of my knowledge, there was no product," I repeat. "Ray Sasso walked away clean. That's what happened. I fucked up, and I'm sorry but that's what happened."

Her voice slows down as if maybe we're not speaking the same language, and she wants to make certain that I understand her.

"Officer Lamb, we have the product in our possession. It is top-grade crystal methamphetamine, enough to cause a great deal of damage to a great many people. And you are going to testify that you watched that amphetamine exchanged by Mr. Sasso for ninety thousand dollars in used bills with Mr. Sipriani. Then your job will complete."

"Are you so desperate for Ray Sasso that you've got to set him up?" I ask, looking at Morgan. "Come on, man, you know this is not right."

Jane Carroll is hanging on like a pit bull. "No," she answers. "What's not right is you. You are an officer of the law, and yet you seem to be having a conflict of loyalty."

"No," I argue. "It's a conflict of truth."

She turns to Morgan James.

"Will you give us a minute alone, please." It's an order, not a request.

In the middle of all this, I start to see the colors swirling round her head, coming back like a display of fireworks. Everything is red, like hair extensions, teased straight up. I can't help but stare. Her colors seem to correlate to her mood, and my gut tells me it's anger.

Morgan notices that I appear in some kind of distress. He walks a couple of steps closer to where I am lying.

"You okay, Jack?"

I notice how bad he's limping. He is truly lame, which must be a reflection of his state of mind. His face looks haggard, like he's been too long without sleep. I feel sorry for him, because he seems too weak to fight, and he's about to be smacked.

"Mr. James, will you please leave the room."

He turns and glares at her.

That's when I cut in, "Morgan?"

He arches his eyebrows as he looks back at me. "Did you break Barfoot's nose?" I continue.

My question seems to blindside him.

"What?"

"Back in the warehouse in Mount Vernon. You backhanded him. It was a pretty good shot. Did you break his nose?"

Morgan's skin drains of color. He looks as close to white as he ever will. As if he's looking at a ghost.

"How the fuck did you know that?" he asks.

"I was there," I answer.

Hallucination? No, I don't think so. I feel relief and confusion at the same time.

His voice wavers. "You were unconscious, staring straight up at the ceiling." He stops talking and looks at me harder. "You were gone." Then, using the word he has been avoiding, "You were dead—"

Jane Carroll, who doesn't have a clue as to what we're talking about, and couldn't care less, is getting meaner by the moment.

She steps between us, right in Morgan's face.

"That's enough," she declares.

Morgan stays with me long enough to ask once more, "How the hell did you know about Barfoot?"

Jane Carroll's voice is sharp and nasty. "Leave this room now, Mr. James."

He starts walking, stops, turns, and looks at me with a crooked smile.

"Yeah, I broke it."

At that point Jane Carroll makes a sound that resembles a growl, and Morgan is out the door.

It clicks shut as she turns on me, lining me up with her small, mean eyes, proclaiming, "Raymond Elliot Sasso is a hoodlum who heads a conspiracy of organized crime."

I don't argue.

"I want him locked up, and I am going to see it done."

Still no protest from me.

"You are going to sign an affidavit that states that Raymond Sasso sold James Sipriani two kilograms of methamphetamine and that you witnessed tills exchange. If you are able you will also testify against him in a court of law. That is your duty as an officer of the state."

As her voice intensifies I'm fixated by the red streams of light that are literally exploding from her head. It is anger that I see, rising. I'm convinced of it. I remain silent, sensing danger.

"Mr. Sasso is going to walk free again unless you do as you are told."

Finally, I answer, "I'm not going to lie."

Her anger rises to lap against the ceiling.

"Then, Officer Lamb, you are going to be charged with committing a felony. You'll go to jail, seven years at least, more if I can arrange it." There is no bluff to her voice. It's as cold as her eyes. "At the time of your admission to this hospital your blood levels showed a substantial quantity of amphetamine. You were using drugs at the time of the takedown. How many lives did you compromise?" She hesitates, letting her words permeate the atmosphere of the room. "I also have it on record, corroborated with the testimony of a state police officer who was also working on this case, that you purchased amphetamine drugs from members of the Sons of Fire Motorcycle Club." She stops again. "This will all stick in court, Officer Lamb, be sure of it. You'll go to prison, and Mr. James, your supervisor, will lose his job."

I am no longer staring at her anger; I'm right inside it, engulfed by it.

"It's either that or a commendation for valor. You decide," she says, then concludes with, "I mean every word that I say."

I hold her eyes. There is nothing inside them but pure intent, all of it bad. I don't want to go to jail. I don't want to compromise Morgan's position. Above all, I don't want to lose my family. It's a terrible, lonely feeling and only ends when I shut my eyes, blocking it out. In my mind, I see the playground. I see my daughter Jade, sliding down that blue board, into the darkness, gone.

When I open them again, Jane Carroll is waiting. She looks very defined against the green wall, almost as if she has been cut out of cardboard and stuck at the end of my bed. There is no more anger, no more heat, now everything around us is ice-cold.

"Will Raymond Sasso make bail?" I ask.

"There won't be any bail. With his priors and his associations, I'll prove risk of flight," she answers. "The next stop for Mr. Sasso is up the river."

She means Sing Sing, located upstate, in Ossining. Carved inside a rock quarry out of granite, it's an old prison, and one of the worst.

"Does he know I have a family?" I ask.

She knows she's winning, so she offers me the deal closer. "He doesn't even know your real name."

"Okay. Then this is what I want. I believe you'll find my wife and child in the hospital cafeteria. Get them away from here right now, take them back to where they live, in a plain car. I don't want them in this room or near this hospital. I don't want them close to anyone who looks like a cop, and when this is all over I want to join them and never see or hear from you again."

"Agreed," she says, extending her hand. I reach out and touch it. Her fingers feel long and bony and transmit the coldness up my arm and into my body. I sit frozen in front of her.

"Thank you, Charlie," she says, her tone sarcastic, smiling her victor's smile, which is self-satisfied and, for a change, unrehearsed.

Charlie Wolf. I feel him with me in the room. He's a liar and a coward. I feel him inside my own skin.

Finally, I break the connection by asking her to leave.

~ 14 ~

LYING AWAKE. CAN'T SLEEP. Telling myself that's it's always like this after a takedown, with the doubts and the self-analysis, when the façade is dropped and the adrenaline stops pumping, but that's bullshit. It has never been like this. I have never used drugs before, never been ordered to perjure myself, never been threatened by my employer. And I have never died and come back.

What if I had kept going? What if I had joined Robert in the sea?

Robert, with the blond, surfer looks and the street smarts, the older brother I talked to when I needed to make a hard decision or was confused.

I close my eyes and think of him, the last time I saw his face. He was lying on a gurney in the morgue of Stony Brook Hospital, with an ugly gash running from his right ear to his Adam's apple, mugged for a hundred bucks and a Visa card in Riverhead, New York. His skin was nearly blue. The memory carries an overwhelming sadness. Then I recall another face. It's coffee-colored and pretty, marred only by the scar from a Stanley knife, running like a worm along the length of its left cheek, through its upper lip. Smiling a fuck-you smile as it walks past me, up the aisle and out of the courthouse, free on a technicality. The face belongs to Bramwell Coker, crack head and street-corner dealer, the man who killed my brother. It was Coker who inspired me to become a cop. I wore a uniform for five years before making it to detective. Biding my time. Long enough for Coker to graduate from the street corner to the lowlife bar and nightclub circuit.

I was good undercover. Pretending to be a weekender, down from the City, slumming it, out for some music and some action. With my short hair under a baseball cap, designer shades, and a three-day stubble of beard, I looked the part.

Coker's last transaction took place in an alley, in the back of a club called the 24-7. I handed him 180 bucks in twenties, and he handed me a brown paper rap about the size of a postage stamp. I opened it and looked inside.

"This isn't even half a gram," I complained. Then I dipped the tip of my index finger in and touched it to my tongue. "And it isn't cocaine, it's baby laxative."

I felt his eyes burn into mine. His pupils were already dilated, so I figured he was using anyway, and my impersonation of big-city arrogance just added fuel to his fire.

My finale was to tip the rap, letting the white powder spill to the ground.

"Fuck you," I said. "Give me my money back."
That did it.

The Butterfly knife came round from behind him, both blades dropping to lock in the middle, but by that time I already had my gun in my hand.

The first 9 mm round caught him in the left shoulder and sent him back against the wall. While he was staring at me, half in shock, I told him I was a cop. The next blew away a piece of his pant leg, leaving the material smoking and a messy hole in his right kneecap.

He hit the pavement squealing, about lawyers and doctors and how much it was going to cost the city to pay him back while I stood above him and said calmly, "Don't worry, I'll be your doctor."

That's when I introduced myself, talking about my brother, reminding him of the court case, all the while stepping down hard with the heel of my shoe, feeling the bones in his knife hand turn to mush as I slowly ground them into the concrete.

I read him his rights while we were waiting for the ambulance.

While Bramwell got fourteen years to convalesce in a New York jailhouse, I went on to become the star of the Narcotics Division, chalking up six more busts before I got headhunted by the DA's Office in Westchester County. Jane Carroll was in need of a fresh, unknown face. Someone with experience.

Neither Carolyn nor I knew what my new job would demand, the time away, the frustration, the danger, but more than any of that, the ability, like some form of controlled schizophrenia, to become someone else for a sustained period, a year at first, then two. And neither of us would have ever guessed that I'd start using.

***

My head has begun to ache, as if the pressure of my situation has all lodged in my right temple, like a toothache in my brain, a constant throbbing. I feel vulnerable and on edge. Even if I get through this and make it home, after so long undercover, what is it going to take to readjust to family life? I'm used to the deception, the danger, and the rush of adrenaline, not to mention the meth. About to press the buzzer for a nurse and ask for a painkiller when the door opens and two men in white pants and short-sleeved shirts enter the room. One of them is pushing a gurney.

"Just came to take you downstairs," the man behind the gurney explains.

The nametag above the pocket of his shirt reads Art Heller.

"Why?" I ask, suspiciously.

"A couple more tests," he replies.

I lie still as they disconnect my monitors and lift me onto the gurney. My drip bag comes with me for the ride.

***

The technician's domain is a large room with an elevated office at the rear and the CT scan machine looks like a squared white doughnut sitting in the center of the floor.

Art and his partner assist the tech in laying me out on the table, in front of the doughnut, where I'm fitted with a small cradle beneath my neck and soft straps to immobilize my head. Then everyone disappears, leaving me alone.

The table moves slightly, back and forth, as the machine makes a soft whirring sound.

Sometime later I'm out, back on the gurney, being wheeled down the corridor. I'm having another problem. Little blackouts. For instance, I don't remember who took me off the table and how I got back onto the gurney.

I nod off to sleep during the EEG, with wires attached to my skull, "to measure the electrical activity in your brain," the technician informs me as he detaches his electrodes.

I can't remember the ride back to the room.

~ 15 ~

TIME-WISE, I AM BECOMING disoriented. My
sleep is sporadic. I know I promised to call Carolyn
and Jade but that was before the visit from Morgan
James and Jane Carroll, which I believe was early this
morning. Jane Carroll promised to get my family out of here,
so I assume that, by now they are safe back home. I trust her
to keep her end of the bargain. She needs me too much to
screw me.

My bedside clock reads 11:05 when I reach across and,
with considerable effort, pick up my room phone, get an
outside line, and begin to dial our home number. Midway
through my mind goes blank. I fumble with the phone and,
for a moment, I don't even know where I am. What's
happening to me? I struggle for composure, get a harness on
my fears, and try again, taking it slow, really concentrating.
My head has begun to ache again.

It rings five times before the answering machine catches
and I hear Carolyn's voice. Her message ends with, "Leave
your name and number at the tone." I don't, as if by
committing my voice to the answering machine I could put
them in jeopardy. I tell myself that they are in Montauk, out
shopping or at the playground and try again five minutes
later. Still nothing. So I call Morgan James at the courthouse
and get his machine, which tells me that it's 11: 15 on the
Fourth of July. It is my daughter's birthday, and I want to be
with her. I leave my name and put down the phone. I want to

make sure my family is safe. That's the best present I can give Jade. Ray Sasso has long arms, and he's got every reason to want to hurt me.

I'm still waiting for a return call from Morgan when Metzler walks in.

"Hello, Jack, how do you feel?"

He's calling me Jack now, assuming a familiarity that I don't share.

"I feel okay," I answer. "Except I'm experiencing some strange stuff that I would like to stop."

"Strange stuff?"

"Short blackouts, loss of memory, headaches."

"I understand," Metzler answers, checking the chart at the end of my bed.

"Plus I see halos."

That catches him off guard.

"Halos?"

"Around people's heads," I reply, breathing a few calming breaths as I study Metzler's, which is a real beauty, like a golden crown, decorated with emeralds.

He laughs. It's a tight, nervous little laugh.

"I'm being serious," I say.

His face straightens as his smile wilts.

"The first things you mentioned, the blackouts, the memory loss, the headaches are most likely symptomatic of your condition, but the halos, well, I've never encountered halos before," he replies.

"You don't believe me, do you?"

He considers my question a moment, then replies, "I think that, just like the Near Death Experience, you believe what you are telling me is the truth, but what is actually happening may be something else entirely."

"Hallucinations?"

"Your EEG showed some abnormal bursts of electrical activity in the right temporal lobe region of your brain. That would correspond with the location of the bullet. My hunch is that it's causing a rare form of epilepsy."

Epilepsy. The word lands on me with a deadening thud. I had a friend once who was epileptic. During an attack on the school playground, I watched as he accidentally bit off the finger of a teacher who was trying to prevent him from swallowing his tongue.

"I'm an epileptic?"

"No, not in the usual way. There are no grand-mal seizures with your condition. Right temporal lobe seizures are usually more psychological than physical. The temporal lobe transients, which is what we call the electrical activity, can trigger visions, voices, even experiences that can be misinterpreted as mystical."

He straightens up. It's the first time I notice how immaculately he is dressed. Howard Metzler is tall and slim, and his suit looks molded to his body, like a lightweight blue gabardine, giving him the appearance of having broad shoulders, tapering to a fine, slim waist. His shoes are like polished mahogany slippers.

He appears to brace himself before he speaks again, "We need to schedule you for surgery."

"But you said—"

He cuts me off. "Your CT scan showed an abscess at the bullet site. It's creating pressure on your brain. We need to drain the abscess, so while I'm in there, barring any complications, I'll try and take the bullet out, since it's obviously the bullet that's causing the abscess." He checks his watch, like he's in a hurry.

"When?" I ask.

He looks at me as he considers.

"Have you been having any other trouble in the last day or so, sweats, anything unusual?"

I study his head for a moment then let my eyes wander down along the line of his body. Something about his attitude rubs me the wrong way.

"I'm experiencing something unusual right now," I answer.

"I'm being serious, sir," Metzler retorts.

"Blue's a good color for you," I continue.

He looks annoyed.

"The main color in your halo is a yellow gold, and blue goes with it really well."

He glances at his watch impatiently while my eyes linger on a dark gray streak which seems to be coming up from his right shoulder like a ribbon of smoke.

"Everything looks good, except for your right shoulder."

I watch his eyes focus on me, as if it's the first time since he's entered the room that he's actually seen me.

"What do you mean?" he asks curiously.

"There's a streak of gray coming up from your shoulder. It's murky. Maybe something's wrong there."

"Like what?"

He sounds cautious, and I sense his fear instantly, feeling bad for having started this going. It was an ego thing. Now I can't pull out. I focus my mind.

"I don't know. It just doesn't look as vibrant as the colors around your head," I reply. "Have you been having trouble with your shoulder?"

He clears his throat, and answers, "Yes, in fact I'm going down in about fifteen minutes to have a biopsy done on a cyst."

Now I feel small. Metzler was nervous, not dismissive, and here I am frightening him to prove a point.

"I think you'll be okay," I say, trying to lighten my tone.

"How do you know that?" he asks. Our roles have reversed. He's the patient, and I'm the man who knows. I feel his vulnerability.

"I'm not sure, not exactly," I answer. "Certain colors seem to trigger certain feelings, like moods. Maybe it's intuition, but I don't think you're in any serious danger."

He stands, silently, looking at me for a few more seconds.

"I'm sorry," I apologize. "I didn't mean to take it that far. I just wanted you to believe me."

I watch him weigh his words carefully. "Your experiences could be caused by the increased electrical activity in your right temporal lobe, stimulated by the pressure from both the bullet and the abscess. We ... " He hesitates. "Western medicine is still speculating about the various functions of that region in the brain."

"Whatever's going on, it's scaring the hell out of me," I answer.

He shakes his head, and I see compassion in his eyes. Suddenly we are just two human beings, doing the best we can in a difficult situation.

"My biopsy shouldn't take long. The growth's not in a crucial area, and it's done with a local anesthetic. I should be fine in an hour. I'll get you down to OR as soon as I can after that," he promises. Reaching out, he places the tip of his index finger gently above the wound on my forehead, "I'll go in here and follow the track of the bullet, suck the abscess dry, then use a set of cupped forceps to pull it out. It is close to an artery, but I'm fairly confident I can do it." His voice is bare of arrogance or attitude.

The idea of surgery makes me very nervous, particularly when I've heard of brain surgery performed while the patient is conscious. I ask, "Will I be awake or asleep?"

"You'll get a neuroleptic anesthesia," Metzler answers. "You're not going to know a thing till it's all over. In fact, you may have a partial loss of memory."

That worries me again. "What do you mean by partial?"

"Brain circuitry is very complex, and when I go in after the bullet I may disturb certain areas that store memory. Your loss, if any, will be relatively short-term. For instance, you may not remember this conversation," he answers.

~ 16 ~

I LIE BACK AND TRY TO relax. Partial memory loss, that bothers me more than anything else, particularly now when I am just beginning to put the pieces of my recent past life together and almost making sense of it. It's like an amputation, a piece of my mind is going to go. But what is my alternative? I turn my head in the direction of my bedside table and check the display on the digital clock. It reads 4:05. They'll be in to prep me soon. In fact, I can hear voices now, outside the door.

A female voice. "The doctor does not want him under any stress."

Answered by another female voice, one that I know well. "We'll be brief."

The door opens.

"Hello, Jack," Jane Carroll says as she whisks into the room, followed by her assistant, Dwayne Dillman.

Her voice sounds a little more manicured than usual, but if I remember correctly, she is taking elocution lessons in preparation for her fifteen minutes of fame.

Contempt fills me. "What do you want?" I ask.

"The doctor tells me you'll be having surgery in a couple of hours."

"Yes," I reply.

"He says there may be a slight gap in your memory after that," she continues.

Her voice and no-nonsense demeanor have the effect of
a chiropractic adjustment to my mind. I snap into a defensive
attitude.

"I don't know about that," I answer.

"In any case, I want your signature now," she says. Mr.
Dillman will be the authorized witness."

Dillman nods in my direction. He's one of Jane Carroll's
sycophants, wearing a wide Regis Philbin tie in navy blue,
which matches his tiny halo, and a cheaper version of his
mentor's pin-striped suit.

"Hi, Jack, good luck this afternoon," he says without
actually lifting his eyes from the heels of the Ms. Carroll's
slingbacks. His face is youngish and could be attractive in a
soap-opera kind of way if he'd splash out for a chin implant.

I bypass him, directing my attention to our boss. "No."

She answers with equal sharpness. "You know the
alternative."

My head begins to throb.

"Why isn't Morgan here?" I ask, needing an ally.

"I've given Mr. James a few days off. He's been under a
lot of pressure," she answers. "Now, since time is of the
essence, we should get started."

Everything in me says that I should not do this, and all
of that is being squashed by the weight of what will happen if
I don't. My head feels like it's in a vise, being squeezed.

Dillman's voice adds to the tension. "Yes, we should get
started," he says, removing what appears to be a legal
document from his briefcase and a fancy gold fountain pen
from the inside pocket of his jacket.

"My memory is still fuzzy," I stall, as the assistant DA
plonks himself down in the chair to the side of my bed. His
socks are flesh-toned and as thin as tissue paper and as he
crosses his legs I notice that they go up only as high as his
ankles.

"In that case, it's probably a good idea to talk it through
a few times," Jane Carroll replies.

"Make sure everything's tickety-boo," Dillman adds with
a diplomatic smile. A couple of summers ago he spent two
weeks in London and came back calling the toilet the "loo"
and saying "tickety-boo."

I remain silent as Jane Carroll talks the case through. She describes the circumstantial evidence her office has accumulated in the past few years regarding Sasso's businesses, his drug-manufacturing labs, his distribution networks, and their supposition that, as with the biker clubs in the Midwest, most of Sasso's meth labs will be converted to the manufacture of Ecstasy, a more mainstream product, within the next two years. What she's got is basically a scenario of outlaws dealing to and with other outlaws, club rivalries for the control of territories and club muscle used against club muscle.

Finally, she arrives at my part in the fiasco, refreshing my memory as to my own reports, given to Morgan during the time I was working inside Speed Dream. Some of the stuff I remember and other things, the real incriminating things against Ray, I know she has fabricated. I never, in fact, witnessed any direct sales of narcotics by Ray to anyone. When I bought, I bought from a member of the club, in quantities of a gram or two. Hardly a heavy hit.

Then she gets to the actual takedown, and it's nowhere near the way it actually happened.

Dillman is making notes furiously about God know what, and Jane Carroll is recounting a series of fictitious events that she should try and sell the producers of NYPD Blue. During all of this she continues to refer to me as Charlie Wolf, which upsets me. I don't want to be Charlie Wolf. He's the weakness in me, the impostor. He's the bullet in my brain. The pressure inside my skull is building with each of her lies. I'm not going along with this, no way.

Finally, after recounting my heroic efforts to hang on to the hard evidence—which is a plastic-wrapped bag full of meth that was probably nabbed in a previous bust and has been languishing for a few years in a Westchester evidence room—while at the same time subduing Ralph Menzies and taking a stray bullet in the head, she stops and looks at me.

"Of course I've spoken with the commissioner and you will be cited for your valor," she concludes, sealing the deal with fifteen thousand dollars' worth of capped teeth, complimented by a halo the shade of ancient ivory.

Dillman puts down his pen and adds his Ultrabrite grin to the color spectrum.

I wonder how much he knows. Not much is my guess. Jane Carroll would keep all of this on a need-to-know basis, which includes me, Morgan James and Jimmy Sipriani, who planted the evidence. Dillman is an unknowing accomplice to a crime.

I stay with her eyes a few seconds before answering "But that's not the way it happened."

Carroll's face downshifts several gears, and her voice slips a notch.

"That is exactly as your reports to Morgan James read," she counters, looking quickly at Dillman, who is gathering the papers in his hand. She nods and he stands up and offers me the dummied reports.

"You'll notice that we have Mr. Sipriani's signature on the bottom of each document, along with the corresponding date," she continues.

I take them, look down the first page, note a few of the fictitious incidents she has described, and see Sipriani's scrawl. Knowing that he's a convicted felon, I also know that his word means nothing without mine.

She must notice that my smile is gone, replaced by a look of disgust that I share with her. Meanwhile, something is going on inside my head. The bullet feels like it's moving.

She continues. "What we are going to do is run over the events of the day of the third of July and see if we can't come up with a concise and accurate picture of what did transpire."

I want them both out of here, now.

"Do you understand what we need?" she adds, the sarcasm returning to her tone.

I reach for the nurse's call button as Jane Carroll continues to talk, with Dillman making alterations on whatever has already been printed on the legal paper. This time her rundown is more specific concerning the takedown, with exact times and actual dialogue between me, Ray, and Jimmy Sipriani.

I get the button in my hand, but can't seem to find the coordination to press it.

"I don't feel too good," I say.

She ignores me, her voice droning on mercilessly.

I force my voice up an octave. "Please leave!"

That stops the drone.

Jane Carroll glares at me as Dillman places his Mont Blanc down on top of the documents and looks up.

"Sign and we'll be gone," she answers, motioning with her hand to Dillman, who hands me the top three pages of the document before offering me the gold Mont Blanc. I see that D.J.D. has been monogrammed on the front of the clip. I see the pores in the skin of his hand, the tiny black hairs, coiled above the knuckle of his index finger. Everything is in amazing detail, like I'm looking through the lens of a microscope.

"No," I say.

"No?" Ms. Carroll challenges.

"Not going to sign," I mumble, feeling nauseous.

"I'd consider that decision very carefully if I were you," she replies tersely, red flashing like a warning light in the muted yellow around her head.

Dillman moves the pen closer to my right hand, until it touches the top joint of my index finger.

Jane Carroll's voice pushes me to the edge. "You are going to lose everything if you don't," she says. "Do you want to say good-bye to your wife and little girl?"

I grip the pen and line it up with the bottom of the page, watching the black ink begin to form the letters of my name. It looks like a kid's attempt at writing. I can't seem to focus my eyes. Everything is blurred as I continue to write, with the pain in my temple expanding to fill my entire head. Then something bursts, like a balloon filled with hot water, sending a flood of crimson into the sockets behind my eyes. I see the color red, nothing else. Everywhere is red and everything is pain, like an ice pick stabbing the side of my skull, over and over again, timed to the beat of my heart, quickening.

Buzzers and bleepers are going off all around me, someone shouts, "Get a doctor!" Then there are hands on my body. Lifting me up, ripping the gown away from my chest.

I'm above it all, outside my body, looking down, watching dispassionately. Jane Carroll and Dwayne Dillman are pushed aside as three nurses attempt to resuscitate me.

Metzler enters the room and rushes to my body, taking over the CPR.

I watch for another few seconds. Until my attention is drawn to a hole in the wall above my bed. It's opening, like a fissure in the green plaster, growing wider as it becomes a dark, swirling vortex, I am pulled toward it as if by gravity, then inside. At first it's pitch-black, and I'm very frightened, but as I travel deeper into this darkness I can see a light, small at first but growing brighter.

I am certain of only one thing, and *that* I know with every fiber of my being. I've got to reach that light.

~ 17 ~

SOMEONE IS SINGING. The man's voice is familiar, low and gravelly, and slightly out of tune.

The words of the song sound far away as if they are coming from behind a wall or from another room. I try hard to listen, but it's taking everything I've got to keep from drifting off and going back to sleep. The song is about the rain, the sun. Seeing clearly.

I open my eyes. The sun is red and it is directly in front of me. It looks huge through the window of the car like I'm climbing straight up to meet it.

The song continues. "Gonna' be a—"

"Morgan?"

He stops singing and turns his head, looking over his right shoulder into the backseat. He looks pleased to see me, and somewhat surprised.

"You're awake!"

I sit up straight. My head feels thick and heavy, as if I am coming round after a drugged sleep. I look around, trying to get my bearings. To my far right, the New York skyline cuts the blue sky like a page from one of my daughter's pop-up books. Jagged and one-dimensional, the Empire State Building looks surreal through the tinted side window of the old Chrysler New Yorker. Below us, the water is a steel gray sheet.

"Where are we?" I ask, completely confused.

"Going over the Throgs Neck Bridge," Morgan answers.

"Going where?"

Morgan answers. "Home."

"Home?" My voice sounds bewildered.

"Back to Carolyn and Jade," Morgan says, as we come down the far lope of the bridge and take a right onto the connecting road for the Long Island Expressway.

I try to remember something, anything, like where I was before, how I got into this car, what day it is, but everything is tangled, and my thoughts are without formation or sequence. I see flashes of the beach and images of Carolyn in a blue-knit top and Jade in a yellow dress.

The right side of my head is throbbing.

"I'm in trouble," I say.

I see Morgan's eyes in the rearview mirror. They look soft and concerned as he meets my blank gaze.

"What kind of trouble?"

I feel like I've awakened in the middle of a dream and can't get my bearings. I'm lost inside the moment, without a past or future.

"How did I get here?" I ask.

His voice is calm and patient. "You phoned me from the hospital, told me you were checking yourself out and asked me to come and get you. A couple of orderlies pushed you out the door in a wheelchair. You stood up, thanked them, got into the backseat, stretched out, and went to sleep. Simple as that."

Hospital? I lower my head and reach up with both hands, resting my forehead in my palms, pressing in with the heels against my closed eyes, as if I can force the deadness from my brain. The fingers of my right hand rub against a swollen area of hardened skin, scabbed and sensitive to the touch. Beyond that my hair is a short burr. I run my hand over the stubble, as if it hides a clue.

"What the hell happened to me?" I ask.

Morgan answers. "You took a bullet, Jack."

I'm beginning to feel very frightened. There's a hollow space that once held my memory.

"A bullet?" I repeat, but even as I say the word I sense a stirring inside the space.

"Don't you remember?" Morgan continues. "Charlie Wolf. The takedown, Ray Sasso—"

Sasso. The name is a catalyst. I recall voices, like echoes in a cavern. "Down on the floor. Get down now! Down!" Images follow. I see men in combat pants and Kevlar vests, rushing toward me. Someone shouting. "10-13. Officer down!" Then the roar of a motorcycle.

At first I don't know if it's coming from inside my head, or outside, but I recognize the sound. I know this bike. The heavy beat from its exhaust seems to match the pulsing pain in my right temple.

I look up to see Morgan's eyes flash in the rearview mirror. Feeling a surge of adrenaline, I taste fear in my mouth. Then the roar is right on top of me. I look out the window to see the red and black Softail, ridden by a man with long dark hair. He turns and stares, eyebrows arching up as his eyes bore into mine. Raising his arm, he points his finger as if it's the barrel of a gun.

I see the ruby ring, gold and red, flashing in the sunlight. It's Ray Sasso.

"You almost died, Jack," Morgan continues.

I duck down below the window.

Morgan's voice is calm, and again it seems to be coming from another room. "Jack? You alright?"

No, I am not alright. I'm threatened and confused. I come up slowly, looking out the window. Unable to control the panic in my voice.

"What the hell is he doing out?"

"Who?"

"Ray Sasso," I state, pushing back against the seat, trying to make myself smaller. I feel like a target.

Now it's Morgan who sounds confused. "How did you know that?"

"Because I just saw him."

"Where?" he asks.

"Right beside us, on a bike," I answer.

He laughs as if he's relieved and smiles his answer. "No, Jack. That's impossible."

"You must have seen him. He was right beside us," I insist.

Morgan's voice seems to amplify in volume as my doubts increase. "Ray Sasso is in the County Medical Center, in intensive care. Somebody stuck a Plexiglas shiv through his left lung."

"But—"

"Happened in Valhalla. Word is it was an interclub contract. Some people didn't appreciate him letting a cop get as close as you did. He broke a few rules—"

A cop? I'm a cop, undercover. My name is Charlie Wolf. More is coming back, like pieces of a jigsaw puzzle, with sharp jagged edges. Lying in the street while Ray hauls Menzies and Walker off me. Smelling the whiskey on Ray's breath. I smell it now, like he's right beside me in the car.

Morgan continues. "Those guys don't want a drug trial. The publicity would cripple them. Last time it happened they couldn't wear their colors on the street without a bust."

As I stare at the back of Morgan's head, I begin to see colors again, blue, yellow, and green, one layered against the other in a vaporous mist, filling the space between the crown of his head and the roof of the car. The colors trigger a new memory, of a man in wire-rimmed glasses, a tailored suit, and high-polished shoes, promising me that when he takes the bullet out all this stuff will go away. Howard Metzler, that's his name, and I'm furious with him.

Finally, I say, "My mind is a mess. I saw Ray Sasso as clear as I'm seeing you now. I don't know what's going on. I've got no memory of phoning you. No memory of getting into this car. Everything's mixed up. It's not supposed to be this way. Metzler told me that once the bullet was out I'd be back to normal. I don't get it."

"This is normal," Morgan answers. "You've been pumped full of drugs: antibiotics, sedatives, you name it. You've been out of it most of the time. Your memory is not going to come back all at once, it's going to be ragged at first, the chemicals take a while to clear your system." He hesitates, and I can feel him building up for something, bracing himself.

Then it comes. "Jack, they couldn't get to the bullet. It's still inside your head."

His tone is soft, but his words land hard, forcing me down against the seat.

"Why?" I whisper.

"Something happened just before surgery, some kind of internal trauma, there were complications, and they didn't want to risk it. As it is, the doctor didn't want you to leave the hospital but you insisted, and Jane Carroll pulled some strings to get you out against medical advice. I don't think having you there looked too good for her case against—"

"Did I sign that bullshit affidavit?" I ask, recalling her threats.

"I wouldn't worry about it," Morgan answers.

His remark antagonizes me.

"Why?" I feel like a child, always asking the same question, needing answers.

"Won't matter with Sasso dead."

"He's not going to die," I snap back. "Ray's tough. He'll live. "

"I doubt it," Morgan answers quietly.

That's when the guilt hits. I created this situation. I'm responsible. Out of my mind on meth, out of control. Charlie Wolf, Jack Lamb, one's as good as the other. I bury my head in my hands.

Morgan checks me out in the rearview, crosses lanes and slows down, like he's looking for an exit ramp.

"You're not ready for this," he says . "I'm taking you back to the hospital."

I think of Carolyn and Jade.

"No, don't do that; I'll be okay. Keep driving."

"I'm worried about you," he insists.

"I'll be fine," I promise. More than anything else, I want to see my family.

He reaches back and hands me a brown vial. "These may help."

I look at the script on the side of the plastic container, advising two tablets twice a day with food, to control episodes.

"What are they?" I ask.

"From Doctor Metzler, I think they're some kind of anti-psychotic," Morgan answers. "Just in case."

I look at the label again. It says Respiradol. I'm probably full of this stuff right now, mixed like a cocktail with all the other crap in my system. That has to be why my mind is so disjointed, the reason I woke up like a zombie.

"No thanks," I answer flatly, pocketing the bottle. "I'd rather go cold turkey and try to remember the last few—" I stop. "How long has it been? How many days?"

"A week since you were shot," Morgan answers.

"Seven days ... Jesus, it's nothing but a blur," I say.

After that our conversation lapses into silence as, mentally, I attempt to put the pieces of my life back together. I keep telling myself that I'm going home, back to my wife and daughter where I can recover and put all this behind me. Then I look down and see the oil and grease stains on the legs of my jeans, reminders of my life working for Ray. The denim's been washed, but the dark stains are permanent, indelible reminders of who I was and what I've done. Then I feel the bullet, pulsing in my temple, and know that Charlie Wolf is alive, inside me, with his weaknesses and fears, looking for a way to ease his burden. I feel his guilt and cowardice as I pass beyond the thin veil that hides the hope that Ray Sasso will die and I'll be off the hook.

I am craving a line of meth to make me whole again.

I am desperate to be with my wife and daughter.

I am unclear, at this moment, whether it is Charlie Wolf or Jack Lamb who is making this journey home.

~ 18 ~

OUTSIDE THE WINDOWS OF the New Yorker the landscape is lush from the summer rains and full with pine trees and shrubs. Everything is vivid green as we roll along at a steady seventy miles an hour, the car's suspension cushioning the rises and falls in the old highway, lulling me to the edge of sleep. I feel hypnotized, watching the road as the exit signs pass by Ronkonkoma, Stony Brook, and a trepidation as to what lies ahead, going back to a wife and daughter I hardly know anymore.

An hour ago I was without a memory, now I'm surrounded by the ghosts of my past.

There is a teaching hospital in Stony Brook. It was built in the late sixties; I suppose it looked modern then, with its twin black towers, each eleven stories high, loaded with glass windows, joined in the middle by a walkway and supported by giant steel girders, but to me it will always look dark and foreboding. It was in that hospital that I last laid eyes on my brother, when I went to identify his body for the coroner's report. And it was there, a year later, that I saw my mother for the final time. She had become a resident patient in the Towers, which is a nickname for Stony Brook's psychiatric facility. I saw her but I've never been certain whether or not she saw me. After my brother's death, which was followed shortly by my father's suicide, my mother sank into a depression so deep that even electroconvulsive shock couldn't budge it. There was a darkness in her eyes that

spread through the limbs of her body and settled on her soul.
No drug and no psychiatrist could reach that far down, and
by the time of her death, of a massive coronary, she had not
spoken a word or acknowledged the presence of another
person in over a year.

I believe that my mother willed her heart to stop beating.

Some families seem cursed, and until Carolyn I felt that
mine was, too.

***

Route 27 narrows to two lanes east of Hampton Bays. I had
forgotten what the traffic's like this time of year, but an hour
covering the five miles between Southampton College and
the town of Southampton brings it all back home.

Since I learned that I've still got a bullet lodged in my
brain, the conversation between me and Morgan has been
thin to non-existent, but then again, I've had my eyes closed
for a lot of this trip, purposefully keeping a distance between
us. I don't want to be reminded of what I've done, or who
I've been.

Finally, he glances back at me and asks if I'd mind
listening to the radio.

"Not at all," I answer, realizing that he probably feels as
awkward as I do.

He hits the button and Jimi Hendrix fills the gap that
divides us.

The song triggers another flash of memory. The last time
I heard it I was standing in Ray Sasso's shop, wired on meth
and contemplating putting a bullet in Axle Barfoot's head.
Fifteen minutes later, he put one in mine.

"Too much confusion—" Hendrix continues.

That's an understatement.

As Morgan rolls through Amagansett, Stephen
Talkhouse is on our left. It's a shingled two-story building
that looks more like a barn than a nightclub. I met Carolyn in
the Talkhouse, on one of the nights that bluesman Taj Mahal
was playing in town. I was on my own, and she was with a
friend. I spotted her at the bar—actually I spotted her friend

first, a stringy blond, more my type than Carolyn, who was dark, curvy, and less obvious. I made my way to them between sets and tried to start a conversation, which went nowhere with the blonde, leaving me standing in front of them with nothing to say. About to make an embarrassed retreat when Carolyn asked me what type of motorcycle I was riding. It was the first time she'd spoken, and her voice had a certain ring, like she was singing even when she spoke. I was amazed she knew I was on a bike at all, till I remembered that I was holding my helmet in my right hand. We ended up on the sidewalk, looking at the Shovelhead, which I had just polished and which seemed to sparkle underneath the streetlights. She told me that she'd spent a week one summer, on the back of a boyfriend's Harley Electraglide, riding through the Black Forest in Germany. I asked her if she wanted to go for a ride on the Shovel, and we agreed that I'd pick her up at her family's house in Bridgehampton the next morning, on my day off.

It was a big, stucco house, in an expensive neighborhood, south of the highway, a block from the ocean. She was visiting, on her summer break from teaching a special ed class for hyperactive kids in a suburb of Boston. She was also on the tail end of a divorce and got a kick out of the fact that I was a detective and carried a gun. She joked that she should hire me to protect her from her ex-husband, a boozy philosophy professor with an eye for his female students. I remember being relieved to hear that there had been no children in her marriage, although I wasn't sure at the time why it mattered.

I spent a lot of days in Boston the following year. I watched Carolyn teach a few times, and gained a lot of respect for the difficulty of her job and the way she handled it. She loved those twelve kids and projected that love to them, even when they were acting up, shouting and fighting, or screaming uncontrollably. She had patience, which I sometimes lacked, and I was straight and honest, which, after her failed marriage was something she needed. We were a good balance for each other and, from the start, we both knew it could be serious. Still, it was only after Carolyn became pregnant with Jade that we decided to buy the house in Montauk.

"How do you know your way so well?" I ask, breaking another long silence.

"I've been out here a couple of times in the summer," Morgan answers. "It's just a straight line from New York, really."

"I guess so," I agree; it's a straight line to another world.

I feel safer now, as if the life I lived for the past years and the characters in it have no place out here. From this perspective they seem like dinosaurs, stampeding down the asphalt and alleyways of a much less civilized world. This is a world where a million bucks buys into a different kind of club than the Sons of Fire. People here spend as much on a line of evergreen trees to ensure that their neighbors don't see them lounging naked beside the swimming pool as most people in America earn in a year. This is the land of designer sunglasses and baseball hats, where the ATM machine at the local bank dispenses hundred-dollar bills instead of tens and twenties, and the Mercedes SUV is the family car; the Harley is reserved for a quick sprint to the Clam Bar on weekends. This is a place of invisible gates, most of them locked.

Being a local, and raised in a working-class family in Montauk, I resented the rich when I was growing up. They'd come and take over, spoiling the tranquility with their loud voices and their excesses. Driving the prices up on everything from a quart of milk to an acre of land, but on this day I'm glad the place is barricaded by money. It reinforces the feeling that the demons that are chasing me won't catch up.

Another few miles, and the highway divides, with the Old Montauk Highway running off to the right, along the beach, and the new highway continuing straight and climbing to a thousand feet above the sea.

Morgan stays with the new road, and, as we get to the overlook, I can see the ocean on my right and Napeague Bay behind us to the left. The sun has just broken through a bank of clouds, sending a shower of silver light down on the sparkling blue water. Everything looks like a postcard in 3-D.

We come down from the rise, following the road to the right, and Montauk sits directly ahead of us. The town was developed back in the 1930s by Carl Fisher, the man who built the bridge that linked Miami Beach to the Florida mainland. He envisioned Montauk as the Miami Beach of the North and got as far as building a boardwalk before he lost his shirt and died broke and disillusioned.

Today, with its neon-lit motels, delis, and fisherman's bars, Montauk is as close as the east end of Long Island comes to a blue-collar resort. Low and flat, about a quarter mile long from end to end, it's a different world than the manicured lawns, cappuccino parlors, and overpriced stores that line the rest of the Hamptons.

I'm excited now. My wife and daughter are so close I can feel them and, just for the moment, that's the only thing on my mind.

Except the pain. It has come back, like a dull ache in the side of my head.

We arrive at the traffic circle at the end of town. Over my left shoulder I can see the White Elephant, which is what the locals call the four-story redbrick apartment building that sits on the west side of the circle. It was the last thing that Fisher built, a stone's throw from my home.

I could hold my breath for the distance remaining between me and the people I love. I am both longing to see them and frightened of it at the same time.

We are approaching Edison Street when I begin to smell something. It's fresh and sweet, like new green apples. I look around but can't find the source of the aroma.

There's the old schoolhouse on the corner, with what looks like a children's playground in the front of it. I can't remember the playground, not from when I lived here anyway. It must be new, something constructed in the past year or so. Then I notice that the temperature inside the car has dropped. Suddenly it's cold.

"Did you just turn up the air-conditioning?" I ask.

"No," Morgan replies, but his voice sounds sullen and far away while his breath forms a white mist as it leaves his mouth.

Shivering, I wrap my arms across my chest, staring at the back of his head. I know he's done something with the air-conditioning. The cold seems to affect my injury, like it's freezing the bullet, making it burn inside my head. The dull ache has become a hot, stabbing pain. I slide across the seat and find the button that controls the window, then try to move it to the open position. It's locked.

The smell of apples permeates the car.

Something catches my eye from beyond the glass. It's the blue sliding board, right in the center of the playground, beside the red merry-go-round and green-plastic swings.

The car slows to a crawl, until everything is going by in slow motion, without sound, as if we have entered a vacuum, and I am staring out the window, at a place inside my mind. This is the place I first saw in the hospital. I recall Jade's voice.

"Daddy, you're hurting me."

The car is moving so slowly that we are almost standing still. The sweet smell is suffocating.

"What's going on?" I gasp, but my voice feels trapped inside my throat. I can hear the words in my head but can't project them.

Morgan doesn't move.

"Answer me!"

I'm falling. Through a trapdoor, into the black.

~ 19 ~

THERE'S STATIC, LOUD AND grating, followed by a garbled voice, its words high and disjointed.

Concentrate, I tell myself, willing my mind to focus on the voice.

It's a woman's voice. Her words become dear as I listen. She's talking about rain, wind conditions and the West Nile mosquito virus.

Where am I?

Look out the window. We are at the other end of the block, past the schoolhouse and the playground. The smell is gone, and the New Yorker is cool and comfortable moving at a normal speed, and Morgan is twiddling with the knob on the radio. Landing on another woman's voice, this one singing about having dreams and visions.

Then the words break up and turn to babble in the air.

"I can't believe this," Morgan says. "Ninety-six-point-seven ... That's a local station. I shouldn't be losing the signal."

I dig into my pocket, getting a grip on the brown bottle of Respiradol. It feels like a safety net beneath me.

Please God, make this stuff stop. I pray. Don't let me be crazy.

Then, as if in answer, I recognize the voice as Tracy Chapman's as it fills the car, and I release my hold on the bottle containing the drug.

"Number 83, off the highway. Is this it?" Morgan asks.

"Yes," I reply. "This is it."

I'm way beyond asking him what happened back along the road. There's no point. I know this is all going on inside my head. It's my bad trip. Fucking bullet. It's got to be the bullet.

As we go down the long gravel drive and approach the two-story, cedar-shingled house, Morgan hits the button on the radio and, inside, the car goes quiet. Outside, I can hear the tires grinding against the loose stones. I can feel the same grinding in my gut.

My nerves are frayed and raw.

The shingles on the ocean side have turned dark from weather and age, and the house looms large and imposing.

Can't go home like this. I'm not right. This isn't right. That's what I'm thinking when Carolyn and Jade walk from the front door and down the wooden steps that lead to the driveway.

Carolyn is wearing a loose pullover, denim shorts, and sandals, and Jade is in a pair of jeans and a white T-shirt. Her feet are tanned and bare. They both appear to be bathed in a haze of white-and-violet light, surrounding them like a beautiful cocoon. The light is pure and good, but I also feel a sadness associated with it.

I stare from the window until the cocoon dissipates with the light from the sun, vanishing like a mist, and my anxiety is washed away by the joy I feel in seeing them.

Out of the car, it feels like I'm walking in a dream. Hugging Carolyn, kissing her, looking down at Jade. She's tentative, and I'm stalling. I don't want to touch her. She seems uneasy with me, and I'm frightened. Terrified that whatever premonitions I'm having will return.

Carolyn senses the impasse.

"Jade, give Daddy a big hug, go ahead."

I'm standing straight up and rigid, looking down into my daughter's blue eyes, wearing what feels like a mask, not a face. My smile is frozen. I've got to touch her. I cannot allow this craziness to keep me from connecting with her.

Morgan and Carolyn are staring at me. It's obvious that I'm having a problem.

Jade extends her arms.

Forcing the words from my mouth, I say, "I just can't believe how beautiful you are." Bending down, I cradle her in my arms, lifting her to me. Her body relaxes as a familiar scent drifts up, filling my nostrils.

"That smell, what is it?" I ask, telling myself that what's happening is a coincidence.

Carolyn doesn't seem to understand. "Her hair smells like apples," I say. Carolyn laughs.

"Oh that ... " she answers. "It's the Sesame Street shampoo. It is apples, but maybe a little on the sweet side."

"I took a bath today with Mama," Jade adds.

I feel the fear grip me and squeeze Jade tight to my body in reaction.

"Daddy, you're hurting me."

"Sorry, sorry," I say, setting her down. "I'm just happy to see you."

I feel Carolyn and Morgan watching me. I don't look right. I don't feel right. I cover by touching my daughter's head, saying softly, "It's good to be home."

We walk into the house.

The first thing I notice inside are the roses on the dining table. Long-stemmed and sitting in a big glass vase, there's a dozen of them in full bloom. They remind me of something. I don't know exactly what, but it's not good.

"Where did they come from?" I ask.

Carolyn looks puzzled.

"The roses, where did they come from?" I repeat.

"They arrived earlier this afternoon," Carolyn answers. "From Jane Carroll at the DA's Office."

"I don't want them in the house," I say.

"But—"

"Please, get rid of them."

After that, the atmosphere changes, becoming slightly awkward. Finally, Morgan says he needs to get back home, wishes us well, and leaves, while I excuse myself to go upstairs and rest on the bed. Trying to buy some time alone in order to get my head together. I feel a bit of a stranger here, and an unpleasant one at that.

My rest turns into a long, deep sleep. I wake up only once, and by then the house is dark and quiet and Carolyn is asleep beside me. I reach over and touch her arm. She stirs, and I take my hand away, not wanting to wake her. Then I lie for a while, with my eyes open, staring into the darkness, realizing that I am more frightened than I have ever been in my life. I have a bullet in my head. I don't even know why it's still there, but it makes me feel unclean, as if I have a malignancy. I feel small, unprotected, and guilty. I pray again; that's twice today that I've prayed. Twice more than I have since my mother used to haul me off to the church at the bottom of the hill, on the other side of the highway. A sense of peace comes with the end of the prayer, then I drift off into darkness.

~ 20 ~

I WAKE UP ALONE IN THE bed. The clock reads 11 AM and I hear Jade's voice coming from below me, floating up the stairs to ribbon its way into my room. She's singing, accompanied by what sounds like an accordion and a guitar. The song is the old classic, "You Are My Sunshine," and her voice is sweet. She's actually carrying the tune, which gives me a surge of pride. I lie still and listen, letting the little girl's voice fill my head. Close my eyes and her voice builds in volume until I'm immersed in it, lost inside my daughter's voice, as if it is the single thing in my universe. Until the accordion and guitar stop and I hear a click, abrupt, like a tape ending, and Jade stops singing, but I can still hear her, as if she's breathing deeply, close to me.

"Daddy, did you hear my song?"

"I loved it," I reply, opening my eyes.

Shocked, because I'm still alone in the room. Jade's not here. I heard her sing. I thought I heard her breathing, and speaking, but she's not here.

"Jade?" I call, but there is no answer. I must have been dreaming.

I get up and out of bed, still in the clothes I came home in yesterday. I guess Carolyn didn't want to risk waking me to get me undressed. Walking from the room, I go to the top of the stairs and listen. I hear them talking from below. Jade's voice is a sweet echo of her mother's. I have the strangest feeling. It's as if I'm not really here. I'm a ghost. I want to shout down to them. I want them to acknowledge my presence, to tell me I'm actually home, part of them again, connected. Then something else happens inside my head. It sounds like a click, like someone has just thrown a switch, turning the grid to my main power back on. Suddenly I'm alive, vibrating all over. I feel clear. Like I've just done a double line of crystal meth.

Jade arrives at the bottom of the stairs.

"Daddy did you hear my song?"

"'I loved it," I answer, consciously repeating my words from earlier and experiencing the most incredible sense of déjà vu.

Mama bought me a karaoke machine," she explains, as I walk down to meet her. "1 know all the songs."

Her halo is like a sunflower, bursting in shades of yellow-gold and green all around her head. She is absolutely radiant.

"Give me a hug," I say. "Please."

Jade raises her arms and I lift her to my chest. The warmth from her body seeps into mine, filling me with a new strength, a resolve to get well. After all the time that I have been away, half her life, she is so open, so accepting of my presence, I'm humbled. Each of these moments is like a new beginning, fresh and full. Holding her close, silently vowing to keep her safe from harm, forever, I carry her into the kitchen.

Carolyn looks surprised to see me.

"Are you strong enough to be out of bed?" she asks.

"I feel good," I reply, then add, jokingly, "better than I have in a long time."

She smiles cautiously. "You were asleep a long time. I called the hospital. They said it was good, that you should have all the rest you can get. Are you sure you want to be up?"

"I feel fine," I repeat.

Finally, Carolyn relaxes and stands back as if she's appraising me.

"You look much better," she confirms.

I smile. "Are you talking about my hair?"

"It's not a bad cut for you, kind of reminds me of Brad Pitt.

Well," she hesitates, studying me, while I wait for the catch. Carolyn's quick and she's got an acid wit. "Like he did in that final scene from *Fight Club*."

Fight Club was the last movie we saw together, and I recall commenting on Brad Pitt's face, or what was left of it, after he shot himself at the finale.

I laugh and reply, "Thanks," putting Jade down so that I can get to Carolyn. We kiss, and her mouth tastes sweet, like oatmeal and honey.

"Honestly," she says, "you do look much, much better."

"I feel it," I answer, thinking that it must be the drugs leaving my system. Then I think of the meth. The thought is quick, but it creates a pang, sudden and sharp, and the façade gives way, leaving Charlie Wolf staring at my wife and child. I sense danger, like a bomb about to explode.

"Sit down," she says.

Her voice creates normality and removes the threat.

"How does an omelet sound, and a sesame seed bagel with cream cheese, and milky coffee?"

I think about my medicine, upstairs in the pocket of my jeans. Take two twice a day with food. Then I tell myself I don't need them. I can beat this on my own.

"A lot better than a glucose drip," I answer.

***

Later in the afternoon, after lunch and another deep sleep, with Carolyn and Jade out food shopping, I call Morgan James, apologizing for yesterday and acting like an idiot about the roses, although I'm happy that they're gone. Then I thank him for the ride home, before asking him about Ray Sasso.

"He's in critical condition," he answers. "I don't think he's going to make it."

His words drag me back into the ugliness of my recent past.

My voice drops and flattens. "Where does that leave Jane Carroll?"

"She's critical, too," Morgan answers. "If she loses Sasso, she's lost her shot at the title. I think she's phoned the hospital more often than the guy's wife."

The mention of Ray's wife sends another wave of emotion crashing down. I remember Maureen, looking at us like we were two bad boys, while she cooked us pancakes and I played games with their son William, before he gave me the wooden soldier.

"Morgan, keep me posted, I want to know what happens to him."

"You got way too close to this guy, didn't you?"

Morgan phrases it like a question, but it sounds like he's scolding me and I resent it.

"He did me a favor once," I answer, my voice clipped. How's he supposed to know about me and Ray? He wasn't there.

"Jack, he's a fucking criminal," Morgan continues.

"I owe him."

Morgan answers. "You owe him nothing."

I feel anger. This guy is pushing me, and I don't want to be pushed.

"I owe him my life," I reply.

There's silence after that.

Finally, Morgan says, "I'm sorry I can't help you with this one. Sounds like you got a few things to work out on your own."

I retract the bite from my tone, and reply, "Morgan, I'm not asking you to help me."

"I know that," he responds, as we reach a truce.

"Just let me know what happens to Ray," I say in closing.

"I will."

After the telephone call I want to walk, to breathe the air outside and clear my head. Without Carolyn and Jade the house feels big and unfamiliar, and after the time I've spent living in the basement cell in Mount Vernon I feel I don't quite belong here. There is still conflict inside me, something deep and unresolved.

Charlie Wolf and Jack Lamb have business to settle between them.

I stand up from the sofa and walk to the front door, turning to look back at the room. The afternoon sun is streaming in from the open curtains on the north side and pours a rich honey gold on the red-and-blue Turkish carpet and the wide planks of the pine floor. The room is big, almost thirty feet long, with a high ceiling and exposed wooden beams, like an old barn. As soon as Carolyn and I saw it we knew we were going to buy the house. She had enough money for a good-sized chunk of the asking price and with what I made as a cop we could handle the payments on the mortgage. It was our place. We went through hell with the local builders, living in rubble while we renovated the kitchen and bathrooms, then decorated the house with furniture from catalogues, yard sales, and some of Carolyn's family heirlooms. Together, we made it beautiful.

Morgan was right. I need to work things out. Then maybe I'll be able to come home again.

I'm about to walk out the door when the telephone rings. I'm not expecting Morgan again and no one else that I want to speak to knows where I am, so I let it go on the machine.

It takes me a few seconds to recognize the voice, tenor and slightly nasal. Metzler, requesting I phone him to set up an appointment. He sounds very official and very somber.

I wait for the message to click off and register on the machine, then I push the erase button.

Metzler means well, I have no doubt of that, but right now I don't want his medicine. I don't want his opinion and I don't want to go back to the hospital.

I want to take a walk, maybe lots of walks. After that I want to be with my family.

~ 21 ~

THE MUSCLES IN MY CALVES and thighs have gone soft from lack of exercise. I have always been a physical person, confident with my body and reliant upon it and it's hard for me to accept this weakness, harder still to acknowledge that it was brought on by my own abuse. I've been an athlete in one form or another for most of my life; now it's an effort to put one foot ahead of the other.

I leave the driveway and continue for a block down the hill, then left onto one of the narrow side streets that leads to the ocean.

I didn't know where I was going when I left the house, but I do now. I know exactly where I'm going. Passing by mothers pushing baby carriages and men with surfboards, but no familiar faces and no friendly greetings. Maybe it's because it's July and the renters are here, or maybe it's because I've been away for so long, but I don't feel as though I belong to their world. I feel like a ghost, passing through.

Another few blocks, to Fifth Street, before I turn left and continue down a line of run-down bungalows, their shingles black from age. I haven't come here in over ten years, avoiding this place and the memories it holds. But today I feel I need to see it, just once more, as though it might provide the join in my life between who I was and who I am now.

Walking is actually becoming easier the farther I go. My body must have needed this exercise, because it's rewarding

me with a certain lightness, as if I'm being carried on the air
that I breathe. At times I feel I'm almost floating above the
ground.

I go to the end of the street and back through a dirt
driveway. No manicured lawns in this part of town,
everything is weeds, wild and overgrown. Up ahead I see the
remains of a house, a cinder-block foundation and a few
sections of a burned wooden frame. It takes me a bit to
comprehend what I'm looking at. I had no idea that the
house had burned down. I wonder when it happened and
why.

Keep moving, right up to where I remember the wooden
entrance steps used to be, then into the rectangle of cement,
to the area where my bedroom was. All the spaces seem so
small. Out through the opening that was the kitchen door to
the square of dirt that was our backyard. I sense the ghosts of
my mother and father, watching my progress.

Pick up a stick, just like my dad used to do. Scratch a line
in the hard, sandy earth.

I hear his voice in my head, that hint of an Irish accent.

"You get on that fuckin' line, and you don't get off it.
Understand me, mate?"

The old man was a mason, and his hands were strong
and hard from working with stone and mortar. They were
also heavy, like bricks.

"Please, Tom, don't," I hear my mother protest.

"Hurts me more than it hurts him," he would answer.
"I'm gonna toughen this kid up."

Scratch fighting was born in the pubs of Belfast. Two
men, one on either side of a line scratched onto the floor.
Money was wagered. It wasn't boxing. There was no
footwork and minimal defense. It was basically a contest of
spirit and fists, with one man left on his feet, holding his line.

My knees shook when I stood in front of the old man. I
felt like a coward, knowing I was about to be smacked, maybe
my nose broken, or my teeth knocked out.

I was fifteen years old the last time we fought.

"First one's a right-hander, gonna' land on your chin."

He would often begin his lessons that way, by
forecasting his blows. That gave me a chance to evade and

counter. He believed he was teaching me something important. He believed he was making a man of me.

Grunting with his efforts, the stink of rotting gums and cheap whiskey traveling with his callused fists, I reacted more from instinct than training, blocking with my forearms, jabbing out with my left.

I caught him solidly on that last day, flush in the mouth.

"Sorry," I said, petrified of retaliation.

"Sorry? What kind of poofter talk is 'sorry'?" he answered, wiping the blood from his lips. "You don't hit a man and say 'sorry,' you hit him again."

With that he brought his left fist up from the side of his body. I never saw it coming till it dug deep and low into my gut, dropping me.

"There's sorry for ya. Now get up, back on the line. Be a man."

He hauled me to my feet, and knocked me back down, over and over again.

Until finally, out of desperation, I fought back, bloodying his nose and mouth before he stopped me with a short hook to the temple, sending me hard to the ground.

"Get up, you little bastard!" He was out of control by then, his nose gushing, his lips cut, saliva whitening them like the froth from a rabid animal.

He kicked me once where I lay then pulled back for another. I was protecting my face, staring up through my hands at his red-bearded face, contorted with rage, booze and blood, when I saw it coming, like a scythe a flash of silver against the orange sun.

Thunk.

My father's legs buckled as his body pitched forward. He caught himself, remaining on his hands and knees for a few seconds, as if he was praying. His eyes were glazed and dumb, as if he was unable to comprehend what had just happened to him.

My brother, Robert, took another a step closer, still wary, holding the aluminum baseball bat in his right hand. He was barefoot, wearing his surfing baggies, his bare chest muscular and tanned, and his sun-bleached hair hanging long, curled by the salt water.

"Lesson's over, Pop. You want another round, have it with me."

My father rolled to his left and tried to stand but toppled over. Robert encouraged him. "Come on, get up on the line. Be a man. Let's do it."

Dad lay back down as Robert hovered above him. "You never touch Jack again, ever, you hear me?"

This time Robert prodded him with the tip of the bat, above his shoulder, in the same place he'd hit him.

"Somethin's broke," my father murmured.

"What goes around, comes around," Robert replied. Then he walked over to me and helped me to my feet. "You want to learn to take care of yourself, I'll teach you."

I can see them both now, clearly in my mind. My father's eyes, blue and wasted, full of the pain he suffered as a child and as a man. I recall the stories of his own father, who whipped him with a leather belt while he lay naked across his bed, of a mother too scared to protest the beatings. He had survived borstals and the streets of Belfast, and somewhere deep down, distorted by the lessons of his own life, thought he was doing me a service. In his mind, he was teaching me to survive. Maybe, in some way, he succeeded. But it was Robert who looked after me.

I feel Robert's presence in the charred bones of this old house. Hear his voice echo from the earth and sand beneath my feet.

Robert was the one I could talk to. He was my surrogate father, and now I am overcome with a desire for his presence and his strength, and for the security he gave me.

I need my brother.

~ 22 ~

THE WAVES CRASH AGAINST the shore on the other side of the Atlantic Terrace Motel as I round the corner and walk the black macadam that leads to the short boardwalk. There is a line of surfboards leaning against the railings to either side and groups of people scattered over the beach. Stepping down into the sand, I keep looking out at the water. Searching for him.

The waves are moderate in size, but breaking too close to the shore for a decent ride, and there are only a few surfers out past the break. All of them are wearing wetsuits, shiny and black against the gray-green. I walk closer, struggling to see their faces, as if he's actually going to be there.

Robert feels near to me, as if by returning to this place, I have summoned him.

"Sit down and cool out," I say to myself, but it's my brother's voice I'm listening to.

I turn from the water. Still talking to myself as I head up toward the dunes, past a couple of teenage girls wearing bikinis and lying in the shade of a bright yellow umbrella. They must hear me mumbling because they giggle as I walk by.

I get to the rise, with a hill of sand to my back and the Atlantic Terrace behind the hill. Sitting down, fifty yards from the girls, and more than that from the next blanket full of late-afternoon sunbathers.

My monologue continues. "Whatever you've done in this life, whoever you've been, that's what you bring with you to every moment."

Robert's there, right on the button. "Tell that to Charlie Wolf."

I think a moment before I answer. "That's my problem."

"What do you mean by that?"

"I'm still thinking like him, paranoid, looking over my shoulder. I'm full of fear."

"Then get rid of him."

"How?"

"Face him."

I stand and brush the sand off the back side of my jeans. The bikinis are looking in my direction. One of them is pointing at me. Skinny and pale, with my short hair, gesturing with my hands, ranting to myself, I must look like a raving lunatic.

I stare in their direction long enough to cause both of them to lower their heads. Probably frightened that eye contact could lure me to their blanket. It's the kind of subservience that only a brush with insanity inspires.

I move on, back to the boardwalk and onto the driveway that leads out to the road. I walk straight for two blocks, turn left, find a cross street, and walk the last block to Edison Street.

My heart is pumping, my mouth is dry, and I'm sweating, not from the exertion of the walk, but from what I am afraid I will find.

The school building is ahead of me on the left, the playground directly in front of it, on the highway side. The air around me seems to have cooled, or is that my imagination? I'm doing my best to keep a bridle on my thoughts, but they are galloping. What happens here, at this place?

Why is it getting cold?

Finally, I see the swings to the front of the building, green-and-yellow plastic, hanging by chains from the metal bar, and the red merry-go-round sitting in the center of the dirt-and-grass yard. It's just as I imagined it to be at the hospital, just as it appeared from the window of Morgan's car.

My body has changed temperature in the space of a minute. I was sweating, now I'm shivering. I look up at the sky. The sun is gone, vanished behind a set of thick clouds that seems to have blown in from nowhere. Everything in me wants to turn and escape from this place. Except Robert—he's in me, too, and he is saying to keep on going.

The playground is deserted as I enter through the front gates, and there appears to be no one in the school building. It's locked and deserted.

I walk straight to the blue-plastic sliding board and place my hands on the metal rails leading to the top, then close my eyes and try to relax my mind. Let it come. Whatever it is, let it happen now. Robert's right, I need to face my demons.

I climb to the top of the board.

Sitting on the perch, behind me I hear cars passing, and over my right shoulder I see the top of the White Elephant. I look down, to the grass and dirt at the bottom of the slide. Everything's okay.

I can climb down now. I can walk away, go home. I've come, faced my fear. There was nothing here but paranoia. The sun has returned. I remember Morgan singing. He was right. It's going to be a bright, sunshiny day.

Then I catch a glimpse of a face in the window of the school building, staring out at me, and for the first time I'm self-conscious. I must look very strange up here on top of the sliding board, alone in the children's playground.

The man moves closer to the window as if to get a better look at me. I reckon he's probably a janitor or a custodian. The sun is causing a lot of glare against the glass, and I can't make out the features of his face.

I'm about to start back down the ladder when the clouds roll back in, the cold returns, and the glare is gone. I smell fresh green apples, and Ray Sasso is staring at me from the other side of the window.

Impossible, I tell myself, but he's standing there, behind the glass. Nothing else has changed. I hear cars passing, see the merry-go-round, the swings. And I see Ray Sasso.

The fear starts with a twitching inside my bowels as he lifts his arm and points his finger, like the barrel of a gun, exactly as he did on the highway. This time it's different. This time I feel him inside my head, as if he has established a hold on me, a tangible link, a cord between his raised hand and the bullet in my temple. He's stretching the cord till the tension is unbearable.

My legs are trembling as I start down the ladder. I've got to end this. One way or the other, I have to make it stop.

I taste the fear, dry and bitter in my mouth, as my vision narrows and I'm staring into Ray's face. Everything else has become a blur. His eyes are directly in front of mine, pulling me toward him as if they possess an intrinsic and undeniable gravity.

Time stops as I travel forward with the sensation of headlong flight, until there are only inches between us and a single pane of glass to keep us apart.

Ray drops his arm. He appears composed, calm, like he did on that day in the warehouse. He holds my gaze without blinking.

I pull off my T-shirt, wrap it around my hand, bunch it into a fist, and pull back to punch.

Another voice catches me from behind, loud and sharp.

"Sir. What do you think you're doing?"

I hesitate.

"Is there a problem?"

I drop my hand but don't leave Ray's eyes. I don't want to lose my intent. Don't want to give him the advantage.

"Sir, please turn around slowly," the voice continues.

I stay concentrated on Ray Sasso.

"Do it now!"

I hear a sharp snap and recognize the sound as a holster opening.

Finally, I do as I am told.

The tone of the voice suddenly changes, "Jack Lamb?"

I see a uniformed police officer, standing on my right side, about six feet away from me, his hand resting on the butt of his Glock.

His eyes soften as I face him full on.

"I thought you were working in Westchester County," he says, removing his hand from his weapon.

I recognize Lou Collins's voice before I recognize the hazel eyes beneath the visor of his cap, then the small pink mouth below his dark mustache. I've known Lou since we were kids, losing touch just before I met Carolyn. I'd heard he had become a cop, but I thought he worked up Island.

"Look behind me," I answer. "Inside the building."

We both stare through the window and into the vacant classroom.

"What am I looking for?" he asks.

"I saw someone inside," I reply, but even as I do I am having doubts. My mind is back on the Long Island Expressway. I thought I saw Ray then, too.

"Someone you know?" Lou asks. He must be a year or two older than me, but aside from a few extra pounds, he hasn't changed much since we ran track in high school.

"Yes," I answer.

Lou meets my eyes and I detect a flicker of uncertainty. It surfaces then subsides.

"Who?"

He's staring at the wound on my forehead as my self-confidence slowly dissolves.

My voice sounds shaky. "I need to be sure he's not in there."

"Who?" He asks again.

"A guy. I took him down in a drugs bust."

Lou looks at me. I read the compassion in his eyes. He knows something's not right, but this one's for old times' sake. "Let's take a walk to my car."

"But—"

"Come on," he says, taking hold of my arm as we start walking.

He opens the passenger side door and I get in. "Stay put, I'll be right back."

He returns to the building and takes a good look at the windows and doors. A few minutes later he's back, beside me, saying, "Everything's locked up tight, there's no sign of a break-in, and the alarm is on inside the building. Jack, there's nobody in there."

"You sure?" Even as I ask, I know he's speaking the truth.

"Trust me," he answers, studying me. "What's going on?"

"I don't know." Which isn't good enough for either of us, so I fill him in as much as I am able to about the Sasso case, without revealing the details of my perjury, my hallucinations, or the bullet in my head, or for that matter, the color of his halo, which is predominantly light blue, highlighted by streaks of red which subside as his eyes grow calm and settle on mine.

The blue drifts outward from his head, filling the space between us like a fine mist, and as I observe it, I sense his sincerity and gain a feeling of trust for him.

"Thanks, Lou," I say, finally. "I appreciate you not calling this in. I just got home, and it's the last thing I need."

After that he gives me a lift back to the house and we talk a little about the old days, and where we are now, agreeing that once I've had a bit more time to adjust that we'll get together and have dinner. He's never met Carolyn or Jade, and I've never met his wife and kids. It seems like a good idea, but even as we discuss it, I have a feeling that it isn't going to happen anytime soon. It's too real, too normal.

By the time we turn up my driveway the sun is setting, the air has cooled, and I see by the clock in the car that I've been gone for a little over two hours.

I notice Carolyn's Jeep in the driveway and wonder how long they've been home. Probably long enough to be worried about me.

I thank Lou again and apologize for not asking him inside the house, telling him that I've been gone so long that I need to readjust, and so do my wife and child. He's working anyway, and he understands, so I take his phone number, stuff it down the back pocket of my jeans, and get out.

The front door is half-open, and Carolyn is watching as I mount the steps. Jade is hanging on to one of her legs, looking up.

"Daddy, why were you in that policeman's big car?"

"That policeman is a friend of mine. He just took me for a ride."

"Can I go for a ride, too?" Jade asks, stepping out from behind Carolyn's thigh to watch Lou Collins back out of the driveway. "I want to ride in that police car, too."

"Maybe I could ask him, but not now," I answer.

"But I want to go for a ride," Jade insists.

"Later, Jade," I answer. "I'll ask him another time, I promise."

"But I want to go in the policeman's car now."

Carolyn steps in. "You heard what Daddy said, if you're a good girl, he will ask the policeman if you can ride in his car."

"But I want to go now."

I reach out to touch my daughter's hair.

"Go away," she says, pulling back. "I want to go in the policeman's car."

"The answer is no," Carolyn says firmly.

Causing tears, which escalate quickly to a tantrum.

"Do you want to go to your room for a break?" Carolyn asks.

"No!" Jade shrieks, throwing herself down on the floor. "I want to go in the policeman's car!"

"That's it," Carolyn says, picking her up and walking her toward the stairs. "Time-out."

I feel useless. Wondering if this is normal behavior or if it is happening because of me. Jade's screams echo from the landing. Her high-pitched wails seem to get right inside my head, battering my skull. I walk to the sofa in the living room and sit down.

The pressure increases. I feel the bullet, like a bunched fist. I close my eyes, trying to shut out the pain. I think of the medicine in the brown-plastic bottle—take two with food, for right temporal lobe seizures, or more delicately put, episodes. Wouldn't a line of meth be more to the point, just for that brief euphoria?

The telephone begins to ring.

Maybe I should take the medicine and become a zombie again.

"Daddy! Daddy!"

Ring. Ring. Ring.

Will somebody please answer the phone.

"Daddy!"

What the hell does she want me to do?

"Daddy!"

I can't keep her safe.

Ring.

Where is it? Where the hell is the phone? I turn and see it on the table. Reach for it. Pick it up.

"Yes?" I sound angry.

Jade's voice fills my head. "Daddy, you're hurting me!"

"Stop it!" I shout back, slamming it down. It rings again. "Stop it!" I'm not shouting at Jade. I'm shouting at the telephone. I'm shouting at the voices in my head. "Stop!" I'm shouting at everything I don't understand.

Then I'm on my feet, running to the stairs and up. Toward the voice, toward the voices in my head. I smell roses. My feet are banging loud and heavy against the oak treads. I smell apples.

"Stop it! God damn it, stop!"

~ 23 ~

CAROLYN LOOKS FIERCE, HER jaw set and her eyes digging into mine, blocking my way at the top of the landing. Her feet are planted firmly, her shoulders squared, and there are the most incredible red-and-orange flames fanning out from around her head. She looks impenetrable, like a forest fire.

Her voice is strong and without compromise. "Stop right where you are." Each word is spoken dearly and deliberately, making it feel like a door has just been slammed shut in my face.

I stop. The voices stop. The smells stop.

Carolyn continues, "I want to know what the hell is going on with you."

For a moment there is the most perfect silence as Carolyn's halo flickers, then subsides to a more peaceful blaze of yellow and blue.

"I think we'd better talk," I say softly.

"Yes, so do I," she answers. "I'll go check on Jade. I'll see you downstairs."

She turns and walks back toward Jade's room, leaving me standing, feeling that I have just been snapped back into frame, like a motion picture that has been pulled into focus.

I turn, walk back down the stairs, and return to the sofa. I can breathe again, my panic is gone. If only I could stay like this, with a guarantee that none of the strangeness will ever return. I relax into the soft cushions.

Carolyn joins me a few minutes later.

Before I can ask how Jade is, she says, "She's asleep. She was exhausted. I think it's all the excitement of having Daddy home."

I look at her in silence for few more seconds, then tell her I'm sorry for going out without leaving a note. Explaining that I didn't know I'd be gone so long, but once I had started walking I just kept going. I tell her I needed the exercise, I needed to think, to clear my head. She listens until I'm all talked out. I've said everything and nothing. I haven't even touched on the truth, and she knows it. She remains silent, waiting, as the pressure inside me builds. She's my wife. I can trust her. I need to talk to somebody. She's still waiting. Finally, when the dam behind my skull feels about ready to break, I open up, spilling the truth about the things that have been happening to me since I was shot, starting with my out-of-body trip to the beach and visit with Robert and including the fact that I now see halos and have seen Ray Sasso twice in the past three days. It feels good to talk, like I'm releasing poison from a sore, even though I realize that what I'm saying makes me sound certifiable.

Carolyn listens without reacting one way or the other. When she does speak it's usually to rephrase something that I've told her, which has the effect of making me reflect on my own words and slowing me down. Calming me.

As we talk I'm aware that Carolyn has a masters' degree in special education and is probably giving me the same treatment that has been previously employed on hyperactive nine-year-olds. I don't care. It feels good and necessary.

At the end of my story, which climaxes with Lou Collins saving me from a possible breaking-and-entering violation, she says something which surprises me.

"Why don't you talk to Simon?"

There are no nerves to her voice, none of the panic that I thought my story might cause. Instead, she seems calm and surprisingly prepared for what I've told her.

Simon Barr is a retired psychotherapist and a family friend. I should qualify that by saying he's more a friend of Carolyn's than mine. In the past, I've always found his philosophical and spiritual views a little far-fetched, bordering on the unbelievable. He's also a member of Carolyn's meditation and yoga group, which, since I don't practice either discipline, puts another gap between us.

Carolyn continues. "He's worked with a number of people who have had a Near Death Experience. I'm sure he'd be interested in your story, and I think he'd be helpful."

I feel the residue of past negativity regarding the Hamptons' two-hundred-dollar-an-hour guru circuit begin to surface, then it gives way to the fact that one way or another I know I'm in trouble, and Simon's a friend. As long as he's not going to ridicule me or ask me to chant with him I'm willing to talk. It would be good to have an opinion other than Howard Metzler's.

Jade sleeps, during which time Carolyn and I continue to talk. I had forgotten how insightful she can be, and how patient. I had also forgotten how much I missed her and how much I am attracted to her in a sexual sense. She is sitting against the side of the sofa, nestled into one of the soft green cushions with her sandals off and her legs pulled up so that she's sitting on her heels. Her short pink-and-white-striped skirt is even shorter now, and if I tilt my head back and to the side, lowering my eyes, I can see that she's wearing pale yellow underpants. It dawns on me that I haven't had sex with anyone but myself in more than a year. It also dawns on me that I am spending more and more time with my head back and eyes lowered and that my train of conversation has veered off in the direction of how much I love her and how good she looks.

Carolyn seems to relax and go along with me, and if I'm not mistaken her legs have just moved a little farther apart. I now have a noticeable bulge running down the right side of my thigh, easily visible through my jeans. Then I begin to notice something else; it's like a warm pillow pushing against me from the front, as if there is a cylinder of warm firm air between me and Carolyn. I also see that Carolyn's halo is ruby red, with what looks like a circle of orange embers spilling from it. It is those embers that are pushing against me, like an extension of Carolyn. It's not anger. This is a different feeling, steady and gently pulsating.

She looks down at my stretched jeans, and asks, "Are you still packing a gun, or are you just glad to be home?"

I laugh, watching as the color around her head grows in intensity and the warmth connecting us turns to heat. "I don't know if I should be doing this," I say, mostly joking. "After all, I am convalescing."

"Your doctor told me that sex is a necessary part of your recovery," she answers with a straight face.

I slide across the sofa, and the warmth wraps us in what feels like a cocoon, tingling with tiny pulses that attach to every nerve in my body. I think of Jade. What if—

"Her door's closed and the floorboards in the upstairs hallway sound like they need oil," Carolyn answers, reaching out for my belt, unbuckling and loosening it before attacking the buttons on my jeans. "Do you want to risk it?"

I stand up like a billboard for Viagra. She looks down at me, and says, "I'll take that as a yes."

Her pants come off easily, sliding down over the soft skin of her legs.

I kiss her as I enter her. Everything is unfolding in the most wonderful wet, soft warmth. Her body seems to open. Accepting me, taking me in. I can feel her heart beating, close to my chest. I close my eyes, and there is light everywhere, the most magnificent light, almost white but without glare. I am traveling backwards, into a womb of security, where love is free and unconditional. I am wrapped in it, humbled by it. Safe again, because of Carolyn.

"I love you," I whisper.

~ 24 ~

THE PHONE IS RINGING. I'm asleep, but I can hear it, as if it's digging through layers of consciousness, drilling down, trying to get to me. I want to answer, but I can't move. My body's paralyzed.

The phone is ringing.

Inhale, exhale, inhale.

Wake up, I tell myself. Wake up. Answer the phone. But everything is numb, from my head to my feet, thick and numb. Come on, move, reach out, do it with your mind. Your mind can move your body. Reach out. My arm is like pulp and there is no sensation in my hand as it grips the handset.

My voice is thick and groggy. "Hello?"

"You were right, Sasso's a tough guy."

I recognize Morgan's voice, even before I understand what he's saying.

"He made it," he continues.

Ray is alive. The news seems to bring life to my own limbs. I can feel again, and the thing inside me that is at war with my lower, baser desires, shines a little bit brighter. At least I'm not a coward, not at that level anyway.

"He won't be the same as he was before but he'll live."

Not the same? Now I sense a hurt, like I'm hearing about some proud beast, a lion, who has been maimed.

"What do you mean, not the same?" I ask.

"The punctured lung collapsed. He'll eventually get off the ventilator, but he'll never do another round in the ring,"

Morgan answers. His voice sounds harsh and cavalier, without respect, like he's talking about something a little less than human.

I remain quiet, thinking, recalling one night in the gym. I was on my knees at Ray Sasso's feet. My nose was gushing blood and my head was spinning.

"You all right, Charlie?" Ray asked.

"I'm good," I answered, but it was my pride talking. The truth was I was only half conscious, all but out. I could hardly remember my phony name. "Charlie?" That didn't sound right.

I struggled to my feet, reeling around the elevated boxing ring like a drunk, saying, "Let's keep moving." Trying to get my gloves back up in front of my face.

"No, it's over," Ray said, stepping toward me. "Let me take a look at that nose."

The three-minute buzzer sounded, officially ending the round as he pulled off his gloves.

"Breathe out," he ordered.

I exhaled a load of blood as he pinched and pulled down, snapping my cartilage back into a straight line.

"That ought to give you some character," he said, stepping back to examine his cosmetic work.

"Have we sparred yet?" I asked. I honestly didn't remember.

"Yes."

"How'd I do?"

"You walked right into one," Ray answered. "Never saw it coming. It's always the ones we don't see coming that nail us."

***

Ray walked into one, too, the day he met Charlie Wolf, and now he's a cripple. I can't imagine it. Then my mind switches to a more practical level and a lesser instinct begins to surface.

Morgan's voice breaks the silence.

"You wanted me to keep you informed, didn't you?"

"Yes, I did," I reply. "So how's this going to affect the case?" Hoping that it will somehow end the reality of a trial and, with it, any participation on my part.

"If he can breathe, she'll get him into that courtroom," Morgan answers, shattering my hopes.

"How long do they figure he'll be in the hospital?"

"Depends if there are any complications, but if he heals, we can get him into a segregated unit in Valhalla. Keep him safe there till the big day."

My voice dips. "So it's full steam ahead?"

Morgan's tone is resigned. "Oh yeah, I think Ms. Carroll has upped the voice-and-drama coach to twice a week. Don't worry, the media will be on full alert."

I think of myself as Charlie Wolf on the witness stand, face shaved and scrubbed to shine, hair short and proper, wearing polished shoes, a smart suit, and a silk tie with a quarter gram of meth rampaging through my brain. Staring into Ray Sasso's eyes while I lie about him under oath. The thought takes away any feelings of reprieve or salvation that yesterday with Carolyn gave me.

Morgan fills another hole in our conversation. "How are you doing, anyway?"

That makes me laugh.

"Good, never felt better," I answer, unable to keep the bitterness from my voice. "I should have got this bullet put in my head a long time ago." Then I think of Morgan on that day in Mount Vernon, bending over my body, willing me back to life, and my heart softens. He doesn't deserve my contempt. "Sorry, Morgan. I sound angry, and I'm not, not with you anyway. I'm all right. It's just a little strange being back here, but it was time I came home. I missed my family. It was time."

"I understand," he answers.

Finally, I say, "Thanks for keeping me posted," and we conclude our conversation.

After breakfast, which revolves around bribing Jade to eat a bowl of oatmeal and a half a banana with promises of a trip to the lake to feed the ducks, Carolyn tells me that I have an appointment with Simon Barr at four o'clock this afternoon. My nerves suddenly escalate. I don't know if I really want to discuss my Near Death Experience with anyone other than Carolyn. It seems deeply personal. I don't even know if I can.

Suddenly I get a taste of paranoia. Is this just a way of getting me into some kind of therapy? Does Carolyn really believe I'm nuts? "Is this like an official appointment?" I ask.

"What do you mean by official?"

"I mean are you paying money for this?"

Carolyn shakes her head. "Simon's retired," she reminds me.

"These days he sees whom he wants to see, the people who interest him. The experience that you had is something he's been studying for years. He just wants to talk to you about it."

~ 25 ~

SIMON BARR LIVES IN AMAGANSETT, on a bluff, about eighty feet above Gardiner's Bay. From his back deck we can see the mile-long strip of green that is Gardiner's Island to the northeast and, on the southeast side of the finger of land that runs from here to Montauk, the Atlantic Ocean. At night he tells me that he can see the beacon from the lighthouse at the tip of the island, going round and round.

The weather is unseasonably cool and the humidity is low. It's paradise here, at least it feels like paradise, as Barr brings me a glass of Perrier water and invites me to sit in one of the teak chairs lining his deck.

He sits facing me, about two feet away. His hair is short and steel gray, and he's dressed casually, with khaki-colored shorts, flip-flops, and a loose white T-shirt. He has a long face, partially hidden behind a full beard, with wide hazel eyes and a mouth that looks like it's smiling even when he's just looking at me. His halo is a gentle shade of yellow, easy on my eyes, streaked with blue and several shades of green, ranging from vibrant to pale. The sun behind his head adds size to this display of colors, making them appear to fan out like a rainbow against the pale blue sky. But it's the lighter shade of green, like fresh new apples, that attracts me, filling me with a sense of well-being. I know that I have come here to talk, but I feel no expectations, no urgency with Simon Barr, as he sits relaxed, with a glass of whiskey in his hand.

"Glenmorangie," he says, looking down at the honey gold liquid. "It's a single malt from the Scottish Highlands. Would you like some?"

The idea appeals to me. I haven't had a drink since I've been home, not since that afternoon with Ray in the clubhouse. Not since I was Charlie Wolf and needed to take the edge off.

"Yes, thanks," I answer.

Barr stands up. He looks more like a triathlete than a shrink, with that lean, long-muscled type of build that I associate with runners and swimmers. His demeanor is self-assured, like he's comfortable inside his body, and it's difficult to tell his age. But I know, from Carolyn, that he's in his late sixties.

"Are you on any medication?" he asks.

"I'm not taking any," I answer, figuring he's concerned about me mixing alcohol with whatever drugs I've been prescribed.

"Good," he replies. Then he's gone, returning with the whiskey.

A few sips and I do start to relax, and so does he. In fact, it's Barr who begins our conversation.

"Jack, just from the little bit that Carolyn has told me I'm willing to guess that you're fairly confused about what happened to you."

I meet his eyes without answering, but I can feel a spark between us, a mental connection.

"Let me start by telling you about my own experience," he continues. "At least you'll know you're not alone. The power of the mind has always been my obsession, and I am convinced that, in the West, certain aspects of it have been overlooked or discounted. In the early seventies I went to India on what amounted to a personal quest to witness some of the things I'd heard and read about as a student of philosophy and psychology. I wanted to witness miracles. I wanted to talk to an enlightened master. I wanted wisdom, but more than that I wanted to believe that there was more to my existence than the three-dimensional world that Western science terms reality. But India can be a tough place, especially if you are not prepared for the change in diet and the rigors of travel. Before I got to do or see any of the things that I went there for, I got sick. It was in Delhi. I contracted hepatitis, which some people say is a very spiritual disease because it robs you of every ounce of physical energy you've ever had. In my case I didn't have the strength to lift a spoon or fork to my mouth, to drink a glass of water, or lift my body out of bed. I almost died. Maybe I did. I felt like I was sucked down a long, dark tunnel. At the end I could see the most wonderful light. It was white, without glare and totally peaceful. But to get there I had to cross a ruby red line, which cut across the darkness like a laser beam. I wanted to keep going, to get to that peaceful place. I had been in terrible pain, and I wanted it to be over, but I knew that if I crossed that line I would never come back. I had a wife and baby son who needed me, I had a clinical practice with patients who relied on me, and I had my research to do. My life was unfinished. So I turned around and went back to my body, and struggled to get well. It was the hardest thing I've ever done, and the experience has haunted me for nearly thirty years. Now, do you understand why I wanted to talk to you?"

"Yes," I answer, feeling as if I have just found an invaluable ally and, in my heart, I thank Carolyn for bringing us together.

Barr seems a mixture between wise man and child; open to everything and completely nonjudgmental. Listening intently as I tell him about my death experience on the third of July and of some of the things that have happened since.

When I'm finished he looks at me, and says, "Death is like taking a walk through your mind."

It takes me a moment to understand what he means.

"You enter here," he says, touching his forehead, "and come out here." He raises his hands to the sky. "Life is the dream in between living and dying."

Opening up to Simon Barr makes me feel lighter inside, as I expose my doubts and anxieties, knowing that I'm no longer alone with my experience. The whiskey feels good, too, warm and secure in my belly.

Barr is fascinated by my ability to see halos, which he calls auras, and informs me that what I am able to perceive has been documented scientifically, by certain types of photography and computer imaging. The aura is the energy body that surrounds the physical body and is as real as the chair I'm sitting in. He tells me that there are people so skilled in working with this energy that they use it as a diagnostic tool in treating disease, interpreting the color and size and, in some cases, manipulating it to heal the illness. As he talks I remember my own experience with Howard Metzler, when I noticed the gray area around his shoulder.

He's also intrigued by the fact that I have a bullet in my head, more particularly, inside the right temporal lobe region of my brain. He doesn't buy the hallucination diagnosis. "They don't know everything," he says, speaking of Western doctors in general. "They're the best in the world at surgery and the worst at treating the whole human being. The fact that you see auras is proof that you are not hallucinating. My guess is that the placement of the bullet is acting to heighten your consciousness."

I mention my bottle of antipsychotics.

He considers a few moments, then answers, "I guess they're good to have as a fallback, but the more you can do without them the better. You can learn a tremendous amount from this experience."

The right temporal lobe is his pet subject. He calls it our link with God, or the Universal Mind, which he describes as the collective consciousness of all things, from human beings to subatomic particles. He believes that everything is conscious at some level, and everything is interconnected.

"The right temporal lobe is like an underworked muscle," he explains. "The left side of the brain is the one we primarily use, to accomplish the tasks that constitute our survival, while the right side, the seat of our intuition, is ignored. Western science claims it to be important mainly for the processing and interpreting of memory and emotion, but that's just the tip of the iceberg. When the right lobe is fully accessed, those things that we call miracles become within our control. Ten years ago, in southern India, I videotaped a sixty-four-year-old holy man by the name of Sai Baba, who was able to make material objects manifest from thin air."

I smile at this point in our conversation, and Barr interprets my smile as disbelief because the next thing he does is hold out his hand and show me a ring that he is wearing. The ring is a band of heavy gold, inlaid with tiny rubies.

"A gift from Sai Baba," he says. "I watched it materialize in his palm."

This is a little too much for me, although I do reach out and touch it. "Did you ever think that the guy just might have been a good magician?" I ask, but even as I do I sense that there is something unusual about the ring, it seems to vibrate subtly beneath my fingertips.

Barr shakes his head and smiles, not at all bothered by my question. "If Sai Baba's a fraud, then he's the world's best, because he's been fooling doctors and scientists for twenty years."

All of this stuff would have been worth nothing more to me than a bit of speculation and probably a laugh a year ago, but I'm not laughing anymore. If an Indian holy man can make a gold ring materialize from the concentration of thought, could it be possible that a part of my mind is causing Ray Sasso to appear? Am I actually creating some form of parallel reality?

I ask Barr and he doesn't discount the possibility, leaving me deep in thought as he goes to get me a glass of water.

I gaze out from his deck across the bay. It's a magnificent view, with Gardiner's Island, emerald green, to my left and the sandy beaches of Devon to my right, winding in a semicircle, all the way to Napeague. Across the thin strip of land that leads to Montauk I can see the Atlantic Ocean, shimmering blue. Then I get a strange feeling. I'm not here at all. I'm looking at a picture in my mind. I'm lost in the moment, disoriented, floating in deep space, clinging to voices and memories.

"Jack?"

Barr's voice stabilizes me.

I turn to see him, standing with the glass in his hand. "Here you go," he says.

As my fingers connect with the cold, hard crystal I feel the bullet begin its little dance, tickling at first, then itching. I reach up to touch the skin above it. Pressing in as the itch gives way to a stinging. Then a quick, sharp pain, causing me to drop the glass. It hits the deck with a thud. It doesn't break, but the water spills, forming a tiny silver lake, reflecting the sun like a mirror.

"I'm sorry," I say, embarrassed by my clumsiness, bending down to retrieve it just as the bleeper starts.

Bleep. Bleep. Bleep. Bleep.

The noise makes the pain worse.

"Are you okay?" Barr asks. His face is serious, and his eyes concentrated on me.

The bleeper continues with an urgent rhythm.

Bleep. Bleep. Bleep. I feel somehow connected to it. I try not to listen. *Bleep. Bleep.* I know that sound, like it is always there, in the background, in my head. *Bleep.*

"Jack!"

Bleep. Bleep.

"Jack!"

Barr's voice snaps me back.

I jolt upright.

"It's that sound," I say, although it seems suddenly distant and muted. "What is that sound?"

Barr smiles, removing the small black-plastic pager from the waistband of his shorts.

"Officially I'm retired," he answers. "But I still do some work with the hospital." Pressing a button, he stops the noise, then checks the numbers on the display. "It's not an emergency. I can take care of it later." He looks up at me as if he's just made a big decision.

"Have you got another hour?"

"For what?" I ask.

"Let's get out on the water," he replies. "I think it would do you good."

"Swimming?"

"No, paddling," he answers with a smile. "In a boat. Can you handle that?"

"I'll probably drown," I answer, only half-joking.

"Trust me," he says. "I won't let that happen."

~ 26 ~

THERE ARE 109 STEPS LEADING from the top of Barr's bluff to the sandy beach, or so he informs me as we head down.

"Lucky we got a cool day with a breeze off the water," he adds. "Horseflies will take a chunk out of you this time of year."

I am following behind him, wondering just what's supposed to happen on the water, when he asks if I've ever been in a kayak.

As he asks I spot the three overturned boats that line the bulkhead at the bottom of the stairs.

"A few times," I reply. Carolyn and I used to rent kayaks and paddle around the lake in Montauk, about five years ago.

"Good," he answers, as we reach the bulkhead. There, he flips one of the boats over to reveal a paddle with pale red blades. Picking it up, he hands it to me. "This one's nice and light."

Then he pulls a white paddle from beneath the next boat in line and we slide two of the kayaks down from the bulkhead, across the narrow sandy beach, and to the water.

"Do you remember how to get into one?" he asks, as I remove my trainers and socks and roll up the bottoms of my jeans.

"I think so," I reply.

My kayak has a white deck and a blue hull. The name
Calypso is stenciled on its side. Barr's, which has a polished
wooden deck and fiberglass-coated hull, is called *Third Eye*.

"Hop in, I'll push you out," he offers.

I manage a reasonable entry, propping the paddle at the
back of the cockpit to ensure that if the boat tips, there's a
blade to hold it up and I don't land with my ass in the air. I
slide my feet inside and locate the foot braces.

Barr gives the *Calypso* a shove, and I'm on the water,
which is clear enough to see the schools of tiny fish darting in
and out from beneath my boat and with just the hint of a
chop from the breeze.

I hunch a little bit forward to take the strain off my
lower back, shift my balance to stabilize the boat, and paddle
a few strokes. The *Calypso* cuts right through the water. The
air is cool against my skin and smells fresh and salty.

He reaches my side and we head out, away from the
bluff.

"How do you feel?" he asks.

"Good," I reply. Actually I'm very relaxed, probably
because of the whiskey.

"Think you can manage as far as Cartwright Island?" He
indicates a small patch of white sand about a mile in front of
us. It appears to sit about even with the waterline.

So far the exercise seems effortless.

"I'll tell you if I'm in trouble," I answer.

"Cartwright's a great place to sit," he adds, increasing his
stroke to leave me in his wake.

I briefly ponder his use of the word "sit" as I continue to
paddle, trying to keep my strokes long and not dip the blade
too deep in the water.

The nearest boat I can see is a small white day fisher,
way down along the southwest side of Gardiner's Island.
Other than that Barr and I are alone in the water. I pick up
the pace and cut to his port side so that I'm only about a half
boat length behind him. Gradually, as the muscles of my back
and abdomen warm up and get used to the exercise, I start to
get into it, matching my breathing to my stroke, digging in on
the out breath. We're going at a moderate pace and the
farther we travel the more concentrated I become. Pretty

soon there is just the breath, the stroke, the brief tension in my shoulders, back, and abs, and the sound of the water rushing by.

Then I begin to get that feeling again, that spatial disorientation. As if I am caught somewhere in the flow of a dream, not here and grounded but in some imagined place. I stop paddling and try to get my bearings. About to call out to Barr, to tell him I'm turning around, when a trickle of sweat, rolling down from my brow, across my cheek and stopping on my upper lip, tickling, until I flick my tongue out and taste it, warm and salty, snaps me back into frame.

I'm here, on the bay, paddling a boat. With that simple realization comes a sense of security. No one else knows exactly where I am. For the time being, I've left Charlie Wolf behind. Ray Sasso can't reach me. I'm protected. Simon Barr is my protector. I feel safe with him. His voice calms me. His manner makes me feel secure. With that, I start paddling again.

***

Cartwright Island looks a lot farther from the water than it did from the shore, and there's a current pulling us to the north, away from it. I figure we've been paddling for about fifteen minutes when we pass a red buoy and a couple of channel markers. Our destination looks more like a sandbar from this vantage point, extending in a long narrow ribbon all the way to the evergreens, shrubs, and grass where it connects with Gardiner's Island. This far out, at about the halfway point, there are whitecaps and small waves breaking over the bow of the *Calypso*, sending a spray of water into my face and into the cockpit.

Another quarter of an hour and the latissimus muscles of my back feel pumped, like I'm midway through a set of pull-ups on a high bar. This is more exercise than I'm used to, and I'm breathing heavily, dipping the blade too deep, tipping the boat. For a second I think I'm going in, but it rights itself, and I continue, paying more attention to the way I use the paddle.

I start counting, four strokes to a breath, keeping them
shallow, pulling long, two strokes, then I've got the rhythm
again and I'm just pulling away at the water as fast as I can,
maybe fifty yards from the shoreline, watching as Barr glances
back at me once before heading in. There's plenty of water in
my boat, and it's shifting like a cork, but I'm shifting with it,
connected by the seat of my pants. I can hear the bottom
scrape against the sand and shells as I hit the shallows, pulling
hard for the beach.

"That was incredible!" I say, meaning it.

We get out, dump the water from the boats, and pull
them up onto the beach.

"How do you feel?" Barr asks, as if he's gauging my
response as the situation progresses.

"I'm good," I answer.

"Tired?

"Not at all—" I answer, hesitating. "My body feels good.
I feel alive."

"Great. Follow me," Barr says, turning to walk up
through a small mountain of broken shells to the higher
ground. A flock of seagulls take flight as we approach,
squawking their protests at our intrusion.

My hands are callused from working in the machine
shop, so the paddling was no problem, but the soles of my
feet are baby soft, and every shell and stone feels like a nail in
my flesh.

He reaches the center of the small patch of sand and sits
down.

"This is where I sit," he says. He motions with his hand
for me to join him. "Peaceful, isn't it?"

I inhale and relax a little bit more.

Barr continues. "I came here at five-thirty in the morning
one time last May. It was still dark outside, and the place was
covered in seagulls. They looked like an army, pretty
formidable, and I had second thoughts as to whether even to
land the boat, but as I did they all took off at one time. It was
like one big white umbrella opening, and the sound of their
wings, all beating in unison, was amazing. I kept looking up at
them, hoping they wouldn't decide to come back and get rid

of me. Then I walked up on the beach to this spot, same place I'm sitting now. After a while the sky over there turned from deep blue to pink—" He points to the finger of land, behind Napeague and, as he speaks, his words create vivid pictures in my mind. "It was just a glow at first, then it began to streak with the most amazing colors of pink and gold. Gradually the sky turned orange. Then the real show started; at first all I could see was a blood red rim, rising up from out of the ocean."

I remain still, breathing deeply, allowing his voice to transport me to the place in his mind.

"It was like this great living thing, this vast shimmering energy, so big and powerful. I felt like I was the only human being on the planet, and I was witnessing the original hour of creation. I felt empowered by it and humbled at the same time. It's hard to describe, but for a time Simon Barr ceased to exist. When I became conscious that I was thinking again, the sun was full in the sky. That's when I looked around and saw that all the birds had come back to the ground. Covered it, except around the patch where I was sitting. I felt accepted."

After this he sits quietly, his legs folded in front of him and his spine straight. He keeps his eyes open, looking west, back in the direction from where we'd come. It's late afternoon, and the sun is hanging low in the sky, reflecting off the windows along the shoreline, making it look as though every light in every house has been turned on. All I hear are the distant cries of the birds and the small waves that break against the shore. Pretty soon I'm simply sitting and watching my thoughts pass, trying not to chase after them. It's like I am taking a break from myself and this drama that has become my life. I don't feel pressure. I don't feel Charlie Wolf. I don't feel hunted.

I feel at peace.

Time passes, and the gaps between thoughts grow wider.

Then I forget about the gaps and seem to drift, almost as if I'm on the cusp of sleep, as my eyes slowly close.

I get that feeling again. Not really here at all, on this tiny patch of sand in the middle of a bay. I am somewhere else

entirely, surrounded by warmth. I hear voices, soft and
muted. I can't make out words. It's more like a gentle
vibration, raining down upon my head. Light fingers stroke
my forehead. I feel cared for, guarded, and looked after. I
don't want to open my eyes. Don't want to break this spell.

I sit for minutes, an hour, I'm not certain. Until I feel a
coolness all around me.

"Beautiful wasn't it?" Barr says, breaking the trance.

I open my eyes. Did he feel it, too, this sensation of
being in a dream within a dream?

"I come out here at least once a week during the season
to watch it set," he continues.

He's talking about the sun, I'm communing with angels.
We're in very different places.

"I wasn't watching the sun," I say.

He looks at me, puzzled.

"I was in another place, warm and safe. It was a long way
from all the craziness that's been in my life lately."

Barr looks at me. His eyes are shadowed in darkness, and
his head is nodding almost imperceptibly.

"What do you think is happening to me?" I ask.

"I think you are getting glimpses," he answers.

"Of what?" I ask.

"Of waking up."

While I'm contemplating just what that means, Barr
stands up and looks back toward the bluff. I follow his eyes. I
can barely make out the beach and the steps leading up to his
house. The wind has picked up, and the water is choppy.

"You're a lucky man, Jack. I know all the words, read all
the books, I've had a taste, but you're actually having the
experience."

"Some of it's not so great," I reply.

"Yes, it's a rough path," he concludes.

I follow him back to the kayaks and climb into the
Calypso, using my hands to push off the beach and back into
the water. The sky is a rose-colored canopy above our heads
as we push off.

It's fairly rough offshore, and it takes a few strong
strokes to turn toward the main beach but after I'm straight
and under way, pulling hard and fast with my paddle, the thin,

pointed hull breaks through the water, showering me with a cold spray. This time it's Barr who stays back and I who lead the way for the entire time it takes to get back to the other side. When we finally get in, pull the boats up and back on the bulkhead, Barr turns to me.

"I've been thinking," he says. "You'd get a lot out of our yoga class and some meditation."

A part of me rebels at his suggestion. I've always harbored a mild disdain for the socks-and-sandals brigade. Judging them as impractical and academic, spouting esoteric babble and paying therapists to keep their heads running in a straight line. It's probably a throwback to my working-class upbringing. Even now I tell myself that I'm not one of them. I don't want to get spiritual and holy. I don't need to stand on my head or balance on one leg. I've seen Carolyn do it—it's okay for her—but I've got a heavy bag hanging in the basement. I can get my exercise punching and kicking.

"It might give you some control over what you're experiencing," he adds.

Control. He hits the magic word, because I know that control is what I need, over my body and my mind, even over this judgmental side of my nature.

I decide to give Simon Barr's medicine a chance.

~ 27 ~

METZLER CALLS TWICE IN THE NEXT week, finally managing to speak to Carolyn, who makes me promise to return his call and confirm our appointment. It's another promise that I break. I want to give myself the opportunity to heal without him.

I spend a lot of time with Jade, walking the beach, playing with her in the sand, digging holes, making castles, and reading her stories at night, before she sleeps. *Curious George, Franklin, Peter Pan, Mr. Jelly, I Spy.* Her library is extensive, and I have established a routine. She has her bath with her mother, gets into her pajamas, brushes her teeth, and it's story time. Daddy lies on the floor beside her bed and reads. There is never a night when she doesn't try to squeeze an extra book out of me, and rarely a night when she doesn't succeed. At the end of my reading she always asks if I'll lie with her for a while, then she sticks her warm little hand out from her bedcovers and touches mine. We usually stay like that till she's asleep. She knows I'm a soft touch, particularly when she tells me that she loves me as big as the ocean and as high as Montauk Lighthouse, which in her mind is even higher than the sky. I get misty-eyed when I think of her growing up, becoming a woman, when I'll look back on these days, when my little girl will have become a memory. I've already missed so much, and my time with her now is the most valuable thing I have. My great hope is that I can stay around long enough to help her grow and look out for her while she does.

My relationship with Jade has solidified my relationship with Carolyn. We're close again, almost like we were before I became Charlie Wolf. A couple of times I've nearly told her the whole story, about the planted evidence, the faked affidavit, but I can't do that to her. I don't want to make her an accomplice.

Still, Carolyn is insightful. She knows that, deep down, something is eating me up. Whenever we're alone, talking about what happened and the effect it has had on me, she asks the same question, pressing the same button. "Who is Charlie Wolf?"

At first I couldn't figure out what she meant. After all, she knows who he is, or was.

"Charlie Wolf is the name I went by for two years," I answered, knowing that she was asking for more.

"Yes, but who is he?"

It took some time, but once the question was planted in my mind, I couldn't shake it. I lived it and slept it. Who is Charlie Wolf, and why do I feel him clinging to me? It is as if he is still attached, like a phantom limb.

"Who is Charlie Wolf?"

Finally, I began to understand. Charlie Wolf is me, every weakness and every bent thought, brought to life. Every day he is alive inside me, struggling to break out. The silver bullet, which should have killed him, didn't do its job, not completely. His guilts and his fears still vibrate within the white metal, projecting deluded images and feelings outward, like some kind of sick, malfunctioning transmitter.

While I read the books on Near Death Experiences that Barr has loaned me, and practice *asanas*, or yoga postures, Ray Sasso sits in an eight-foot-by-ten-foot prison cell in the segregated unit of Valhalla. According to Morgan, who is my only contact with that world, Ray's in bad shape, stick-thin and unable to walk ten steps without gasping for breath.

While he sits there, I bend and twist and stretch my body, or sit cross-legged and silent in the corner of our bedroom, attempting to quiet my mind and find some peace.

I practice these disciplines every day, often with my daughter singing inspirational lyrics over her karaoke machine.

Jade is my sunshine.

Then, one afternoon, after an hour of yoga exercise, I had what felt like a revelation. This pain was cleansing me. Every drop of sweat was washing Charlie Wolf away. Like a release valve for my guilt and my fear, working as much on my emotional system as on my joints, muscles, and bones. It was my purge. It was also connecting me to a part of myself that I had not been connected to in many years, the part that yearned for balance and simplicity, to go back to basics, with no more lies.

After that I began to alter my diet, beginning with a forty-eight-hour fast to get rid of the garbage that has sustained me for most of the past two years. By the end of the fast I felt as if the entire mechanism of my mind had been taken down off the shelf, disassembled, dusted off, and polished.

My guilt had diminished and my paranoia subsided. I thought that I could finally see the end of my nightmare.

For a time, I was clean.

***

It's nine o'clock, an hour before yoga class. Carolyn is coming with me and April Summers is staying here with Jade. April lives with her parents, a five-minute walk from here, and looks like her name. She's twenty-two years old, about five feet seven inches tall, and between the sun and the peroxide her hair is as white as Jade's. She's got the kind of legs that are slim at the ankle, round and muscular at the calf, small again at the knee and long and smooth up top, a tiny waist and stand-up breasts. In fact, with the exception of a small gold ring through her right nostril, she looks like a Barbie doll. Her face is heart-shaped, her lips are full, and her eyes are big, blue, and not quite innocent, with long, dark lashes. She calls me Mr. Lamb, and her voice is sort of husky, with a strange little giggle in it that sounds like a squeak.

April is training to be a professional day-care worker, and Jade loves her. They relate. I suppose it's the Barbie doll thing. Carolyn has used her to babysit for the past two years. She trusts Jade with April Summers, which is more than I do, but that has nothing to do with April, it is simply the way I have become in the past weeks. I am very possessive when it comes to my daughter; I like to know where she is and what she is doing at all times.

"She'll be fine," Carolyn assures me, as we walk from the house and toward the Jeep. I can hear Jade singing in the background, her voice echoing and breaking as it comes through the small speaker. Singing a gospel number this time, almost in tune.

"Mr. Lamb?" April's voice catches me from behind, just as I'm about to open the driver side door and climb in.

I turn.

"There is a phone call for you. A man by the name of Mr. James. He says it's very important."

I haven't spoken to Morgan in a few days and wonder what he wants. A part of me hopes it's to say that the lawyers have reached some kind of plea bargain, but I realize that's unlikely, on either side.

There is a sense of foreboding as I look at Carolyn. "Could you wait for me a minute?"

She looks concerned. It seems every time Morgan phones I go into a depression for a day. "Go ahead," she replies. "I'll be in the car."

I walk back into the house. Jade has hit her stride with her performance, and I ask April if she can turn the volume down a bit. Then I go into the kitchen, as far from the rest of them as I can, and take the phone from the wall. I feel bad about this call, and I'm not sure why, till Morgan says, "He's out."

"What do you mean he's out?" I ask.

"Sasso made bail at eight-thirty this morning," he answers flatly.

"Jane Carroll told me that would never happen," I argue. I feel betrayed. Everything is closing in on me. The kitchen feels small and claustrophobic, and I'm looking out the window into the driveway as if I expect to see Ray roll in on his bike. My head aches. I smell roses.

"Jane Carroll didn't know he was going to end up with one lung and a contract on him," Morgan answers. "Listen, Jack, in his condition he's not exactly a threat, and he's sure as hell not going to run."

"Wouldn't it be safer for him inside?" I answer, looking around the kitchen.

"Maybe, maybe not," Morgan replies. "He's got a hardship case now and he's not posing any risk of flight."

I see them, half a dozen roses, all red, in a vase on the windowsill.

My head is throbbing. "This is not the way it was supposed to happen," I say feebly.

"None of this is the way it's supposed to happen," Morgan counters. "I just wanted to keep you informed."

"Thanks," I answer.

Another track starts on the karaoke machine, and Jade kicks in with a country and western tear jerker.

"Call me if anything develops," I say. "I want to know everything that's going on."

"You got it," Morgan promises.

I put the phone back, pick the roses up from their vase, and walk from the kitchen and toward the door.

"Was that a nasty phone call?" Jade's voice echoes through the cheap speaker.

I stop at the door, turn, and walk to where she's seated on the sofa. April moves over to let me get close to my daughter. The music track crackles in the background as I hover above them.

An instant later the vertigo hits and I'm looking down at the top of Jade's head from what feels like a hundred feet above her. Everything around me is ice-cold. I'm having a panic attack. I drop the flowers on the floor and watch them scatter as I pull back, away from them.

April Summers's voice is shrill with nerves. "Mr. Lamb—"

I turn on her, my eyes wild. "What do you want?!"

She pulls back, frightened.

I step toward her. "I asked you a question!"

Her voice is so meek I can hardly hear it. "Are you okay, Mr. Lamb?"

Jade is staring up at me with a terrible look in her eyes, like she's just seen a monster. I feel ashamed.

"Sorry ... Sorry ... " I fumble.

April looks down at the roses.

"They're from my mother's garden. I brought them for you and Mrs. Lamb."

"Sorry," I repeat, then walk to the front door and out into the driveway.

Carolyn is sitting in the Jeep, with the window down, looking at me. I know I've got that asylum look in my eyes, intense to the point of glazed.

"What's happened?" she asks.

"Sasso's out of jail," I answer.

"Out of jail? I don't understand," she says, sounding confused.

The last I spoke to her about Ray he was in a solitary cell in Valhalla, under a twenty-four-hour police guard.

"He made bail."

"I thought that was impossible," she continues.

"He's out," I repeat angrily, letting my nerves beat me.

She counters with her calm. "So how does that change anything?"

"I don't like having him on the outside."

Carolyn firms up, getting straight to the point. "Are we in danger?"

I think of Ray, barely able to breathe, let alone walk. Jane Carroll will have him watched so closely he won't be able to shit without spectators.

"No," I answer.

Carolyn relaxes. "Then get in the car and let's go."

"You go on your own," I answer. "My head hurts."

She looks at me for another few seconds, assessing my condition.

"Jack, you can't keep doing this. You're like a yo-yo. Every time Morgan calls this house, you react. You get depressed, you get manic, you go silent. The truth is you're going to have to learn to live with whatever has happened. So let's just get on with our lives."

"Please, Carolyn, go without me," I answer. I'm so close to spilling the truth that I'm afraid to talk. "I'll be better when you get back. I promise."

She hops out of the passenger side, walks around, and stands in front of me. "I don't have to go either," she says. "April can stay with Jade and we can take a walk and talk things over."

I firm up again. "But I want you to go. I want to be by myself. I need to be."

"You've got to get over this," Carolyn persists. "These mood swings are no good for anybody. It's upsetting me, and it's confusing to Jade." She looks me in the eyes, and I can see her resolve. "Maybe it's time you got some help. I know you've spoken to Simon, but maybe he's not the right person."

"I'll be okay," I insist stubbornly. "I'm sorry for what's going on, but I can work this through by myself."

"Have you returned Dr. Metzler's phone calls?" she asks. The fact is, I haven't. On top of that, and another thing that Carolyn doesn't know, is that I've purposefully missed two scheduled appointments.

I'm becoming agitated. "I don't need antipsychotic drugs," I state. "I don't need to walk around like a dead man. I want to be alive. I need to go through this on my own."

"The problem is," Carolyn replies "that we're all going through it with you." Then her eyes soften and her tone lightens. "Tell me what I can do to make it easier."

I feel the divide in me between the truth and the lie. I can see it in her eyes. I want to cross over with Carolyn there, waiting on the other side, but I can't take the first step. Then, for a moment, I think that maybe she wouldn't care that I'd lied, that I'd signed the trumped-up papers that started all this stuff in the first place. She doesn't know Ray, other than that he's a criminal, an outlaw who's getting what he deserves. But that's not it either. This is about me, living with myself, who I am and who I'm not. This is about Charlie Wolf and Jack Lamb.

Finally, I reach out and pull her toward me. Hugging her tight to my body. She feels strong and warm and safe.

"You could give me a ride down to the beach," I say.

~ 28 ~

THE TEMPERATURE IS IN THE low eighties the waves are building, and even though it's still early morning, there are a flock of surfers out on the water. I take off my trainers and socks, leave them at the end of the boardwalk, and walk down to the ocean, then right, following the shoreline for a few hundred yards until I'm absolutely alone, with the steady pounding of the waves and the cries of the gulls above me. Another hundred yards and I veer back toward the bluff, finding a spot where I'm fairly certain that I can be without being seen or disturbed.

I sit down, fold my legs in close to my body, place my hands on my knees, straighten my spine, lower my head a little, and force myself to begin one of the breathing exercises that we practice in class. It's pretty simple stuff, a long inhalation, a retention of the breath when the lungs are full, followed by an equally long exhalation, intended to relax me and quiet my mind.

But I don't relax. I keep thinking about Ray Sasso, out of prison, home with his wife and son. What does he tell them? What does he think of what has happened to him? I know what he thinks of Charlie Wolf. I can feel his hatred. I believe it is that hatred that provokes the panic attacks, like a dark energy between us. I've read enough of the books that Barr has loaned me to believe that reality is created by the mind. I'm proof of that. We are all connected, like frequency bands, or vibrational fields, and the things that happen to us are attracted by the field that surrounds us. We are magnetic. Light attracts light, dark attracts dark. It's the lie that clings to me. It's Charlie Wolf who won't release his hold. Dragging me down, into the lower levels, back into that basement where he'll always live.

I sit here tormented, with the wind blowing sand in my face, while my wife chants *ohm* and my kid sits at home, next to a full-sized Barbie doll with a pierced nostril. The irony makes me laugh, but it's not a good laugh.

My thoughts are negative, turning black.

My head is pounding, as if the bullet has a heart and pulse all its own. I feel the cold creeping in, all around me. I sense my enemies close by and feel defenseless against them. Books and postures, meditation and prayer, they don't mean a thing if I am just going through the motions. I've got to make this change inside me real, yet at this moment, nothing seems real, except the lie and the reality that the lie is creating.

I stand and brush the sand from the seat of my pants. Then I turn and begin to walk in the direction of the water, against the wind.

I see a figure walking toward me. I'm not sure where it has come from, but it is suddenly there. There is still fifty yards between us, and the wind is getting stronger, but I recognize the walk, the way the body shifts, the shoulders wide, arms hanging relaxed but ready, long hair blowing forward, obscuring the features of his face. I veer to one side, and he follows my movement, like a mirror. Walking purposely toward me. He's coming. I can feel him in my heart as it slams against my ribs.

Ray believes in justice.

He raises his head. His eyes are piercing, and black with rage.

"Jack?"

The voice comes from another place, faint, as if it's struggling against the wind.

"Jack!" Stronger now and more urgent.

Sand batters my eyes, and I blink reflexively. When I open them again, Ray is gone. I turn, searching, and see Carolyn behind me.

"Where have you been?" she asks.

There is a cloud of mist above her head, descending like a sheer black veil in front of her face.

Her voice is distant. "Come back home."

~ 29 ~

I RUN TOWARD HER, FEELING fear projecting from her body in strong steady waves, pushing out at me until it seems I am swimming against it, fighting for each breath struggling to reach her, until finally I am by her side.

"Something bad has happened" she says.

"What is it?" I ask, looking around for Ray but knowing, inside, that he's gone. I don't feel him anymore.

"Let's go back to the house and talk."

I'm right in her face, breathing the chill that surrounds her.

"Tell me now," I demand.

She studies my eyes as I fight back the first stabs of panic.

"Morgan called." Her voice trembles. "There was a car bombing in Mount Vernon."

Am I seeing ghosts?

"Is Ray Sasso dead?" I ask.

Carolyn drops her eyes. The next words seem particularly hard for her to say. "No. It was his wife and seven-year-old son. They're dead."

My throat constricts. I feel like I'm being strangled. "Morgan thinks it was some kind of revenge killing," she continues.

"Revenge?" I repeat.

"I don't know all the details. He wants to come out here and—"

"No," I say, cutting her off. "I don't want Morgan here. I've already told him that. I don't want him anywhere near us."

"Then let's go back, and you call him," she answers, putting her arm around my shoulders, trying to get me moving again.

I stall, staring at her. "Did he say anything else?"

The darkness that I perceive around her creates shadows, hardening her features, making her appear frail and brittle, aging her. Her eyes, at this moment, remind me of my mother's, watching me from the kitchen window as I take a beating from my
father; they are helpless and frightened. I look down at the sand.

"This is bad, isn't it?" she asks.

"We'll be fine," I lie, pretending to sound confident and committed, causing her fear to retreat.

***

Jade is seated, with April Summers, on the living-room carpet, assembling a Sleeping Beauty jigsaw puzzle. She jumps up as I enter, running to me. I lift her to my chest and hold her tight in my arms.

"Daddy, where were you?"

"I was on the beach," I reply.

"Swimming?"

"No, Jade, I was walking," I answer, smelling the apples in her hair.

"Why?" It's a word I've grown used to in the past weeks. Every sentence has a why? attached.

"I was walking because I needed to think."

"Do you have to walk so you can think?"

"Sometimes," I say as I carry her to the sofa and sit down.

"Why?"

I let that one go and turn to April, suggesting that Carolyn pay her for the morning so she can go home.

Carolyn and I both thank her at the same time, our voices forming an anxious chorus, then we sit in silence, listening to her footsteps recede down the gravel drive. I pull Jade a little bit closer, vowing to myself that I will protect her forever. I feel Carolyn looking at me, her eyes searching for mine.

"Those poor people," is all she says.

"Yes," I answer. I feel hollow inside.

"You should call Morgan."

Jade is quiet, staring up at me. She knows something's wrong and looks confused. Carolyn reaches out and lifts her to her lap. "Use the phone in the kitchen, I'll stay here."

I get up and walk to the kitchen. I'm in a daze, walking through a nightmare. I can't even remember the number for Morgan's cell phone. Standing there with the telephone in my hand, my finger hovering above the digits, drawing a blank. Then it comes, like an automatic motion, and I tap in the numbers. Listening. Three rings and I hear his voice.

"Charlie?"

Did he say Charlie? Why did he call me Charlie? "It's Jack," I say. "Jack Lamb."

"Oh, sorry, Jack, sorry, I was expecting somebody else. Sorry."

It sounds like he's covering up for something and I'm about to ask who the hell he knows named Charlie, except Charlie Wolf, but what's the point?

"Bad scene up here," he says. "Very bad." His tone is somber.

I use every reserve to pull myself together. "How did it happen?" I ask.

"Sasso'd only been out two hours, home with his wife and kid. Two hours, and they went after him."

"Who was it?"

"Don't know, not for sure anyway. They used a plastic explosive, military stuff, wired to the ignition of his Range Rover. The state police still think it's an inner club thing, like the stabbing, but nobody's really certain. The guys that hit him in Valhalla aren't talking. Whoever did it knew he was out and knew where he lived." Morgan's voice hardens.

"Bastards murdered a seven-year-old kid and a pregnant woman."

"Pregnant?"

"Fourteen weeks," Morgan answers.

I feel another knot in my throat. My brain's going numb. I think of Ray's son William, with his face scrubbed clean and his silky black hair combed and parted, wearing his blue jean overalls, ready for school. Laughing at my jokes and giving me his toy soldier.

I hear Jade's voice in the next room, asking Carolyn what's the matter with daddy. "Is it the boo-boo on his head?"

"Where did it happen?" I ask.

"In his driveway, in front of his house. His kid had a dentist's appointment at eleven-thirty and Sasso was going with them because the little boy was scared of the dentist. Since Sasso's not too well, his wife was at the wheel of the car. The kid left something back in the house, so Sasso went to get it and his wife started the car. Bang. That was it."

"Where's Ray?"

"In Valhalla on a material-witness order," Morgan answers.

"Protective custody, twenty-four-hour lockdown."

"Is there going to be a funeral?" I ask.

Morgan hesitates. "Jack, things are still happening here. Nobody's thinking about the funeral yet."

"I want details when you do think about it."

"Why, you gonna send flowers?" he asks.

"Fuck you, Morgan."

A few hours later he calls back to tell me that there will be a family funeral.

"Is Ray going?" I demand.

Morgan hesitates. "Yes," he answers. "He'll be there."

"When?"

"Three days from now."

I get this feeling, like a compulsion, that I should be there, too.

"Where is it?"

"At St. Joseph's in Mount Vernon. Unfortunately, there's going to be as many cops as mourners," Morgan replies.

"What time?"

Morgan hesitates. "Why, what are you thinking about?"

"What time is the service?"

"It's at three o'clock in the afternoon. Listen, Jack, I'm sorry about my remark earlier. I was beat and I wasn't thinking straight. I shouldn't have said it."

"That's okay," I answer. "Forget it."

"I was wondering about taking a drive out there," Morgan continues. "We could sit down and talk."

"We've got nothing to talk about." My words have a sharp edge, which I cover by saying, "Sorry Morgan, but it's not a good time. Why don't we wait till this is all over. Okay?"

"I really think we should talk," Morgan repeats.

"Later," I answer, and put down the phone.

~ 30 ~

I HAVE NO PEACE OF MIND. There seems to be no higher ground for me, only the escalating consequences of my past actions. I can't get to sleep at night, and when I do my dreams are violent and graphic. I see the takedown, over and over again. I watch the bullet fly in slow motion toward my head. Feel it burn its way through the flesh and bone, into my brain. Then I jolt awake. In that long, cold moment I am Charlie Wolf, back in that basement in Mount Vernon. It's all about to happen again, and again, like a tape loop in my mind. That's my hell.

Carolyn is losing patience. She has phoned the hospital and spoken with Metzler and knows that I've missed appointments and not returned calls. She knows I'm frightened. She also knows that I haven't been taking my medication. I feel her looking at me when she thinks I can't see her. What she doesn't know is that I see everything. I have eyes everywhere. If I am standing in the kitchen with my back to her, I can watch her come into the room. Watch as she opens the refrigerator and takes out a carton of milk, watch as she fills a glass or makes a sandwich. It's the same kind of seeing that I did when I died. It has nothing to do with my physical eyes. The best way I can describe it is to say that my spirit is often separate from my body, and that my spirit has eyes.

Carolyn had it right when she asked me, "Who is Charlie Wolf?"

The problem is I don't know the answer. Don't know where the divide between Charlie Wolf and Jack Lamb is, and I don't trust either of them.

On the morning of the funeral in Mount Vernon, I am particularly withdrawn, unwilling to communicate with either Carolyn or Jade. My guilt is so extreme that it seems to trigger paranoia in every direction. I expect retribution.

Finally, after a breakfast during which I eat nothing and sit fixated on the wall clock, counting the hours and minutes till the funeral, Carolyn suggests I call Simon Barr.

"You told me that you trust him," she says. "I think you need someone to talk to."

I look into her eyes. They have lost their luster and have what appear to be long, faded bruises beneath them. It's terrible to watch someone you love die slowly, which is more or less what Carolyn has been doing since I got home. It's breaking my heart. Enough is enough.

"Okay," I agree. "I'll phone him."

At least Barr is not judgmental. I can be as crazy as I feel with him, and he won't walk away.

I catch him on the way out the door and he suggests I stop by later in the afternoon, after lunch.

***

The sun is bright and warm, pouring through the bay front window of Simon Barr's house, bathing us in a light that seems to shrink my nighttime fears and bring new perspective to what I am experiencing. He is sitting, facing me, in a tan-leather club chair, his back to the window, while I sit straight-backed against the firm cushions of a beige sofa, with a coffee table between us. The table is rectangular, made of dark-lacquered bamboo, and the small rolls in its polished surface are glowing with the reflected sunlight.

I have told him about the car bomb and about my compulsion to be at the funeral service. I have told almost everything, and even though there is sense of confidentiality with Barr, I will not trust him with my lie. The lie is the single thing that I keep separate, embracing it so tightly that it has become what I am.

"Do you feel responsible for what happened to Ray Sasso's family?" he asks.

"Yes," I answer.

"Why?"

This is my chance to confess, to own up about the planted evidence and the false testimony, but I don't have the guts to accept the responsibility. I don't have the strength to bear the weight of what has happened. All I manage is a half-truth. "My written testimony against him set all these events in motion."

"But that testimony was part of your job," Barr replies.

"I'm still sorry I signed the affidavit," I answer, feeling the lie like a sickness in my belly.

Barr raises his head and looks at me. There is a flicker in his eyes, like an animal awareness as if he has just heard something in the distance, the snap of a twig or the warning cry of a bird.

"You're holding something back."

He's right on the button, pressing. I can feel the pressure in my head, as if the bullet is about to move.

I meet his eyes and try to conceal my secret.

"Must be tough," he continues. "You are so open now in a spiritual sense, right on the cusp of a real understanding and this one thing is stopping you."

"It's the bullet in my head," I say as if that is the one thing he's talking about.

"Do you think so?" he asks.

"Got to be," I continue.

"Maybe you're having a spiritual crisis," Barr suggests.

"What's that?"

"A time when you need to redefine who you are," he answers.

I think of Charlie Wolf, down in his basement in the dark.

You're obviously going through some changes," Barr continues. "You should spend some time on your own. Go somewhere and sit. See your life from a different perspective."

Time on my own? He hits another button.

"I can't do that," I answer.

"Why?"

"I've been away from my family enough. I don't want to go anywhere else."

As I speak, I am thinking that I need to be around to protect them from Ray Sasso.

"I'm talking about now, right now," Barr continues, turning to look over his shoulder, through the window and out at the water. "Take the kayak, paddle over to the island, and sit for a while. It did you good last time, maybe it will work again. Have a talk with yourself." Barr stands up.

The steps down to the beach seem long and demanding, but even as I take them I realize that the struggle is with my mind, not my body. Barr doesn't seem to notice, or is being too polite to mention my slowness, although at the end of the near-vertical drop he saves me the effort of trying to drag the kayak off the bulkhead and down to the water by doing it for me.

I'm wearing a light cotton pullover, with a hood. I tighten the drawstrings around my neck as I look across the bay at the small pedestal of sand that is Cartwright Island. There is a light breeze, so the water has a little chop, although no whitecaps. I think I'll be okay, if I take it easy. Still, the notion of paddling a mile or more to sit by myself in silence seems daunting.

"Maybe I'll take a rain check on the boat ride," I say. "I'm liable to drown out there."

Barr bends down and dips his hand into the water.

"I doubt it. Water temperature must be seventy degrees. You could float for hours, hanging on to the boat."

With that reassurance he watches as I climb into the shell, then he pushes me into the water. I back paddle to turn the boat around, toward Cartwright Island, and, noting as I did last time that it looks a long way from the vantage of being almost level with the water, take a few strokes, looking back once to see Barr halfway back up the steps.

I reckon it's a little after two o'clock in the afternoon, probably less than an hour till the funeral service. I paddle harder for the next few minutes, as if I am late for the event, like it might be taking place on the island and I've got to get there to pay my respects. I think of Ray waiting for me, and, as I do, I look down and see a flash of white below the surface of the water. It's quick, but enough to cause me to stop paddling.

I'm in the channel now, and the water is deep. Dark and deep, with something swimming in it, below the kayak. Maybe a bluefish? I see it again, but it's just the reflection of sun off the shiny skin. It's big, and fast, and right beneath me. Look around. There's not another boat in sight. I'm alone on the water. I've heard about an area of the Pacific near Carmel, California, where the bottoms of kayaks have been mistaken for seals by Great Whites, and the shark has taken the entire boat down with a single bite. I've seen documentaries featuring the survivors of those attacks, stared at their shredded limbs.

The waters off Montauk are a breeding ground for the Great White.

Here I am, out here alone, with only myself to rely on, and I don't trust myself.

The white flash moves the opposite way, from port to starboard. It's big, nearly the length of the kayak.

Staring down, not paddling, I am fixated by whatever is down there. I feel my muscles tightening as my heart dances a wild rhythm in my chest.

Once, when I was a kid, I saw a family of seals get hit by a ten-foot White on the ocean side of Napeague along the shore. I still remember the sounds of those seals, like the bellows of cows being slaughtered, as the big fish tore chunks of flesh from their sides, causing the tide to run red with their blood, dragging them back to the sea, one by one.

I imagine the pink gaping mouth, the white triangular teeth, shaped like daggers, razor-sharp, tearing through the flesh from my body.

I see it coming, rising fast, getting bigger, that great tail thrashing the water, turning it to foam, its wrinkled mouth opening. Breaking the surface.

I pull back against the opposite side of the boat, tipping it.

Bleep. Bleep. Bleep. The sound breaks through my consciousness like a warning. My mind stops.

Something inside me knows.

This is a dream.

This is not real.

Bleep. Bleep.

I blink, and stare down at a reflection of my own eyes in the water, looking up, straight at me, glazed with fear.

The sight triggers a sense of separation. I'm down there. I am this reflection, looking up at the scared man in the boat. This is not really happening at all. I'm living inside my head. Walking through my mind.

The bleeper stops and I snap to, turning away from my reflection, looking ahead to the island. Forcing my arms to paddle as I will myself to the shore.

Telling myself that there was no shark. There is nothing but my mind, throwing images out like the images from a projector, projecting my fear in a hundred different forms.

I get to shore and step out of the kayak and into the sand. The tide is coming in, making the strip of land even smaller than it was the last time. It's covered in a gray-white hill of clamshells and crab shells that the gulls have picked from the bay and dropped from up high, over and over again, till the shells crack open, giving access to the soft flesh inside. The shells dig hard and sharp into my feet as I walk over them to the clean sand at the center of the island. Heading to approximately the same spot that I found before, there I sit down, looking back toward the shoreline of Amagansett. The sun is out, the temperature is somewhere in the seventies, the wind is moderate, but I'm still shaking.

I stand up and begin to walk, back across the jagged shells, to the shoreline and then up along the island until it narrows, forming a peninsula that joins with Gardiner's Island. I'm walking fast, my feet in the water, the cuffs of my jeans getting soaked, really going through it, ranting, shouting, cursing Jane Carroll, Morgan James. Cursing Charlie Wolf.

Cursing myself, for my cowardice.

My voice sounds big and clumsy, out of place with the rush of water against the shore and the wind as it whistles across the sand.

Knowing all the while as I vent my anger and frustration that Ray Sasso is burying his family.

Finally, I'm on my knees. I don't know how I got there, but I am, looking up at the sky with my arms outstretched and my hands in the air, asking for mercy. My head is breaking, the bullet is burning.

"Please God, help me. Forgive me!"

I close my eyes and lower my head, inhaling the sweet, heavy smell of roses. Everywhere are roses.

I imagine myself in the midst of a congregation of people, kneeling in prayer. Imagination segues into reality as I feel the cushion beneath my knees, the back of the wooden pew against my spine. There are strangers to either side of me.

"Our Father who art in heaven, Hallowed be Thy name—"

Where am I?

Ahead I see two caskets in front of a wooden altar, a crucifix hanging on the wall above, and flowers all around, hundreds of blood red roses.

My voice joins in the chorus. "Thy kingdom come, Thy will be done on earth as it is in heaven. Give us this day our daily bread—"

Ray Sasso steps from the front row of people. His hair looks matted and filthy, his body is skeletal, and his skin is a dead gray. Dressed in a black suit that hangs shiny and loose over his shoulders, he kneels beside the smaller of the two caskets. He is weeping.

"Forgive us our trespasses as we forgive those who have trespassed against us —"

He crosses himself and stands. Turning, he looks directly at me. His eyes are pained and tired. Fixed and staring, they penetrate mine, stripping away the fabric of my lie. I am an impostor. I don't belong here.

I stop praying, but the other voices continue.

"Lead us not into temptation and deliver us from evil."

The sweet smell of roses gives way to the stink of death.

I wake up, alone on this tiny island, with the smell of decaying fish all around me. The air feels cold against my face.

I look to the sky: it's a pale blue and the sun is far away, hovering above the ridge of trees to the west, on top of the bluff. I am here with this strange madness, this feeling of being asleep, yet awake, walking from one dream to enter another.

I get to my feet and make my way back to the kayak, which is shifting sideways in the water, its bow on the beach, stern in the bay. Pick up the paddle and climb in, then using the edge of the blade I push myself out. The *Calypso* bobs and tips as I turn and point it west. Waves break over the bow as I dig in and paddle.

***

Simon Barr is sitting on his deck, watching me climb the last of the steps leading to him.

"I was beginning to get worried," he says, as I walk closer. "You were gone a long time." He looks out at the bay, and adds, "The wind kicked up, and the water got rough." Then he notices that I am wet from spray. "Let me bring you a towel; how about a whiskey?"

I decline.

"Did you get anywhere?" he asks.

I turn to him, lost for words. Finally, I confess. "I feel like I'm dreaming and can't wake up. That's where I got. That's where I am."

Barr studies me for a few seconds, gauging his answer. Finally, he reaches out and pats me gently on the back, saying, "I know it's tough right now, but hang in there, Jack, don't give up."

~ 31 ~

I SEE THE BLACK CHRYSLER New Yorker as I pull into our driveway. It's an older car and a bit run-down, sort of the thing I associate with a gypsy cab, an observation I have shared with Morgan James more than once. I know it's him because I recognize the license plate, J 45 9 MM. He swears the 9 MM is a coincidence, but I've always doubted it. The thing I don't recognize is the small Wells Fargo trailer that is hooked to the rear bumper, its door secured by a padlock. I wonder what's inside, but more than that I wonder what Morgan James is doing at my house. I'm angry as I open the front door and enter. It's the kind of feeling that rocks my equilibrium. I've certainly made my wishes clear to him and the idea that he would come here infuriates me. It also makes me nervous. Morgan is no asshole. He wouldn't be visiting on a whim.

I walk in to find him seated on the sofa. His aura is tight to his head, a deep purple and barely visible in the light of the room. There's a full cup of coffee in front of him, still steaming, so I assume he's just arrived, although Carolyn and Jade are not with him.

He looks up as I enter, and his colors change, a yellow flickers in the blue then dies, followed by a spark of red.

"Hello, Jack."

At least he's calling me Jack and not Charlie, but his voice sounds edgy, and his eyes are intense, slightly glazed, like he's bone tired but there's one last drop of adrenaline keeping his lights on. This is definitely no social call.

"Morgan ... "

"Yeah, I know. You weren't expecting me, and you're not happy to see me."

That' not exactly true. It's good to see him, I'm just not comfortable about our connection anymore. He reminds me of something I don't want to be reminded of.

He waits another few seconds till it's obvious that I'm not going to say any more, then he drops the bomb.

"Ray Sasso's missing."

I feel my stomach tighten, and my mouth goes dry as Morgan continues. "It happened during the funeral service."

My next question is a reflex. "Where are my wife and kid?"

"Upstairs," he answers. "Carolyn's with Jade, putting her to bed."

I nod. Okay, that much is good. Everybody is safe.

My palms are moist, and there are beads of sweat gathering on my forehead. They should have had maximum security around Ray. This should never have happened.

"How?" I ask.

"I don't know for sure. Nobody knows. Maybe he'd planned it, maybe it just happened. It's more likely that he set it up."

I'm getting impatient. I want details.

"Set what up?" I ask.

"From what the state cops tell me, Sasso was very upset in the car on the way to the church. Spent most of the ride with his head down, his face buried in his hands. Not exactly crying, but making these funny little noises, like he was catching his breath. They figured it was his lung giving him trouble. When they arrived at St. Joe's, they walked him right up to the front of the church. I was there, and there must have been half a dozen agents to the other side and behind us. I felt sorry for the guy. He couldn't even have his grief in private. A few minutes into the service and he got up, made it to the caskets, and said his goodbyes. When he came back he started wheezing again, louder this time. I thought he was going to die. A little while later he whispered that he felt sick and asked to go to the toilet. We walked him out into the foyer. He went inside alone and shut the door. I know somebody should have been with him, but given the circumstances we let it slide. When he didn't come out and the door was locked from the inside I knew we were in trouble. We broke it down and he was gone."

"How?" I ask.

"Through a tiny window at the back side of the building," Morgan answers.

"But Ray was a cripple, how the hell did he crawl out of a window?"

"He must have had help," Morgan answers.

"Who?" I ask.

Morgan looks at me in an uneasy silence.

"Who?" I repeat.

"Jack, the story gets a little strange here, a little crazy—"

I'm impatient. "Tell me what happened," I demand.

"Were you anywhere around Mount Vernon today?" he asks.

His tone is abrupt.

"What?"

Morgan raises his hands. "Look, man, I'm sorry, but I've got to ask. A few of the people we interviewed saw a guy inside the church who fit your description." He hesitates, studying me. "Right down to the gray shirt you're wearing. Nobody knows who he was. Seems he just disappeared, a little before Sasso did."

"Are you crazy?" I ask him. "Coming out here to accuse me of—"

"Hold on, I'm not accusing you of anything. I just asked you a question."

"Do I need an alibi?" I ask.

"No," he replies. "Your word is good with me."

I settle down. "Okay. At three o'clock this afternoon I was sitting by myself on a patch of sand called Cartwright Island in the middle of Gardiner's Bay. If you need me to, I can prove it." Simon Barr is my proof, but I'm also reminded of the experience I had while I was on the island, when my imagination seemed to flow into reality. Is there a connection between that and what people saw at the church?

"You don't need to prove anything to me," Morgan states. "But I would like to notify the local cops, just to keep an eye on things here."

His words and tone send a chill through me.

"You think he'd come after me?"

Morgan reaches out and grips my arm, squeezing my biceps.

"No, not out here, but I don't want to take any chances."

"And I don't want a bunch of uniforms hanging around outside the front door," I reply. "It's hard enough around here without an audience."

"I was thinking more in terms of a patrol car, driving by maybe half a dozen times a day."

"That would be fine," I agree.

Morgan continues to stare at me. His eyes don't blink, and his lips barely move when he asks, "What's happening to you, Jack?"

His question catches me off guard.

"You seem distant," he adds.

"I'm going through some changes," I answer, reminding myself that this mess is not his fault.

He looks at me and nods. "So am I, but we can't take back what we've done, can we?"

"No," I reply with resignation.

Morgan holds my eyes for a few more seconds in silence.

Finally, he says, "I've got to go," and stands up from the chair.

"There's a spare bedroom upstairs, you're welcome to stay," I offer by way of apology for being so difficult.

"I can't," he answers. "I've got to be back in town early. Thanks anyway."

I get up and show him to the door. It's a strange, awkward moment, like we've both entered an understanding, that whatever has been set in motion is now charting its own course. It has changed our relationship, and it's changing our lives.

"One more thing," Morgan says, stepping out into the overcast night.

"What's that?"

He walks to the back of the trailer, takes a key from his pocket, and slips it in, opening the lock.

"I've had this since the day of the takedown," he answers, pulling the crossbar to the side. "I know how much it means to you. Belonged to your brother, didn't it?"

He opens the doors.

I follow him to the back and look in. It's dark, but I can still make out the silhouette of the Shovelhead. I've wondered what happened to it, but with everything else that's gone on I've never asked.

"Yes, it did," I answer.

"It's been in my garage," Morgan says, as I step up into the trailer and hold the handlebars steady while he removes the straps that secure it; then we roll the bike backwards down the ramp. It feels strange touching the old rubber handgrips. Again I feel connected to Charlie Wolf.

Even in the darkness I see that the motorcycle has been cleaned and polished. With that observation comes another wave of feeling, taking me farther back in time. I sense Robert's presence, remembering the day he rode the newly purchased bike home from Westhampton Beach, bucking along slowly in third gear, like he was afraid it was going to take off and throw him. After he'd shut down the engine and climbed off we walked around the Shovel like it was a work of art.

"Who did the polishing?" I ask.

Morgan smiles, his teeth white against the darkness. "Even used a toothbrush on the spokes," he answers.

"Looks great," I say. "I was wondering if I'd ever see it again." Then, looking down at the bike, "There's a lot of sentimental value to that old ride."

"I know," he says, and for that moment we're friends again, like before, with nothing between us.

I extend my hand. "Good luck, *amigo*." We shake, and he's gone.

I watch as his car backs down the driveway, its headlights casting lonely spots on the leaves of the trees. Then I roll the bike to the garage and put it away.

Finally, I go back into the house and walk into the study, which is a small room off the hallway leading to the stairway. Inside, there is an old school desk, which looks like a flat oak table, and a brown-leather office chair. Carolyn's laptop sits on top of the desk. Beside her computer is a bent-arm reading lamp and a telephone. I sit down in the chair and listen to the sounds of the night. I assume that Jade is asleep and Carolyn has gone to bed, in order to leave me alone with Morgan. She'll probably be waiting up for me, wanting me to fill her in on what's happened in Mount Vernon. I know that Morgan wouldn't have said anything to her. He's always good at playing the cards close to his chest.

I pick the phone up and tap in Simon Barr's number, listening as it rings once, twice. Before anyone answers I replace it in its cradle. I can't keep running to Barr for answers. I've got to find them within myself.

I remain still long enough to hear the pine floor creaking. From beyond the walls of the house, the wind whines as it blows through the branches of the trees, and from somewhere far away I hear chimes, plaintive and lonely. The air is thick and heavy, and smells of rain.

Carolyn is awake when I get to bed.

"Is it bad?" she asks, as I settle in beside her. There's a tremor in her voice.

I want to tell her the truth, but I don't want to frighten her. "Sasso's run bail," I answer, trying to make it sound like an everyday thing. "He's sick and he's grief-stricken, and they'll probably get him back in the morning."

Carolyn's voice sounds small and far away in the darkness of the room.

"Jack, does he know where you live?"

"He doesn't even know my real name," I assure her.

I hear a roll of thunder in the distance, then the sound of falling rain against the windowsill.

"We're safe?" she asks softly.

"Yes," I lie again, because tonight I don't feel safe, not even inside my own skin.

~ 32 ~

I HEAR THE PHONE RINGING from somewhere far away. Ringing. I'm coming up, closer to the surface. The ring is louder sharper, right beside me. It hurts my head. Why doesn't somebody answer it? Where's Carolyn? I can't wake up and it won't stop. Come on, I tell myself. Roll over, open your eyes. The clock says 7:30. Who's calling at 7:30?

"Hello?" My voice sounds groggy.

"Jack?" It sounds like Morgan.

"Yes?"

"Talk to me."

I sit up in the bed. "About what?"

"Face-to-face," he answers. "This is too sensitive to get into over a telephone."

"What's going on?" I ask.

"There's a diner in New Rochelle, on Old Post Road, a couple of blocks up from the hospital. I think it's called the Meridian, it's a long silver fifties-style place. Can you get there?"

"Why New Rochelle?" I ask.

"Cause that's where I've got to be, visiting someone," Morgan replies.

"Is it Ray Sasso?"

He doesn't answer my question.

His voice crackles like it's coming from a car phone. "Can you be there in three hours?"

"Yes," I answer, not stopping to think.

The connection goes dead.

I get out of bed. Where's Carolyn? I listen for a few seconds, then call her name.

"I'm in the bathroom with Jade," she answers from the room down the hall.

Pulling on my jeans, I shout back, "I've got to meet Morgan in New Rochelle. I'll need the car for most of the day. Is that all right?"

"Are you okay to drive that far?" she asks.

Recently, the extent of my driving has been local, with Carolyn beside me in the car.

"It's important that I go," I reply. "I'll be fine."

Her voice becomes anxious. "Has something happened?"

"Don't know. He won't talk on the phone, so I'm assuming something's gone down."

Carolyn appears in the doorway, with Jade right behind her. They are dressed nearly identically, in T-shirts and blue jeans, no shoes.

"Do you think they've got Ray Sasso back?" she asks.

"I don't know," I repeat.

"Will you phone me when you do know something?"

"I will," I promise.

"While you're there, I think you should stop and see Dr. Metzler," she suggests. "His last message on the machine sounds pretty urgent. I could phone him and let him know you're coming."

I have a moment of doubt. Is this some kind of setup between Carolyn and Morgan to get me back into the hospital? If it is, I don't want to go. Not while Ray Sasso is loose. I need to be right here, protecting my family.

"Don't phone him. I'll take care of it," I answer.

"Promise me that," she says.

"If I have time," I answer.

"Make time. It's important, and be careful," she adds, kissing me lightly on the lips

***

I'm on the L.I.E., about ten miles east of Stony Brook, when I notice it for the first time, three cars back, about a hundred yards behind me. The car is black with a squared grille. At first I think it's Morgan James, but this car doesn't have a front license plate and this car has tinted windows. I know only one car that looks like that, the black Lincoln that belongs to the club.

I accelerate, cutting across two lanes of the Expressway, and the black car follows, closing the gap between us by fifty yards. It is directly behind me now as if it has just slipped out from cover. I reach across the seat and get hold of Carolyn's cell phone, punching in Morgan's number. I hear his voice say "hello" before the connection begins to break up, and I'm shouting, "Morgan, I'm in trouble! Being followed—" Then I shut up.

I hear Morgan's voice, "Is that you, Jack?"

Carolyn and Morgan, they are the only ones who knew where I was going. My mind is racing, but it keeps arriving at the same place.

I toss the phone down on the passenger seat and the connection breaks. I get a crackle followed by Morgan's voice again, garbled this time, "You a — right? — Can't hear you. Where — ?"

No, I'm not alright. I've been set up, and it's got nothing to do with a visit to see Howard Metzler. Somehow, for some reason, Morgan James has pulled me into a trap.

"Jack? —"

The Lincoln is no more than a car's length behind me. I look in the rearview mirror, desperate to see the driver's face. All I get are fast glimpses of a man with shadowed eyes. Maybe he's wearing dark glasses. I hear the whine of an engine as he screams to within inches of me. My mind flashes to the rider on the red-and-black Harley. Morgan was there, too. Taking me away from the hospital. Telling me I'd been drugged, that I had amnesia. Morgan, my friend, my sole source of information. It has to be Morgan, playing with my head.

His voice is tinny in my ear. "Where are you?"

The Lincoln hits me. My tires squeal against the road, and the Jeep shimmies as I jolt forward, restrained by the seat belt. I'm looking around. Where the fuck are the police? I'm doing 110 miles an hour and I've got a maniac banging into me from behind. Where's the highway patrol? Another whine from the Lincoln. I hear its fan belt slip and scream. I've got the pedal flat to the floor—120. Still it's coming, like the shark in the bay, mouth opening, that big grille rolling forward. It hits and I'm skidding, out of control, my rear end smacking into the dividing wall as sparks fly from the fender. I fight the wheel, and the front end slides, my wing mirror sheared off, my side window shattered. The Lincoln locks on to me, its grille biting into my rear bumper, sounding like a tractor, straining with a load, pushing me mercilessly up the highway. I've got to get clear. It's my only chance. I whip the steering wheel hard to the right, squeezing the last out of the six-cylinder engine. Enough to rip me clear as I veer back across the highway, skidding in front of a pickup truck, its horn blaring and driver shouting curses, waving his fist.

That tinny voice again, far away, "I can't hear you. What's happening?" Morgan is listening. He's got to be listening. Waiting for the end.

"Fuck you!" I shout back at him, aiming the Jeep for an exit ramp. Where are the cops? I need the cops. I'm going ninety by the time I hit the first bend. The Jeep skids as the road banks and I feel the wheels on my side leave the ground. I'm going over. Then it flattens and I bounce down. The smell of gasoline and burning rubber seems to seep up through the floor of the car, jamming my nostrils. I wrench the wheel to the right, skidding onto a two-lane blacktop, bouncing and sliding like the suspension's shot. There are no highway signs, no sign of a service station, no public phone, no other cars, no sign of life.

"Jack, are you still there? Talk to me, Jack," Morgan continues from the seat beside me. His voice is calm, soothing. Maybe he thinks I'm already dead. I reach down and hit the end button on the cell.

"Talk to—"

I see it on my left, just off the main strip. It looks like a dirt road, wide enough for a car. I check my rearview. I'm still alone. I slow down, one eye on the highway, the other behind me. There's pressure inside my head, enormous pressure, like a wedge splitting my skull. Then I begin to get that feeling again: I'm separating, my mind and body are dividing, and for an instant, I can see everything from above. I'm out of the car, like a bird in the sky, watching the blue Jeep all alone on an unmarked stretch of road, nothing ahead and nothing behind. I panic. If I'm up here, who's driving? The thought snaps me back behind the wheel.

Slow down. Make the turn. Branches scrape the side of the Jeep as I drive slowly up the path, across potholes and puddles, deeper into the woods, looking for a place wide enough to pull over. I need rest. My head aches, my body feels weak and heavy.

There it is, like an oasis, a patch of clear land, a picnic table and a waste bin. I keep telling myself I'm okay, going to get through this. I drive into the clearing and shut off my engine. My cell phone is ringing, high and shrill, over and over again. I lift it from the seat.

"Hello?"

Morgan James's voice is clear and close, like he's right inside my ear. "Jack?"

I don't answer.

"Jack, are you listening?"

In the background, through the broken window of the Jeep, I hear another sound. It's the low drone of a car's engine, the screech of a fan belt slipping, tires mulching branches and earth, coming closer.

"I'm listening," I reply.

The volume of his voice increases.

"I'm right here with you."

He knows where I am. He's put a bug on the car. That's why he came to see me last night. It's all starting to fall into place.

"Let me know you can hear me," he continues.

I see it through the spider's web of broken glass, low and black, with that square metal grille, long and alive, feeling its way along the ground, like a predatory animal. It has no

license plate, and the front sun visor is pulled low so I can
only see the big, bearded jaw of the driver, his lips hiding in
the dark bush like a thin shadow.

This is it, payback time.

The Lincoln pulls close alongside me and stops, blocking
my exit.

"Come on, man, I know you can hear me. Talk."

Finally, I speak. "Where are you?"

"I'm right here, beside you—"

I hear the click as our contact is broken, leaving me
frozen with the phone against my ear, straining to see
through the darkened windows of the Lincoln. Staring at the
blackened reflection of my own fear. What will Ray do to me?
What will he call even for the wrong he's suffered? I imagine
myself naked, emasculated, hanging from a tree. Still alive as
the blood trickles down my thighs. Calling for my wife and
daughter. Praying to die. I feel the fear begin to slow my
thoughts, threatening to freeze my mind, crystallizing my
imagination to form a terror. I've got to fight this. Think. Got
to think. The doors of the Jeep are locked, but that's like
taking shelter in a house of glass. I could crawl to the
passenger side, and out. Make a run for it, into the woods,
but another voice tells me that there is nowhere to run. This
is my test. This is the place I find out who I am, what I'm
made of.

Seconds pass, and each of them feels like a wire spanning
the distance between my thoughts, taut and stretched, about
to snap.

The Lincoln doesn't budge, its windows remain closed,
the driver's face set and grim, without animation. I feel the
pressure building in my skull.

I want a resolution. Demand it.

Sliding my right hand along the console to my side,
opening it, searching inside for a weapon, anything that I can
use to hit or to cut. I feel a resolve firming my spirit, coaxing
it to rise from the ashes of my guilt and fear. I am going to
war. My fingers find a solid metal tube. I know it's a key ring,
about six inches long with a sharpened point at one end.
Called a kubaton, it was given to Carolyn by her instructor

during the first week of a jujitsu class that she did not continue. It's a weapon. I can break a window with it. Break a skull. I lift it from hiding and remove the key, then clutch it so that the spiked end is downward, extending a few inches below my hand.

The cell phone is ringing again. Morgan? Is he in the Lincoln, along with Ray, watching me squirm?

I place my left hand on the handle of the door, pushing against every fear inside me. Willing my hands and fingers with the full force of my mind, I open it.

The air outside the Jeep is humid and still. It's like swimming through warm, dirty water. My muscles are tight, and my lungs are contracted. Breathe, concentrate on the breath, I tell myself.

The engine of the Lincoln is idling. There's a trail of white smoke snaking up from its exhaust, toward the patch of gray sky that hangs like a canopy above the thick branches of the trees.

I'm out of the Jeep, using the door for partial cover, turning to face whoever is inside the car. If they want to kill me, now is their time. I'm on offer.

Still nothing from the Lincoln.

I drop down, low to the ground, then lunge toward the rear window of the black car with the kubaton raised above my shoulder like a knife. My intention is to break the glass and get inside. My intention is attack.

The Lincoln moves in time with my body, lurching backwards like a startled animal, throwing dirt from its rear tires as I continue my charge, running, following it down the path and to the highway, where the big car careens onto the main road and, still in reverse, doughnuts backwards. When it's fifty yards from me it screeches to a halt. I am directly in front of it, standing in the middle of the road, heaving for breath. We remain like that, facing each other. The car has become alive, taken on the minds of its occupants. Its headlamps are its eyes, the grille its mouth. I hear the growling begin, low, building to a roar as it heads straight for me, covering the distance with a single beat of its huge metal heart.

I drop the kubaton, dive to the shoulder, and roll into the shrubs as it screams by at arm's length.

Squealing to a halt. I look up and see that the rear window is open. I hear a song, coming from inside, a thin, tinny musical track, then a girl's voice, singing. It's Jade.

An arm protrudes from the opening. My vision narrows, and I see the heavy band of gold, wrapped round the thick index finger of the extended hand, with the blood red ruby set inside it. The hand opens, dropping something to the ground.

The engine revs, the gears engage, and rubber screams against the asphalt, leaving a trail of smoke as the Lincoln disappears down the highway.

Silence fills the space it leaves behind. Cautiously, I walk across and look down at the ground. At first I don't see anything. Getting on my knees I continue to search, all the while listening for the drone of the engine, hearing nothing but my own heart, straining to fill the hollow.

I've got a feeling.

I've never had such a strong feeling. It's creeping up my spine, soft and cold, insinuating with its intimacy, like it knows me as well as I know myself, where to touch and probe, where the nerves lie exposed and raw. I'm all alone in this place, all alone with this feeling, out here on a highway that I never knew existed.

I smell it, sickly sweet, like something spoiled.

The rose is half-buried in the dirt and gravel, its petals a deep purple, almost black, torn and broken. I lift it by the stem.

"You are my sunshine—" Jade's voice fills my memory as I squeeze it between my fingers, feeling the thorn.

The pain is deep and quick. A trickle of blood runs down my index finger like a tear.

Memory collides with reality, and I'm crushed between them.

Bleep. Bleep. Bleep.

I am transported to another room in my mind, with a clean white bed and cool sheets. There is something in my mouth, running down my throat. It feels like a long tube, pumping oxygen into my lungs. Wires attached to my body, monitors to either side of me, lights blinking and graphs charting the beat of my heart and the waves of my brain. Needles jumping all over the place, leaving sharp, jagged lines. I hear Jade singing her song.

Bleep. Bleep. Bleep.

I'm walking, sliding. Slipping from dream to dream with nothing to hold on to. Listening to voices in my head. "Hello, Jack. Wake up, Jack. We love you, Jack."

Then I'm back on the road with the black rose in my bleeding hand.

Everything is amplified, from the cries of the birds and high-pitched chortles of the squirrels to the dried leaves rustling in the trees. I keep listening for my daughter's voice, singing to me, while my eyes search the highway.

Other feelings come, waves of loss and sorrow, sudden and overwhelming, hitting me again and again, sweeping me to a cold, desperate loneliness.

Please don't take my sunshine away. I drop the rose to the ground.

~ 33 ~

THE SUN IS RED, SITTING low in the western sky. What time is it? I thought it was morning. How did I lose the day? Move, I tell myself. Take a step, find the car, but I am disoriented, like I have awakened in a place without familiar boundaries of any kind. I turn slowly as my eyes focus. The dirt road is directly in front of me.

I command my feet to walk.

Up the road, to the Jeep.

The door is halfway open, the way I left it, which must have been hours ago, and the cell phone is still sitting on the passenger's seat. I climb in and pull the door shut. Some of the spidered glass breaks loose and falls into my lap. I brush it to the floor and pick up the phone. It takes me a few seconds to remember the number of my own home. My fingers are trembling, and I forget to include the area code on my first attempt, ending up with a recorded message from AT&T. My next try is successful but our line is busy, so I reverse the Jeep down the path, ramming tree stumps and bushes, scratching the paint. It doesn't matter. Nothing matters but Jade. I've got to get to Jade. I swing back onto the main road and head west in the direction of the Expressway. Picking up the cell I press redial. This time I get through. It rings once, twice, three times. Another ring and it will go to the answering machine. Come on, God damn it, Carolyn, answer the phone.

Halfway through the fourth ring there's a click, then her voice.

"Hello?"

There's no panic in her tone.

"Carolyn?"

"Jack, where are you?"

"Where's Jade?" I ask.

"Are you alright? You don't sound too good."

"Where is Jade?"

"I can hear you, you don't need to shout. She's sitting here with me on the bed. We're drawing in her book."

The next voice I hear is my daughter's. "Hello, Daddy."

Tears fill my eyes as I get myself together enough to speak. "Hello Jade. I love you. I love you very, very much."

"I love you, too, as big as Montauk Lighthouse."

"Montauk Lighthouse? That's very big. I love you that big, too ... I want to talk to Mama again, okay?"

Carolyn's voice comes back on the line. "Jack?"

I feel my control returning.

"Where are you?" Carolyn continues.

"Coming home," I answer.

"Did you see Morgan?"

"I never got there," I reply.

"We've been worried," she continues. "Morgan has called here three or four times, trying to get hold of you. Is something wrong?"

"I had a problem," I answer. Did Morgan set me up? Now I'm not so sure. At the moment I'm not too sure of anything.

"What kind of problem?"

I drive below an underpass then take a right onto an entrance road for the L.I.E. Doing seventy-three when I spot the white-and-blue police cruiser, sitting on the center verge, hidden by a cluster of pine trees. He's got his radar cone up, aimed at me. I take my foot off the pedal and roll by at seventy, then check my rearview. There's a law against driving and using a handheld phone at the same time. The last thing I need is to be pulled over. "Carolyn, I see a cop, I've got to go. See you." Then I toss the cell down on the seat.

Morgan? What kind of paranoid fantasies am I having? Who was in the black car? I feel the fear again, climbing up my spine, spreading through my arms and fingers like a cold chill. Where did the time go? Am I insane? I slow down to fifty-five, as if the speed of the car and the speed of my thoughts are connected.

Slow down, get control, I tell myself. It's the bullet, it must be the bullet. I feel it all the time now. I think of Howard Metzler, phoning our house, concerned, and I haven't answered one of his calls. Haven't kept a single appointment, and he's probably the only hope I've got left. I'll phone the hospital. I'll go see him. I check the road ahead, check the rearview, then pick up the cell, about to punch 411 when I hear a voice coming from the receiver. I must have forgotten to press end. Maybe Carolyn left the phone in the house off the hook, or maybe Jade's been playing with it.

I recognize Morgan's voice, low and gravelly. "Do you think there's any chance he can hear us?"

"I don't know," Carolyn answers. "Sometimes I think he understands everything that's happening to him."

I don't believe my ears, not at first.

"How about Jade?" Morgan asks.

"She's tried, too, but it upsets her so much that I don t push it," Carolyn answers. "I don't want to tell her the truth." Her voice breaks. "I don't want to tell myself the truth."

The truth? What are they talking about. What is the truth? I want to shout down the line. I want to tell them that I'm listening, but I can't get my voice to clear my throat. It's stuck down there, as if everything around it has contracted and seized.

"Got to go now," Morgan says. "I'll be back later."

I hear what I believe to be the sound of a kiss, the smack of lips parting from flesh. After that the phone lies silent and dead in my hand. I drop it on the seat and continue to drive.

I feel as if the bottom has fallen out of my life, as if everything and everyone I have trusted and believed in has been a lie. I have no place to grip, no one to hold on to me as I spiral down into an abyss of fear and doubt.

I am trying to get home, to the truth, but I don't know where or what home and truth is anymore, so I continue to drive, following the road without really knowing where it will lead me.

**

I park beneath one of the big oak trees. The house looms like a shadow above me. I am confused and sad, deep in my soul.

Carolyn is standing in the doorway. I look at her, my eyes questioning. What is it that she knows but can't tell me? What is this secret that he shares with Morgan, and Jade?

"What happened to you?" she asks, her eyes wide with worry.

"You tell me," I answer, without challenge.

Her eyes leave mine for a moment and go to the Jeep. "Did you have an accident?"

My memory is disjointed. The whole thing with the black Lincoln, the chase along the Expressway, the missing time; it all seems distant and without sequence, like a half-forgotten dream.

"A little bang," I answer. "Nothing serious."

"Are you alright?" Carolyn asks, walking toward me, putting her arms around my back, holding me close. Her body feels warm against mine.

Her voice is soft. "Jack, tell me what happened."

"I sideswiped a guardrail," I answer.

"Where?"

I feel myself breaking down. I want to trust her. I need to. Still, I'm wary.

"On the L.I.E. Then I got lost and missed the meeting with Morgan."

"Lost?" She sounds disbelieving.

Finally, I own up. "The bullet's causing problems," I say. "I need to talk to Dr. Metzler."

I see her mouth tighten as she looks at me. She's scared, too, but she's trying not to show it.

"What kind of problems?" she asks.

"I think I'm having episodes, or some kind of seizures."

"How about your medication?"

"Yes, I need to take it," I answer. "I also need to see Metzler. I can't keep going like this. Look, I'm sorry about the car—"

"The car's not important," she answers. "Not now."

We walk into the house. I look around, half-expecting Morgan to be there, but the place is empty.

We walk to the sofa and sit down.

"Where's Jade?" I ask.

"She waited up for you as long as she could. We got through the *Dumbo* video and almost the whole book of *Harry the Dirty Dog*," Carolyn answers. "She wanted me to tell you that she loves you as deep as Gardiner's Island."

That gets right to me. I didn't even know Jade knew about Gardiner's Island. I want to go see her, but first I've got to clear my mind.

"How long ago did Morgan leave?" I ask.

Carolyn appears confused, and her aura begins to change colors, from yellow, green, and blue, it begins to cloud as the colors mix.

"Or is he still here?" I can't keep the suspicion from my tone.

"Morgan's not here," Carolyn answers. "We've spoken on the phone, but he hasn't been here since you last saw him."

"Don't lie to me."

My words hit her like a slap in the face. She looks stunned, and the murky wash of color ignites with flames of red and purple. I sense rage.

"I heard you two talking," I continue. "I know he was here."

"What are you saying?" she asks, pulling back and away from me.

"I'm saying that somebody left the phone off the hook; and I heard you two talking about me. I'm saying I know he was in this house."

"And I'm telling you he wasn't," she bristles.

"What's going on, Carolyn?" I demand.

"Nothing," she states. The pupils of her eyes are tight, and her jaw is set firm.

The silence between us is rigid.

I stand up. "I'm going to see Jade."

"After that I think you should call your doctor," she says softly.

I dismiss her suggestion with a "yeah, sure."

"And please, try not to wake her," Carolyn says, as I leave the room.

I feel dizzy for a moment, like my blood pressure has taken a sudden drop. I recover before Carolyn notices or says anything more. Got to keep on going, I tell myself. Can't give in to this.

I walk up the stairs and take off my shoes before I enter Jade's room, stepping quietly across the thick wool carpet, getting halfway to her bed before I stop.

The moon is full, streaming in from the east-facing window of her bedroom, casting a cold blue-white glow over everything it touches. Jade's hair, spilling out from under her duvet and falling down over the side of the wood-framed bed looks like a blanket of silver. She is not only surrounded by light, she appears made of it, as if her body is glowing from the inside.

I walk, closer, watching the duvet rise and fall with each of her breaths, and with each respiration the light inside and surrounding her grows brighter, then dims with a perfect rhythm. She sighs faintly as she exhales. Her face is turned sideways on the pillow, looking away from me, and her arm is draped over her favorite teddy bear. I hover above her, in awe of the gentleness that I feel, as if her room is a sanctuary, created by her innocence. I kneel beside her bed, inhaling the light that bathes us, and in that moment I have all the courage in the world.

She rolls over as if she senses my presence. Her St. Christopher's medal reflects the moon. It looks alive and glowing, lying against the skin at the top of her chest. Her eyes open slowly, looking up.

"Hello, beautiful," I whisper.

She doesn't answer or move. Her eyes don't waver. She's still half-asleep. I don't think she even sees me. Anxious for a moment, I reach down and gently stroke her forehead, caressing her skin, like a warm silk. Still, she doesn't respond; her eyes seem to look through me, making me feel light and transparent, as if I am not there at all.

"You go back to sleep now," I say softly. "See you when the sun comes up."

Her eyes close again and she rolls to the opposite side, this time her face is turned away from me.

"God bless you, little girl," I whisper, before I stand and leave the room.

~ 34 ~

I GO BACK DOWN AND JOIN Carolyn on the sofa, where I apologize for my accusations and promise that I'll call the doctor first thing in the morning. After talking for a while we go upstairs, where I head straight to the bathroom, open the medicine cabinet, and take out the brown-plastic bottle. Unscrewing the cap, I place two of the small pink pills in the center of my palm. I look at them a moment, thinking of Simon Barr and feeling a sense of defeat. Then I put them in my mouth and swallow before walking back into the bedroom.

I don't know how long the Respiradol will take to come on, but I do know its effect is cumulative so I don't anticipate turning to stone, not tonight anyway.

Sitting on the side of our bed, I watch in the dim light as Carolyn takes off her clothes until she is standing by the dresser, in front of the wall mirror, wearing just her bra and pants. The white-cotton bikinis cling tightly to her high, rounded hips, puffed out at the front with her sandy blond mound of hair. She has two dimples at the base of her back, just before her ass begins. I love her dimples. She's not trying to be sexy. I imagine that sex is the last thing on her mind, but something in the way she moves, without any self-consciousness, as if she's all alone in the room, captures me. Tonight I need her. There is a desperation in me as I study her, like maybe we're in two different places, on different sides of a divide. I need to grab hold of her, to pull myself over to her side. By the time she's brushed her teeth and put on a nightdress, I'm aching for her, lying in the dark, waiting.

She gets into bed, turns off the light, and rolls toward me so that we are face-to-face, only inches apart. I feel the heat of her body and place my hand on the back of her thigh and stroke gently up and over the swell of her hips. Her skin is flawless, and my hand glides over it with hardly any friction.

"Are you serious?" she asks, her breath warm and flavored with the faint aroma of mint.

I reply by pulling her closer to me and pressing myself against her.

There isn't a lot of foreplay, simply a long deep kiss as she lifts her leg closest to me and uses her left hand to guide me along the underside of her thigh and inside her. It starts like that, warm and shallow, kissing, tasting her tongue as I pull her onto me. The skin of her neck smells of faded perfume, like a musky incense. After we find a slow rhythm she turns on her side, bends her knees, bringing them up closer to her stomach so that I am directly behind her, going deeper while feeling the full heat from her hips as they nestle into the lower part of my abdomen. I wrap my arms around her, listening to her breath as it deepens. She moans quietly as she exhales. The changing pattern of her breath seems to signal the beginning of a transformation, as she becomes something that is tender but at the same time wanton and primal. It is a part of her that is held secret from the world, known only to me. I guard it jealously, this intimacy between us. It is the reason, since we met, that I've never wanted another woman. Carolyn completes me.

I am about to increase the tempo of my hips, thrusting harder, when she pulls away from me, disconnecting our bodies before crawling on top of me, pushing my shoulders down onto the sheet and straddling me. Taking me in her hands then putting me back inside her. I have been trying so hard for control in the past weeks, this surrender feels right and necessary. I look up to see her above me, a silhouette against the darkness of the room, her breasts swaying gently as her hips grind down into me with a strong, circular motion. Her back is arched and her head is tilted backwards as she breathes through her mouth. I arch up to meet her, to take more of her, reaching with my arms, gripping her shoulders. At first I think I have lost sensation in my fingers because I feel nothing. No sense of her body. I can see her, or the shape of her in the darkness, but I can't feel her. My hands have gone to sleep, my fingers are cold and numb, dead-heavy and thick, sending their deadness outward. I feel nothing but space all around me, vacant and cold. The feeling seeps from my body to my mind. Followed by a moment of complete disorientation when my thoughts split apart, fragmenting like the pieces of a jigsaw puzzle, flying away from any kind of order into this deep space, leaving me confused, frightened, and lost. Is this the effect of the drug? I need a reason. It's the drug. It must be.

"Carolyn?"

There is no answer.

"Help me." I don't know if I am thinking or speaking the words.

Then I hear her voice from far away, as if I am down a well and someone is calling my name from above. "Jack?" It reverberates inside the darkness.

"I'm here," I reply, clinging to the thought of her.

"Jack, did you say something? I think he said something. I think he said my name."

"Daddy?"

It's Jade. The realization of my daughter pulls me back from nowhere, re-creating an attachment, a picture in my mind. I don't want Jade to see us like this, naked and aroused. It's not right. I cover myself with the duvet, pulling it high to my neck. Turning toward Carolyn, who is sleeping beside me. That's when I know that I've been dreaming.

Jade is standing a few feet from the bed. Wearing her nightshirt, embroidered with red and green flowers, like a Mexican wedding dress. She looks so delicate and small, like a leaf from a tree, fallen from the sky, a shadow in the dark.

"Daddy, I can't sleep," she whispers. She knows she's not supposed to leave her bedroom till morning. It's been a family rule since she graduated from her crib to a bed. "There's a monster in my room," she adds in a very serious tone.

I smile, reaching out to touch her hand, making sure of her presence, answering, "Jade, there are no such things as monsters; it's only in your mind." I know that Carolyn would take her back to her room. Carolyn would maintain the discipline.

"But I saw this monster," Jade insists. "He was mean."

I slide over and lift the duvet, whispering, "Come on, get in before you wake up Mama."

She climbs in and cuddles up close to me. I feel safe again.

"You won't let that mean monster get me, will you, Daddy?"

"Never. I promise. No monsters. Now go back to sleep. See you when the sun comes up."

~ 35 ~

I OPEN MY EYES. MY head feels thick and heavy and my memory of last night is blurred as I reach out, expecting to touch Jade, but my fingers find only the edge of the bed. I turn toward Carolyn and see nothing there but a pillow, fresh and unruffled, as if it has never been used. Then I hear their voices, coming from downstairs.

"Eat your French toast, all of it, then you can have your chocolate milk. That's the way it works."

"But I don't want French toast," Jade answers.

"Then why did you ask me to make it?"

"I want chocolate milk," Jade insists.

Carolyn firms up. "French toast first, then chocolate milk."

Jade begins to protest, and Carolyn cuts her short with, "Eat your toast."

After that it's quiet below. I wonder what time it is and how I managed to sleep through both of them getting up, getting dressed, and leaving the room. Then I remember taking the Respiradol, the zombie pills. I roll over and see that the clock reads 8:15. I lie still a few moments, trying to organize my thoughts. Having quick, jagged recollections of car chases and panicked phone calls, of making love with Carolyn, all jammed together without sequence, like a dream. I have what feels like a fence inside my mind, containing things that scream to spill over and grow wild. I do my breathing exercises, inhaling, suspending the breath, exhaling slowly, thinking of Simon Barr, trying to reach an equilibrium. Straining to hear more from below. Needing the reassurance of normality, of French toast and chocolate milk, but there is silence all around me now, and I feel deserted. Sitting up, I'm shocked to see that I'm wearing a green hospital gown.

I get out of the bed and look at myself in the mirror above the dresser. I have no aura, none at all. I have noticed this before, in other mirrors and I have explained it by telling myself that the colors are of such delicate vibration that they don't reflect in the glass, but today my entire head and upper body seem to be composed of a flesh-toned vapor, undulating in waves, coming in out of focus. The only thing that appears solid is the gown, standing out from the rest of me, as if it exists in a different dimension. I tell myself that it's my eyes, playing tricks, influenced by the drug.

I remove the gown and drop it to the floor, then walk into the bathroom that adjoins our room and step into the shower, using a soapy sponge, scrubbing my neck and shoulders, turning the tap to cold and letting the water cascade against my face, as if I can rid myself of the effects of the Respiradol and the confusion it's causing. Suddenly the shower stall feels like a coffin. I want out. Turn off the water, step onto the bath mat, grab a towel. Got to get downstairs to where things are sane, to familiar faces and familiar voices. I dry off quickly, then go to the closet and grab a T-shirt from one of the shelves. There's a pair of old jeans lying on the floor in the corner, dirty and greasy. I pick them up, thinking that it's not like Carolyn to leave them lying around. They smell of oil and gasoline. It's a strangely comforting aroma and reminds me of motorcycles, rubber and steel, a way to escape. I pull them on, then, carrying a pair of boots, walk back into the bedroom.

Where's the gown? I left it lying on the floor. Where's the green gown? I get down on my hands and knees and search for it, under the dresser, underneath the bed. It's gone.

Every fear and bit of paranoia fights to return, restrained only by the drug, like a soft-padded wall around my mind. Should I take some more? Then I think again. What if someone is playing with my head, attempting to drive me mad? Someone close.

I finish dressing and go down the stairs two at a time, finding Carolyn alone in the kitchen, sitting at the breakfast table, sipping a cup of tea with a slice of brown toast on the plate in front of her. It looks like a stage set, and she looks like an actress in a play. Nothing seems real.

"Where's Jade?" I demand.

She raises her head. There's a strange quality to her face. Her features seem set, half in shock, half in sorrow. Maybe it's because she can't believe I'm still here, functioning, not giving up.

"I heard you talking to her where is she?"

"Jack, why are you so angry?"

"Don't answer my question with a question. Where is my daughter?"

She sits back in her chair looking frazzled.

"Jade is with April."

"What's she doing with her?"

Carolyn answers slowly and patiently, as if I am impaired.

"They have gone out for a walk."

"Why aren't you with them?"

"Because I want to be with you," she answers. "Till this is over. Do you understand? Is that okay?"

"What did you do with the hospital gown?" I ask. Her passivity is enraging me.

"What gown?"

"The green hospital gown that I slept in last night," I reply.

"You had your boxer shorts on in bed," she answers patiently.

I study her eyes, looking for the lie.

"Did Morgan James come to this house yesterday?" My voice is sharp and full of accusation. "What was he doing here?"

She trains her eyes on mine. "Jack, have you called Dr. Metzler?"

"I'm talking about Morgan James, not Howard Metzler," I retort.

She continues. "Isn't it time you did?"

"Where is the green hospital gown?"

Her face softens, and I see tears welling, then a single
tear spills from the corner of her right eye and slides slowly
down her cheek. If she's acting, she's very good.

Her voice has the beginnings of desperation. "Jack,
please listen to what I am saying. I want you to understand
what is happening."

"Somebody's fucking with my head," I answer. "That's
what's happening." I feel fear crawling toward me like a
snake, coiled, ready to strike. "I heard you talking to Morgan
yesterday. I was listening. I heard what you said, talking about
telling me the truth. What is the truth?"

"Listen to me," Carolyn says. She's standing in front of
me, so close I can breathe her, but I can't remember her
getting up from the chair. Colors are pouring out of her, like
billows of red-and-black smoke. I feel a mixture of danger
and fear. My mind seems to be shutting off, then switching
back on. Off. On. Off. On. In waves. She continues to speak,
her voice becoming stronger inside my head. "I think we
should call Dr. Metzler."

If this is some kind of elaborate mind-fuck, I can't think
of a reason for it. The only person with grounds to hurt me is
Ray Sasso. Carolyn is my friend, my ally. She reaches out and
touches my hand.

"You know I'm with you, Jack, all the way, I'm not going
anywhere. "

I feel so small, so pathetic, with my anger and my rage.
It's my mind. I'm not well. I should rest, stay quiet, get hold
of Metzler; the sooner he fixes me, the better.

"I'm sorry," I answer. I want to squeeze Carolyn's hand,
to let her know that I'm with her, too, but I'm going to cry,
and I don't want her to see my tears. Turning, I walk from
the kitchen and back up the stairs, into the bedroom, closing
the door behind me.

It takes my eyes a moment to adjust. Then I get that
feeling again, of déjà vu. It's as if I am seeing memories. The
green gown is folded neatly and lying on my bed.

~ 36 ~

I PICK IT UP, SQUEEZE THE fabric with my fingers, lift it to my face, and smell it. I can smell my body in the cloth, my sweat and my fear. This is it. Proof that something's happening, that someone is playing tricks with my mind, trying to drive me over the edge. That's not going to happen. I've been through tough times before. I don't break. I won't. With the gown in my hand I go back downstairs and into the kitchen. The table is clear, and Carolyn is gone. There is no note to say where, nothing. I call her name a few times, then search the downstairs of the house. The place is vacant. I look outside the front door. The Jeep is in the driveway, exactly as I left it yesterday. I look again. No, that's impossible. The window has been repaired, the hood and sides repainted. It looks new. Maybe it's another car. I check the license plate. It's ours, the same car I was driving. I think it was yesterday. How long have I been asleep?

"Carolyn!" I shout her name. "Carolyn!"

Back into the house and up the stairs, where I search the guest room, closets, and behind the doors, then into Jade's room.

By the time I get to our bedroom I notice that I'm no longer carrying the hospital gown. Where did I leave it? I'm about to head back downstairs when I hear footsteps, coming up from the living room.

I close the door and turn the lock above the handle. The footsteps come closer, till they are right outside. I stand very still and listen, barely breathing. I watch as the doorknob turns, then see the slight movement of the door inside the frame before the lock takes hold.

"Jack?"

It's Carolyn.

"Why have you locked the door?"

I don't answer.

Her voice gets louder and more anxious. "Can you hear me?"

I'm right next to her, with maybe an inch of wood between us. I don t even need to raise my voice.

"Who's with you out there?"

Open the door," Carolyn answers.

"I asked you a question."

"There is no one with me. Now will you please let me in," she demands.

"Where's Jade?"

"Jade is with April. I told you that before." Her voice softens, as if she's digging into her last reserves of compassion. "She'll be home in a little while. Now open the door. I need to get to the bathroom."

"There's a bathroom in the hall," I answer.

"Yes, but it doesn't have my Tampax in it. Now for God's sake open the door!"

I reach across and turn the small oval knob, stepping back and to the side as the door opens.

Carolyn enters, carrying the folded gown in her hands.

"What are you doing?" she asks.

There is pity in her eyes, but also anger, as if she has been pushed to her limits. I don't answer so she walks past and to the bathroom, closing the door behind her. I wait a few more seconds before going to the bedroom door and looking out into the hallway. Nothing unusual in the hallway, nothing unusual anywhere upstairs. By the time Carolyn's come out I am more relaxed, vigilant but at ease. The hospital gown is still in her right hand. There's some explaining for her to do.

"Why don't you just get back into bed and rest," she says gently. "Have you taken your medication?"

"Should I put my gown back on?" I reply.

She follows my eyes to her right hand, where the evidence waits.

She smiles, which infuriates me.

"I doubt if it would fit," she says, holding up the folded gown so that it unfurls. "It's even getting a bit small for Jade," tossing the small, frilly nightdress to me.

I get a sinking feeling as the cloth touches my hands. I smell apples on the gown. The smell is sickly sweet. There's something wrong. I try to close my mind, to block it out but the feeling won't go away.

"Jack, I think we need to call Dr. Metzler right now," Carolyn says.

"How did you get the car fixed?" I ask, clinging on. Without my doubts, without my anger, I'm lost. "It looks new."

"There was never anything wrong with the car."

"Don't lie to me." My words repeat in my mind. Lie. Everything's a lie. Everyone is lying. Lie. It has become my constant refrain.

She doesn't even acknowledge my remark. Instead she walks to the glass-topped night table beside the bed and picks up the phone.

"That car was wrecked when I drove it home," I continue, as if by persistence I can make her break. What I'm doing feels sick, I feel sick, yet I can't stop myself. "Something's going on around here," I continue, watching as she punches in the number for the hospital. "Somebody's fucking with my head."

"May I speak with Dr. Metzler in Neurology?" Carolyn asks in a pleasant, professional-sounding voice. She waits again while the switchboard connects her. "May I have Dr. Metzler?"

"Are you listening to me, Carolyn?" I demand. At this point it's like I'm not even in the room.

She continues to speak. "Yes, it is an emergency. Yes I want you to beep him." After that she gives her name and our phone number. Putting down the phone, she looks at me. "Why don't you lie down?"

"Why don't you answer my questions?"

"Please, Jack, don't make this so difficult."

"Where was I yesterday?" I demand.

"Right here."

"Bullshit," I answer.

She bends over to pull the bedcover down.

"Please take off your clothes and get back into bed."

My adrenaline has stopped flowing, leaving my stomach sour and a bitter taste at the back of my mouth. I feel physically weak, and the bed suddenly looks good to me, irresistible.

"I'm keeping my clothes on," I answer. The T-shirt and jeans feel like armor.

"But you're filthy," Carolyn protests.

I look down at my hands. I've got dirt under my fingernails. Must be from yesterday, crawling around by the side of the road. I must have missed it in the shower.

"I'm staying like this," I confirm.

She holds my eyes long enough to know that I won't budge.

"Lie down."

It's a gentle order.

I walk over to the bed and sit, one eye on the door to the room, anticipating that it's going to explode inward at any moment. When nothing happens I put my feet up and settle back against the pillow. I'm not going to sleep. I need rest, that's all, not sleep. No sleep, I keep telling myself as I float off. Images form in my mind: green-plastic swings, a red merry-go-round, and a blue sliding board. I smell apples. It's that place. Don't want to go to that place, but the bottom has dropped, and I'm falling. Until my body jerks, my head snaps back, and I jolt upright in the bed. Looking for Carolyn. Where did she go?

I call her name, but my voice is faint and weak. It doesn't seem to carry. She must be in the bathroom. I attempt to get out of bed, but I'm dizzy and keep falling backwards against the sheets. It's the drug, coming back on me.

"Carolyn!" The word doesn't travel beyond my lips.

I need help, right now. I could call Morgan James. No, not Morgan. I don't trust Morgan, not since yesterday. I'm still not clear about what happened yesterday. Everything seems muddled and confused.

The telephone rings. It's got to be Metzler. He's the man I need. I want him to open me up and take this bullet out. Right now, no waiting, send the ambulance, I'm in trouble.

I reach across the bed to the night table. It takes all my strength and concentration to pick up the phone and by the time I get it to my ear all I hear is a busy signal, which means someone else has answered it in one of the other rooms of the house. Looking down at the panel of lights I see that it's been taken in the kitchen. Carolyn must be there. I put the phone back in its cradle and wait. Any second the call will come, Carolyn will transfer me to Metzler. I'll tell him everything, about the hallucinations, the nightmares, the dreams. No more bullshit with auras and telepathy, no more of Simon Barr's on the cusp of awakening rap. As he said, he's not living through it. I am, and I want it to stop.

I listen hard, trying to hear Carolyn's voice while wondering why she hasn't put me through to my doctor. I'm impatient, getting angry. What the hell is she doing, what are they talking about? Then I see the light on the line go dead and hear what I believe are sobs coming from downstairs. It's Carolyn, crying. What has Metzler told her? How bad is it? Am I dying?

Her footsteps are solid and fast against the stairs, like she's running.

The door opens.

I have never seen Carolyn look the way she does at this moment. She seems to have aged twenty years, her face is pale and drawn, her eyes are red and watery, and her hair is disheveled, as if she's been pulling at it. She stands in the doorway staring at me, her arms at her sides, her chest heaving, fighting to control a mixture of fear and sorrow that extends from her body in the most intense display of colors I have seen since I began to see in this way. The vivid reds and yellows that are swirling round her stretch out and mix together, forming a deathly glow of amber that extends until it touches and washes over me like a fog, clouding my eyes and filling my nostrils with the pungent smell of rotting apples.

Somewhere, from beyond the walls of the bedroom, I hear the wail of a police siren.

Carolyn's eyes are locked onto mine. Her lips begin to quiver and move, as if it is painful to form the words. Her voice is barely controlled, flat and unnatural.

She manages to say, "It's Jade," before breaking down again. "Somebody—"

"Somebody what?!" I demand, pushing myself up against the mattress.

She blurts, "Somebody took our baby," then chokes back her sobs.

I stare at Carolyn, feeling all my defense systems kick in at once, working in unison to deny what my ears have just heard. The police siren is very loud. It seems to fill my head, and for a moment I think it is outside the house. In the next moment it has become a cry in the distance.

"She was at the playground with April. There was a man there—" She stalls again.

My strength returns in a single burst. I'm out of bed, standing in front of Carolyn, with my hands on her shoulders, holding her tight, steadying her.

"What playground, what man?"

My presence seems to calm her. Her body stops trembling and her eyes focus.

"The little playground on Edison Street."

I knew it. I saw this coming. I should have said something, forbid her ever to go there. I should have trusted myself, my instinct. Instead, I have trusted no one and nothing.

Carolyn continues. "April didn't see him till she was on top of the sliding board, with Jade. Then she saw a face in the window of the school, watching them. She thought he was a janitor. By the time Jade got to the bottom of the slide he was outside, waiting. He was dressed in black with long hair. He had a hard, chiseled face and dark eyes. April said he looked like the devil. He picked Jade up from the ground and carried her off."

"To where?"

"It was a black car with tinted windows," she answers. "He threw her into the back and got in with her."

"What the fuck was April doing?!"

"She tried to stop him, but he punched her and knocked her down. She was scared—"

"Yeah, I'll bet she was. I'll bet she didn't even try to get up. She let him take my daughter!" I shout. "God damn her!"

"Who did this?" Carolyn asks, her eyes digging into mine. Her question silences me.

"Did you know something like this would happen?" she continues.

I shake my head and answer, "No," as I feel Charlie Wolf stir inside me. Lying, caught again.

"Where is April Summers right now?" I ask.

"At the playground making a statement to the police."

I'm already pulling on my boots "Let's go," I say, walking past her to the door.

~ 37 ~

WE'RE NEARLY OUT OF THE house when the telephone rings. I'm not thinking about who it might be, just that it's important, as I rush into the kitchen and pick it up.

The voice on the other end catches me off guard. Gruff and harsh, it's a voice I will always remember.

"Charlie, is that you?"

It's a voice that knows me as Charlie, and with that recognition, the time and distance between Jack Lamb and Charlie Wolf no longer exist. It is a voice that has power over me.

"Yes," I answer.

"She smells like apples."

I hear the musical track for "You Are My Sunshine," overlaid by a succession of screams, wrenched from deep down in the gut, gasping and primitive, human only in that I can make out the word "Daddy," as if it is being regurgitated and spit out over and over again.

The music ends, and the gruff voice returns, "Daddy?"

"Hurt her and I'll kill you."

Ray Sasso's voice doesn't ruffle or change pitch. It stays low and even, without the strain of emotion. "You did worse than kill me."

Carolyn walks into the room, looking at me with the big question in her eyes, knowing by the expression on my face that the call is about Jade. I lift my hand to ask for her silence.

Saying to Ray Sasso, "This is between me and you, nobody else—"

He cuts me off, his voice suddenly bitter. "Tell that to my family."

The bottom falls out of my anger. "If I could take what happened back, every bit of it, I would, but that's got nothing to do with— "

"How old is Jade?"

"Don t do this," I plead.

He continues, lightening his tone. "She says three but I think she looks older—" The connection breaks up and crackles. It's a cell phone. I can hear the sound of a car horn in the background. "'—ood-looking little chick. My little boy was good-looking too, wasn't he? And my little girl—"

I try not to let his words reach me but I can feel them in the pit of my stomach, spreading out like a slow poison.

"I'm sorry," I say, as Carolyn moves closer, trying to hear what's happening on the other end of the line. I press the phone tighter to my ear, separating her from Ray Sasso.

His next words are loud and clear, like he's right beside me in the room. "Yeah, it was a little girl, that's what the autopsy report said. They recovered the fetus from what was left of my wife. The baby was only about four inches long, weighed a little more than half an ounce, must have looked like a tiny little doll."

"I'm sorry," I repeat, my voice just above a whisper.

The phone crackles again and sounds hollow as he moves farther and farther away from me. "I'll bet you are, Charlie, but not as sorry as you're going to be—"

The door that has been keeping back the nightmare begins to open.

"What do you want?" I ask.

"I want you to spend some time thinking."

"Who is that?" Carolyn demands.

"I want you to understand," Sasso continues. "I want you to learn—"

Carolyn comes closer.

"—what goes around, comes around, motherfucker." At last his emotions break through, and his voice spills pure hatred.

Carolyn reaches for the phone as I pull back, away from her.

"Where are you?" I ask.

"Same place as before—"

"Give me that phone!" Carolyn wrenches it from my hand as the receiver goes dead in her hand. She hits *69 and a recorded message tells her that the number she wants is private and unavailable.

Finally, she looks at me, "Who?"

I shake my head. Even now I can't tell her. Can't let her in on my secret.

"Tell me!"

I lower my eyes, and say, "I don't know."

"What did he say?"

"He's got Jade," I answer. "That's all he said."

"Where?"

My head throbs. I feel the bullet like a deadweight, pulling me down, reminding me of who I really am.

"It sounded like the call came from inside a car," I answer. "I don't know exactly where they were."

Carolyn is surprisingly calm. It's the kind of calm that comes when every fear and uncertainty is pushed aside for the sake of survival.

"They haven't been gone long enough to get past Southampton, and there's only one road out of here."

As she's speaking I hear the sound of tires on gravel from outside the house. We walk to the door in time to see my old friend Lou Collins drive in. There's another cop with him in the patrol car, and April Summers is seated in the backseat, eyes forward and stone-faced. Her aura is blue and black, like a bruise, barely visible as it extends just beyond her hair. She appears frightened, on the verge of shock.

Lou steps out, sees us, nods, and says our names, "Carolyn ... Jack," as he walks toward us. His face is solemn, and I'm very frightened that whatever he's about to say will be bad. His next words, "There's no news yet on your daughter," at least allow me hope. "The state police and the FBI have both been notified. They'll set up roadblocks."

"We just got a call," Carolyn volunteers.

Lou looks at her, and his eyes narrow.

To me, this feels wrong. I sense that Ray is watching, listening to us, waiting for me to make the wrong move. I sense his will. This is ultimately about me and him. I don't see the police involved. I don't see negotiation.

"There was a phone call," I say, hedging. "That's all."

Carolyn turns on me angrily. "What the hell are you doing? Tell him the whole thing." When I don't she turns back to Lou Collins. "The phone call was from the man who kidnapped our daughter. Then she turns on me, staring accusingly. "What's the matter with you? What kind of game are you playing? This is about our child's life."

I turn away from her, to Lou. He looks uncomfortable, like he's too close to something he doesn't want to be close to, or maybe shouldn't be. He drops his head and stares at the ground for a moment. When he looks up his eyes have hardened, and his tone is all business.

He cocks his head a little bit. He's thinking about our last incident on the playground, I can feel it. He's questioning the soundness of my judgment, maybe my mind.

"Do you know who it was?" he asks.

His question is so direct that it takes me a moment to speak. When I do, I lie. I'm trying to save my daughter's life, I tell myself, but I also know that I'm trying to save Jack Lamb.

"He didn't identify himself, and I didn't recognize his voice," I answer. "The call sounded like it came from a car. The line was bad, I could hear traffic in the background, but I could hear my daughter crying."

Carolyn remains silent, but I can feel her eyes boring into me, her mind questioning.

There is a surreal quality to what is happening. I feel like I'm watching it from another place, another perspective, and everything is distorted by the fact that I know something that they don't. I feel the pressure to come clean but hold back, frightened by what a wrong move could mean. Remembering Jade's voice on the phone, crying, "Daddy!"

Collins breaks the silence by saying, "I'm going to need a current photograph of your daughter."

I know the drill. The photograph will be immediately circulated to every law-enforcement agency in the area, ending up with the news media.

"I'll get one from the house," I answer.

Carolyn follows me inside. I walk to the fireplace and look up at the series of framed photographs on the mantel. Pictures of Carolyn and me, and pictures of Jade, pictures of us all together, like moments of frozen time. If I could only have one of them back, any of them, to live inside its security. A single photograph, in particular, catches my attention. I recall having seen it before but not here, in this place, yet not in any place that I can remember. It's a picture of Jade in her mother's arms. She's wearing a yellow-cotton dress and her hair has been bleached white by the sun. The St. Christopher's medal is hanging around her neck, and the sky behind her is clear and blue. Her face is soft and tanned as she looks straight at the camera, straight into me. Did I take this picture? I can't recall, but I feel unusually connected to it. There are other pictures of Jade on the mantel, but none capture her expression in the way that this one does. She seems to be reaching out with her eyes. I feel her touching me. I reach up and grip the silver frame, lifting it down.

"When was this taken?" I ask.

"At the beach on the third of July," Carolyn replies. "The day you were hurt."

"We'll give them this one," I say, removing the print from the frame.

"What's going on with you, Jack?" Carolyn asks. There's no edge to her tone, simply worry and concern.

I turn and look at her.

"Why are you being so hedgy with the police?"

I look at her as if I don't know what she means.

She continues. "Who was that on the phone?"

She's got me, and I know that if I continue to meet her eyes she'll see the lie. I turn away.

Her voice becomes harsh and accusing. "You know, don't you?"

I answer, "We don't have time for this now." Then we walk back outside, where I hand the picture over to Lou Collins.

He looks at it quickly, and says, "You don't have anything with just her in it, like a school picture?"

"This is the most recent," I reply.

Carolyn is behind me, staring at the back of my head. I know I'm going to have to tell her something, and the thing I have to tell her is the secret I've been keeping back since the beginning. It is the thing that's missing between us, the single thing that will either reestablish a trust or blow us apart completely.

"Lou, I need to be alone with my wife for a little while," I say.

Collins eyes us both, like he's assessing my request. He has his own suspicions, I'm sure, regarding what I know and what I'm not saying.

"Sure," he replies, looking back at his cruiser. "But till the FBI gets here I'm going to leave Officer Simms at your house while I run Ms. Summers down to the station and get her to look at a photo array, see if we can put a face on this guy." He looks directly at me. "You know once the Feds get here it's their case, and it's probably going to get ugly with questions and motives and everything else, so it would be a good idea for you and Carolyn to talk and get your facts together." He pauses, then says sincerely, "I'm sorry that this has happened. If there's anything I can do, either professionally or personally, I will."

"Thank you," I reply.

Collins turns as the other officer gets out of the car. "George is a good man."

I thank him again, then walk to the police car and look in through the window.

April Summers meets my eyes. Everything about her looks confused and out of place, one side of her face is swollen and her makeup has run down from her eyes, leaving black streaks along her cheeks. Her lipstick is smudged and looks too red against her tanned skin, and her nose ring is missing, leaving a small circular hole in her right nostril. Her hands, protruding from the sleeves of a fawn-suede jacket, are small, reddened from rubbing down along her face and over her mouth, and trembling. It's the first time I've noticed that she bites her fingernails. She looks at me and pulls back against the seat.

I lean forward, closer to the window. "It's not your fault," I say softly, knowing that she probably can't hear my voice through the glass. She meets my eyes with a look I recognize, her lips tight, her eyes frightened of me. She thinks she could have done more. Could have fought harder. She thinks she let Jade down. I know because I've got that feeling too.

"Believe me," I add, then walk away from the car.

~ 38 ~

GEORGE SIMMS IS A SHORT, stocky man with dark, cropped hair, a flat belly, and carpenter's hands, thick from use and callused. By the crow's-feet and deep lines around his eyes I put him in his mid-forties. His manner is calm, and he appears very capable, asking few questions. He seems to understand that his job is our security, and after a quick but thorough look around the house, to check on locks and access points, he settles in a chair by the front door. We agree that I will answer all phone calls, then Carolyn and I go upstairs to the bedroom. There's a horrible tension between us. I know what I've got to do, what my obligation is. I also know that I have only a short time before a team of Federal investigators swarm our house and take over our lives.

As soon as we are inside the bedroom with the door closed, out of earshot from Simms, I turn and face her.

I keep my voice low. "I'll get Jade back."

She looks at me, and I see a mixture of fear and suspicion in her eyes.

"You don't know that," she answers.

"He doesn't want Jade—"

"He?" she asks. "Who is he? Who was that on the telephone?"

I don't answer, and Carolyn's eyes turn a steely blue. "You're playing with our daughter's life."

I stare at her, cornered. "It was Raymond Sasso, the man I put in prison."

Her voice trembles as she struggles for control. "Is he going to hurt our little girl?"

"No, because I won't let him," I answer, trying to muster all the conviction I can.

"You can't make that promise. You can't—"

"I will get her back," I repeat, trying to make myself believe it.

'Why didn't you tell the police?"

'This isn't about the police," I reply slowly.

"Then what is it about—"

"A debt."

"What do you mean, a debt?"

"I owe Ray Sasso," I answer.

"How can you owe that man anything?" There is scorn in her tone. She knows I work in the gutter, with the scum.

"I betrayed him."

Her voice sounds tired. "That's your job."

"It isn't my job to sign my name to false testimony. It isn't my job to swear to things that never happened. The DA's Office set him up. There were no drugs on him on the day of the take-down. He was clean. The evidence was planted."

Now that the gate has been opened I feel everything flooding forward.

"On the day of the takedown I was out of my mind on amphetamines."

Her eyes don't leave mine as her confusion is replaced with disbelief.

"The doctors didn't tell you because, for the sake of my testimony, Jane Carroll put a lid on it. It started about a year ago. Morgan knew I was using, and so did she, but she wanted Ray Sasso so bad that she left me in. On the day of the takedown Ray Sasso knew I was fucked up, and he was suspicious. He beat us all that day, fair and square. He was walking away from the whole setup when Morgan's team piled in. Then everything went wrong, and I got shot. The DA's Office had nothing on Ray Sasso, but Jane Carroll was so desperate to make her case that she made sure there was evidence. Sasso was framed, and I helped frame him."

Carolyn has the same look that Ray had on that day in the warehouse. Her eyes are wide-open, staring into mine, disbelief mixed with disgust, and lots of hurt. It's like she's seeing me for the first time, finally seeing who I am, but now that I've begun I need to dump it all out. Right now, it doesn't matter what she thinks of me.

"I signed papers swearing that Ray Sasso had product in his possession, and that I witnessed the exchange. I swore to things that never happened. I was going to court to testify against him. Then somebody who didn't want that court case to happen put a contract out on him, but they fucked up the hit. His pregnant wife and seven-year-old son were killed instead—"

It feels like eternity before Carolyn speaks again, and when she does her voice is low and without pity.

"You brought this sickness into our lives. You are responsible for it. If Jade comes to any harm, it's on you. How could you be so weak?"

I feel physically ill as I reply. "It was either lie or go to prison. Jane Carroll had enough to put me away for years." I'm starting to crumble. "I was going to quit after this investigation. I wanted to come home. The idea of seven years in Sing Sing broke me. I've changed since I've been home."

She looks deep into me. "Have you?"

I watch her rage building, like a river of red flowing between us.

"Have you really changed?"

Then she's flying toward me, shouting. "What about my baby?" Striking out at me with her clenched fists, her hands battering my chest. "What about Jade?"

I don't try to stop her. I want to be punished. I welcome it.

"What have you done to her?"

She smacks me across the face with her open hand, tears streaming down her cheeks.

"God damn you. How can you say you've changed when you're still a liar, lying to me, lying to your daughter, keeping your secrets, taking our love—"

"I didn't know how to tell you. I was ashamed," I answer.

"Look what your shame has done."

She continues to glare at me until I'm drained and dizzy. My head is splitting. I bend forward, feeling as though I'm about to fall.

"I'm sorry," I gasp, staggering toward the bed.

I see colors where there should be a floor, swirls of reds and blues. I hear Jade's voice, "Daddy, Daddy."

"Sorry," I repeat. "Sorry." Closing my eyes.

When I open them again I am lying on my back in the bed with Carolyn looking down on me. She reaches and places the palm of her hand against my forehead. The anger has gone from her touch. Her face is soft and her eyes are gentle.

"Please forgive me," I whisper, drifting off, listening to her footsteps fade against the floor.

When I wake up the curtains are drawn, the room is dark, and there are voices coming from outside. They are quiet, like mourners at a funeral, and although I can't make out their words I sense that they are talking about me, and that the things they are saying are not good.

I need to find Jade.

~ 39 ~

I STILL HEAR THEM, LIKE a low, steady drone, as I get up and walk across the room to lock the door. After that I open the window above the back garden and climb out, hanging on the ledge with my fingers before dropping to the grass and fallen leaves below. I try to relax as my feet touch, sending the shock of impact up through my ankles and into the muscles of my thighs. Then I'm moving, staying to the back of the house, walking across the blue-stone patio, then through a patch of shrubbery and over a wooden picket fence. Another fifty feet and I'm beside our small, single-car garage. I enter through a side door. The place smells like a compost of wet wood, dead leaves, gasoline, and oil. The old, rigid-framed Shovelhead sits on its stand, in the center of the concrete floor. All my riding gear, helmets, jackets, and gloves are either lying on the workbench along the side wall or hanging from a series of wood pegs on the wall beside the door. I take down my heaviest leather jacket and a pair of insulated gloves and put them on, then a set of Ray-Bans and a helmet. Half a tank of gas plus the twenty bucks I've got in my pocket should get me as far as I'll need to go.

I open the barn-style door and look outside. Back up the driveway I can see the tail end of a patrol car, blocking the Jeep. I roll the bike out, close the door behind me, then push the Shovelhead down the drive to the road before climbing on to let it roll another twenty or thirty feet down the hill. When it's moving at about fifteen miles an hour I turn the key in the ignition, kick it up into second gear, and pop the clutch. The bike hasn't been run since that last day in Mount Vernon, and the old engine is temperamental, so it takes me another few tries to get it to crack into life, which it does with a belch of black smoke. Then it's chugging and bumping over the joins in the macadam, carrying me toward my little girl.

The stretched peanut tank holds enough gas to keep the bike alive for about ninety miles, so before I leave Southampton and get on to the rough patch of Route 27 that leads to the equally ragged asphalt of the Long Island Expressway, I stop to fill up. The pumps are self-service so I dig inside the pocket of my jeans, pull out a rumpled five-dollar bill, and walk into the building looking for the attendant. I spot him, a redheaded teenager wearing baggy jeans and a plaid shirt, sitting in a folding chair behind a wooden counter loaded with candy bars, plastic-wrapped muffins, and breath mints. He looks up from his magazine, startled, as if maybe I've come in to rob the place.

"Sorry, sir, I didn't see you," he says.

Beside him, on a white-topped table there's a small television. The sound is muted, but I can see my daughter looking at me from the screen. They have taken the picture of Jade and Carolyn, removed Carolyn, and blown up Jade's face. Her eyes reach out to me.

"Please, turn the volume on the TV up," I say.

The kid in the plaid shirt looks as though he doesn't understand my request.

My greatest fear is that I'm too late, that Jade is dead.

I motion to the TV and demand, "Turn the sound up. Please."

He snaps to attention, saying, "Yes sir, no problem," then picks up his remote and presses the button.

The female commentator's voice fills the room. "No news yet on three-year-old Jade Lamb, the little girl who was reportedly snatched from a Montauk school playground at around nine o'clock this morning. Police are asking—"

I put the five-dollar bill on the table, tell him which pump I'm using, and walk to the door.

~ 40 ~

I'M RIDING, SIXTY MILES AN hour, seventy, eighty, with Sasso's words repeating in my head. "Same place as before." Across the ridges that join the macadam as the bike jumps and jolts, punishing my kidneys like short, sharp punches. Continuing for miles, off at exit 30 north, up and over the Throgs Neck Bridge, with the jagged skyline of Manhattan to my left and the cold, gray water of the Eastchester Bay to my right. Through the Bronx, into the concrete jungles where the faces are the faces of my past, the predators and the prey.

Charlie Wolf knows his way around here.

Charlie Wolf knows where he's going.

Back to the place where it all began.

Riding across the railroad tracks, into the south side of Mount Vernon, along Gramatan Avenue. Dismal even beneath the summer sun, the sidewalks are littered and the shops deserted, boarded over. FOR RENT signs and graffiti are everywhere; the people look tired and used, poorly dressed and fed on junk.

The deeper I travel into this sterile landscape, the more I adopt its bleakness. Until finally, as I take the right turn onto Third Avenue that leads to the wood-framed, flat railway-style house that has been headquarters to the SOFMC for twenty years, I have dredged up all the old feelings, rekindling within me the part that was Charlie Wolf. Only the thought of my daughter spans the divide between what was and what is.

I am surprised that there are no police or surveillance vehicles outside the wood-sided corner house with its steel front door and barred windows. I was expecting a police presence, but that's not the only thing that seems out of order. There are no cars or bikes in the short driveway in front of the building. The clubhouse looks deserted as I ride the Shovel to the curb and shut off the engine. Everywhere is silence, and even the sound of the kickstand scraping against the gravel in the road seems loud and disturbing.

I stand for a moment beside the bike. I know that they have a twenty-four-hour guard, an armory of weapons inside, and full-video surveillance on the outside. I'm an easy target, and right now I am being observed, every move I make scrutinized and monitored, so frightened that my legs don't respond to my commands to walk. Only the memory of my daughter's face, looking out from the television screen, her eyes searching for mine, gives me the courage I need.

I watch the tiny eyes of the two wall-mounted cameras follow my steps up the driveway, across the patch of brown lawn and onto the concrete slab that forms the front porch. There is something wrong. I should have been stopped by now and challenged.

The door is painted matte black. It has three visible locks and two more heavy bolts on the inside. I recall the sound of them closing, their absolute finality. I am about to pound on the metal with the back of my fist when I hear one of them disengage, then the other. Another few clicks, and the door opens.

Ralph Menzies stares down at me. Half his face, from his forehead to his jaw, is covered in fresh, ugly scars. His aura is strong and dark, full of purple and gray, like a storm brewing.

Only the left side of his mouth moves when he speaks, and his words are slurred. "Hello, Charlie, wondered when you'd show up."

"I thought you were—"

"Dead?" Menzies asks. With that he reaches forward and grips the lapel of my jacket, hauling me across the threshold and into the front room. There, he pats me down.

Satisfied that I'm clean, he says, "You got a lot of balls coming here without a weapon. Either that or you're a fucking moron."

Inside, the place is a mess. Tables and chairs are turned over, while papers and photographs litter the old wood floor.

"What are you doing here?" I ask.

"I'm here because you're here, Charlie, simple as that." His mouth smiles, but his eyes don't.

"Where's my daughter?"

He grips my right arm, fingers so tight into my biceps that I think the muscle might burst. "Come on," he growls, dragging me down the narrow corridor and into the room that was Ray Sasso's office. Now it's a mess, the drawers from the desk are lying on the floor, their contents spilled. The club colors are gone from the wall behind the desk.

"Your friends came here with a warrant," he explains, finally releasing his grip. "Took everything important." He walks to the door of the closet that used to be the liquor cabinet, opens it, and picks up something from the floor that looks like a black-plastic garbage bag, tied at the top. "Well, almost everything." He hands it to me.

The bag is very light.

"Open it."

I don't want to open it. I've got a very bad feeling about what's inside.

His voice is suddenly clear, his enunciation perfect. "Open the fucking bag."

I fumble a moment with the plastic ties, then open the top. A smell like linseed oil and kerosene wafts up.

Menzies inhales. "Preservative," he says.

The room is lit only by the light from a single window, and at first it's hard to make out what's inside, lying almost flat against the bottom. It appears to be two pieces of paper, like parchment, yellowed and curled up at the edges. Whatever it is, I have an aversion to touching it.

"Pick it up," Menzies orders.

I stare down at the contents. My stomach seems to understand before my mind. It begins to curdle.

"Largest organ of the human body," Menzies continues. "Of course, a kid doesn't have that much."

A kid? Jade? I have to stop myself from falling. I feel as if I have collapsed inside, my knees have turned to rubber.

"Lift it out."

His voice forces me to hold on, backed by the sound of the slide of a pump-action shotgun, snapping a shell into the chamber. I feel the end of the barrel against the side of my neck, beneath my ear, digging in, just like last time.

"Do what I say."

My trembling fingers go down inside the bag and grip one of the two pieces of whatever is inside. It feels hard and brittle as I bring it up, into the light.

It is oblong in shape, maybe eight inches in length, and looks like very old leather.

"Skin," Menzies says.

I'm holding my breath, trying to keep a rein on my thoughts as I turn it over in my hand. There is a marking on the underside. I feel the beginnings of relief. The ink is faded, and the tattoo has shrunken and withered, but I can still make out a black skull and crossbones with the word "DIABLEROS" scrolled across it. I pick up the other piece, it's bigger and more squared, but it is marked by the same tattoo.

These are the tattoos from the two Chicanos. Not the flesh of my daughter. I'm elated, almost light in the head.

"Ray is a very serious man," Menzies states. "He believes in retribution."

I feel I've been given another chance. "Where is he?" I ask. "Go back to your old place," he answers. "There's something there you're going to need."

I drop the skins into the bag and drop the bag to the floor. It lands with hardly any sound. Then, with the barrel of Menzies's gun pushing into the small of my back, I walk to the front door of the clubhouse.

His voice comes from behind me. "Good-bye, Charlie."

The butt of the Remington catches me sharply across the back of my skull, sending me to one knee. I hear the door slam shut behind me and the locks bang into place as I fight the darkness that wants to swallow me up.

Bleep. Bleep. Bleep.

I hear it inside my head, as if it's coming from the bullet, throbbing, but this time the sound is keeping me conscious.

Staggering to my feet, I limp to the Shovelhead and drape myself across the saddle before I kick it over.

I ride past the broken shop windows, past the blank faces of the people, turning down a side street, until everything begins to distort, becoming a blur in my mind.

Only Charlie Wolf knows where I'm going.

He's been there before.

To the old tenement house, with its iron railing and nine steps leading down, to the place where he once lived.

~ 41 ~

WHY IS THE DOOR OPEN? Why is the light on? Why has nothing changed? It seems impossible, but the apartment is just as it was when I left it, with its beige-acrylic carpet, marred by cigarette burns and a wine stain that looks like a rusted quarter moon. The card table still sits in the corner, with my once precious books stacked on top of it, and the small cot bed with its grimy sheets waits against the far wall. The smell of damp and mildew is everywhere. Something's wrong. I sense a trap. All this should have been examined, cleaned up, and removed. It should no longer exist, but here it is, and here I am, with my head thick and my legs like lead. I shuffle toward my old bed, sit down, and rest against an arm, wanting to fold up and die.

There's something there you're going to need.

I force myself to stand and look around. I feel heavy, almost numb. Maybe it's exhaustion, or the drug, or the bang I took from the butt of Menzies' rifle. I'm not sure, but I know I won't make it out of here like this. I won't find Jade.

I've got to wake up.

Yes, there is something I need.

The kitchen area is a journey of about ten feet, but it seems like an hour passes before I'm at the sink, holding on to the countertop. William Sasso's toy soldier sits on the shelf, staring down into the cracked cast-iron basin. I follow his painted blue eyes. Searching. I remember brushing it aside with my left hand, hearing it smack against the metal.

Thinking never, never again. Now I'm praying it's still here. I need it, the same way I needed it then.

My eyes focus on what looks like a small lump of dirt, caught in the strainer, blocking one of the tiny steel holes. I lower my hand, extending my fingers, gripping the piece of hardened crystal, trying for a finesse and delicacy that I can't find. Lifting slowly, desperate not to drop it.

Jade is singing in my head. She is my sunshine.

Hands raised, lips opened, tongue out. It's like taking communion. I remember kneeling beside my brother, waiting for the priest to come with his wafer and his wine, the body and blood. I'm nervous, my eyes are closed, I feel it light against my tongue. I have just enough saliva to taste its bitterness as I try to crush the lump of crystal meth up against the roof of my mouth. It's too hard, so I grind it with my teeth and swallow it.

Turning away from the sink I take a few steps toward the bed as the chemical begins to fill the synapse between Jack Lamb and Charlie Wolf. Coming on me in waves, stronger than I remembered it to be. Maybe it's because I've been clean or maybe it's the dose, but everything is whirling and spinning, my thoughts stretching and losing shape, until I perceive nothing but watery splinters of color and light.

Nothing real to grip or hold on to.

Dropping to my hands and knees, I black out.

When I come to, I am whole again, but something has changed. My perception is altered, as if I have entered a higher, more refined frequency, in which I am more tuned, more alert, aware at a different level. There is no more pain.

Kneeling on the floor, I use one arm for balance while the other is extended with my hand reaching forward, and my fingers wrap around the knurled grip of a Seacamp. Small and nickel-plated, sparkling even in the dull light, I don't know how the gun got here but I know I've seen it before, aimed at my head. I pop the clip, making sure it's loaded, then I stand, focusing on the sounds around me, until there is nothing but sound and intuition.

I hear a car outside, engine idling, then revving. Impatient. I know he's waiting for me. There is no doubt. This is where it begins.

The clock beside the bed reads 2:30.

It's time.

I slide the Seacamp into the pocket of my jacket, walk out the door and up the steps. The black New Yorker is parked opposite me.

It's Morgan. In a way I've always known it would be him. I've felt his presence often since I was shot, like a guiding hand.

White smoke crawls like a wispy snake from his tail pipes as he drives slowly away.

I watch from the saddle of my bike as he stops at the sign, turns left, and stops again.

I kick the Shovel over and ride after him.

Once he can see me in his wing mirror he takes off again, driving purposefully as he leads me through the seedy back streets and out onto the main road, which we follow to Macquesten Parkway.

We continue until we are in front of Speed Dream and the adjacent warehouse. Finally he stops, allowing me to pull up beside him.

He rolls down his window, looking from me to the door of the warehouse.

"This is as far as I go, " he says.

I am beyond judgment or anger. Whether Morgan is a good guy or a bad guy is no longer of any consequence.

"Is he inside?" I ask.

He nods. "Through that door."

I search his green eyes for some kind of answer, some reason for him to be here, doing what he is doing, and for a moment I'm sucked backward in time, lying on the floor of the warehouse, with Morgan looking down at me.

"You're going to make it." His voice echoes the same words he said on the last day. Whispering, "Good luck, *amigo*," before driving off.

I park the bike along the curb, get off, and begin to walk in the direction of the warehouse.

"Jack!"

I turn quickly, sure that I heard Carolyn call my name.

I don't see her, just a long straight road, lined by utility poles and telephone wires. There is no traffic, nothing but the howl of the wind through the wires.

I walk across the pavement, noticing that Speed Dream has been closed and boarded over. My boot heels mark a steady cadence, *click clack, click clack, click clack,* and from somewhere far away I hear a song and recognize Hendrix's slide guitar, his voice singing the first words of "All Along the Watchtower."

There is no way out of here, not for me.

"Jack, please come back," Carolyn calls again.

Jack can't come back. Jack's gone.

I grip the knob and push as the heavy door grinds open.

~ 42 ~

INSIDE, THE PLACE IS PITCH-BLACK. There seems to be no barrier between myself and the darkness. I am submerged in it, part of it.

"Hit the switch, Charlie."

Ray Sasso's voice is everywhere at once, inside and out.

"What's the trouble?" he continues. "Turn the fucking light on."

"I don't know where it is," I answer.

"Sure you do, you've been here before."

I have. Over and over again in my mind, to this place, to this day, wanting to change it, wanting to change myself. I turn and extend my arms, feeling for the wall, finding it, then inching my hands along it like a blind man. Locating the switch. Throwing it.

A light goes on behind me.

"Now turn around."

I turn slowly, my right hand in my pocket, my finger on the trigger of the Seacamp. Don't want to risk a shot through the heavy leather of my jacket, I'll need to get the gun clear before I use it.

"Take it out, it's okay," Ray says. "You'll never get a round off from inside your pocket."

Am I that easy to read? It seems that my thoughts are transparent.

I expose the Seacamp as my eyes adjust to the amber glow of the single bulb that hangs from the ceiling above the man's head. It takes a few seconds to convince myself that it is Ray Sasso. The first thing that strikes me is that he has no aura. I am so used to seeing energy that this single feature unnerves me. I might as well be looking at a dead man.

I see his lips move, but his voice is right inside my head.

"Just me and you now, hey, Charlie?"

He is seated on a chair directly beneath the light, in the same place that Jimmy Sipriani was on that day. Wearing his funeral suit and dark tie, Ray's body is stick-thin and his face gaunt, the flesh around his mouth receded. When he smiles, as he is doing now, his gums and teeth become grotesquely prominent, like the face of a skull. He is leaning forward, supporting himself by means of a carved wooden cane.

I look around. There is no one else in the room.

"Fancy a spar," he continues with that deathly grin. "A few rounds?"

I have both pity and fear of him.

"No games, Ray. I came for my daughter," I reply.

"Charlie, you don't have a daughter."

His words evoke outrage, and I feel my finger tighten on the trigger. Searching for his eyes and finding only two dark slits.

"I'll kill you right now," I vow.

He smiles again, all teeth and gums, untouched by my threat. Saying, "Come a little closer."

I take a few more steps, until I can feel him staring straight into me.

"God damn, look at you, wired again. I told you that stuff was going to beat you sooner or later."

"Where is she?" I ask.

"Where do you want her to be?"

"Out of this," I answer.

He settles forward, both hands pushing down on the silver head of his cane. I look closer and see that the metal has been carved to form the head of a lion, its mouth open, fangs glistening in the light from above us. As I stare at the lion's head, Ray begins to tap a steady rhythm against it with his ruby ring.

Tap. Tap. Tap.

It is the sound of time running out.

Bleep. Bleep. Bleep.

His voice comes from far away. "That's going to cost you."

"That's why I'm here," I reply, taking another step, lifting the gun.

"Easy, Charlie, think about where the meth stops and your courage begins. That's a dangerous line to cross. Of all people you ought to know that."

I stop about three feet in front of him, dropping the gun to my side, speaking slowly and deliberately. "Her name is Jade. She's three years old. She's done nothing to you—" I stall as my emotions overwhelm me.

Ray Sasso stands up a piece at a time, as if there is agony in every muscle and joint, needing slow and deliberate reconnection to form the whole. He looks at me, and for a brief spell I see compassion in his eyes. Then, as he begins to speak, the compassion gives way to stark resolve. He steps away from the chair.

"Sit down," he says. "You look wasted."

I hesitate.

"Sit down!"

I walk to the chair. My mouth is dry and my head has begun to ache again. I turn to find the metal seat, landing heavily on my hips, while the gun comes to rest in my lap.

Sasso stands, looking at me. "Do you know what it's like to lose everything you've ever loved. Everything that matters?"

I think of his family, his health. I think of his freedom. I shake my head slowly.

"I don't want Jade Lamb," he continues. "She can go home, back to her mother. She can grow up, get married, have babies—" He hesitates, his eyes digging deep into mine as the sadness inside him spills out and over me. "My business is with Charlie Wolf. It has always been with Charlie Wolf. That's you, isn't it?"

I feel the meth working my brain, I feel the weight of the gun.

"Yes," I answer.

"Then let's end this thing between us," he says.

I lift the Seacamp.

"Do you understand what you need to do?" he continues.

It will be easy to kill him now, standing there, balanced on his cane, lame like a wounded animal. I take aim between his eyes.

He smiles again, and I see the death's-head in his grin.

His voice is a whisper. "You don't get it, do you?"

My finger feels alive against the trigger, there is electricity between my flesh and the metal.

"You think that's going to make it stop? You think you'll never see me again? Every time you look in a mirror you'll see me looking back at you. I live inside you."

He points at my head, his index finger extended, thumb cocked back, like a gun.

"I saw you in the car that day on the bridge, staring out the window. You were looking for me, same as you were that day at the playground, and at the beach. Every time you look for me I'm going to be there."

He drops his thumb against his index finger, and says, "Bang."

I feel the bullet inside my head.

He continues. "How about the funeral. I saw you there, too. I couldn't even mourn my own family without you watching. Why do you keep searching for me? What is it you need?"

I sit silently, thinking. I need my daughter. I need my life. I need Jack Lamb. I need forgiveness. I need my sanity.

"Do you like walking inside your mind?" he continues.

"Where did you hear that?"

"Same place you did, on the porch of that crazy doctor's house."

"But you weren't there."

"Daddy, I love you as deep as Gardiner's Island," he whispers, smiling again.

My brain feels like it's incinerating. I level the gun, holding it on him with both hands.

"Stop it," I order.

"I can't stop it. Only you can stop it. It's your mind, Charlie. It has always been your mind. Do you really think

you can control it by standing on one leg and chanting *ohm*.
You idiot. You can't stop the thoughts. They're going to keep
on coming, getting sicker and sicker for as long as Charlie
Wolf is alive. I didn't steal that little girl from Jack Lamb. You
did. You made it happen."

His smile ebbs as I lower the gun, turning it over in my
hand, staring down at it.

"What do you think is going on now?"

I feel the weight of the metal in my palm, the coolness of
the grip.

"You can't make this end because you can't let go of
Charlie Wolf," he continues. "You're too fucking scared to let
go, because you think there's nothing left on the other side of
the lie. You've got no faith so the nightmare keeps building.
Until finally, look where you've got us, back where we
started."

He turns and begins to walk away from me. I listen to his
shuffling steps and the clack of his cane against the stone
floor, *tap, tap, tap. Bleep. Bleep.* As my trembling finger tightens
on the trigger, he stops at the door and turns once more,
digging in his pocket for something, lifting it out. Tossing it
onto the floor so that it slides toward me.

St. Christopher looks at me from the polished gold. I
lean forward and pick him up, squeezing the circular
medallion tight in my left hand. It's Jade's medal.

"What goes around, comes around," he says.

He turns off the light, but I still hear his voice.

"Do you want this to end?"

"Yes," I answer.

"Kill Charlie Wolf."

The words resound inside the darkness as the door
slams, leaving me alone, teetering, without balance. Knowing
that I can't go back.

Kill Charlie Wolf.

Raising my arm, I press the barrel of the gun tight against
my forehead, inhaling, holding my breath, clenching my teeth,
willing my finger to squeeze the trigger.

Kill Charlie Wolf.

Bleep. Bleep. Don't think. Don't doubt. Squeeze!

There is a quick, brilliant flash of light.

I hear a scream inside my head.

The bleeping turns into a flat, steady drone.

Then nothing but pain, hot and searing, like a flaming poker through the socket of my right eye, twisting into my temple, melting flesh and bone. Followed by a deep, rumbling sound, like wheels against metal tracks. I'm rolling, like a passenger in a train, traveling through the tunnel and toward the light.

Leaving Charlie Wolf behind.

Free.

I see it in front of me, glowing warm and familiar. After a long, hard journey I am going home.

~ 43 ~

MUSIC PLAYS. VERY SOOTHING, it sounds like a string quartet, filling me with delicate waves of violin and cello swelling and ebbing, like a baby's lullaby. I look down at a body laid out on a table, draped in green sheets, right up to and covering the face, all except a small portion of the head, which has been shaved to the scalp and glistens beneath the incandescence of the light. Tubes and wires are connected to his body and a group of people are gathered around, wearing green hospital scrubs, caps, and masks. One of them is working with something that looks like a small pneumatic drill. I can hear it, like a dentist's air drill, blasting away at a site on the upper right-hand corner of the exposed skull, where the flesh has been cut neatly and folded back, revealing a deepening hole. It looks raw and painful, but there is no movement beneath the sheets that would indicate any discomfort, simply a steady rise and fall in the area of the chest as the body breathes.

The person in charge places the drill on a tray, bends closer and examines his work. His voice is calm and reassuring, pronouncing its words very clearly. "I am going to open the dura now."

I recognize that voice. I have heard it many times. I just can't remember where or when.

He picks up a scalpel, moving surely and with great purpose, as he begins to cut away at the layer of tissue directly below the bone. Occasionally he stops and studies his work, then there is more cutting, while a second man sponges the bloody fluid that continues to seep from the open wound. Finally, a third assistant begins to use a suction tube, drawing off the flood of pus that pours from the entry site.

"Let me have the cupped forceps," the familiar voice requests.

An assistant slaps the long-tonged instrument into his gloved hand.

"Are we clear inside?"

"Yes, we're fine here," the man with the suction tube replies, stepping back.

Then the main man looks up, to the fourth figure, standing beside the patient's head.

"I'm going to go in and get it," he says.

The robed figure checks her gauges, makes an adjustment to one of them, and answers in a soft female voice, "We're in good shape at this end."

The main man positions himself directly above the body, forceps pointing downward toward the hole in his skull. He reminds me of a matador, poised for the kill. Then he's in, pushing and probing, twisting and squeezing, but all with a high degree of finesse and delicacy. It's like a job of fine carpentry, requiring patience and absolute concentration.

An oboe and clarinet enter the mix of music as it builds and he penetrates deeper into the wound.

His voice is finally triumphant. "Got it." He withdraws the forceps, holding a small object between the cupped tips, studying it through the lenses of his glasses.

"Nice one, Howard!" One of the others applauds. He sounds relieved.

The man, now identified as Howard, swabs the object with a piece of cotton and holds it up to the light.

I stare at it, shining like a small ball bearing, polished and clean.

He lifts it till it's right under my nose. As if he knows I'm here, watching.

I see the light again, warm and glowing, reflected in the metal.

"There's your silver bullet, Jack."

~ 44 ~

JACK? JACK? WHO IS JACK? Even as I ask I am pulled backwards, as if the name possesses its own power, drawing me to it, slowly at first as I resist, then faster as my resistance gives way to the feeling of inevitability. Away from the reflection of light, I watch as it shrinks before my eyes, then becomes a luminous speck in my mind, sinking like the setting sun. The light is memory, and I am being sucked through a passage, hard and black like the barrel of a gun, spiraling down through a fissure in time, back to the beginning.

***

Bleep. Bleep. Bleep. That damn bleep never stops. It has always been there, behind everything, like a beating heart.

"Jack?" I hear a voice. "Can you hear me? Squeeze my hand if you can hear me."

"Yes," I want to answer, but my throat is clogged and my mouth is stuffed full with something. *Squeeze my hand.* I want to do that, too, but I can't connect the thought to my body. I try again.

"I feel something," the voice continues, more urgent now. "I think he's listening."

Open your eyes, I order myself.

I feel the muscles strain to lift my lids.

"We love you."

The curtains begin to rise, letting in the light, but it's bright, too bright to see. I close up again, more secure in the familiarity of the darkness.

"Turn off the overhead light, it may be bothering him," a second female voice suggests.

"Jack, open your eyes." Coaxing. "Come on, Jack."

I try again. That is when I see them looking down on me, just shapes at first, outlines against the pale green backdrop, but as my eyes focus they gain depth, color, and perspective. The woman is tall, her hair is dark and long and her eyes are blue. Her face is familiar. She is carrying a child in her arms, a child with long blond hair, curling down to touch the shoulders of her yellow-cotton dress.

"Daddy?" the child says.

I hear another female voice in the background.

"He's conscious. See if the doctor's on the floor."

Daddy? My mind is working, trying to reassemble itself, struggling to make order out of confusion, to give definition to what my eyes see. Trying to remember.

The dark-haired woman bends slightly so that the little girl can touch my arm. I smell fresh green apples in her hair. The scent touches my memory.

"Tell Daddy you love him."

"I love you deep as Gardiner's Island," the little girl says. Gardiner's Island. I imagine a patch of land covered with birds, the wind in my face, the smell of salt air, the sound of waves lapping the shore. I feel the child's small, warm hand against my arm. I sense peace.

Jade. I think her name before I actually know that she is part of me.

"Daddy, we want you to come home now," she says. Daddy. The way she says it, without a grain of doubt. I am this little girl's daddy, and I have never been happier about anything in my life.

Then the other voice, older and less familiar, speaks again in the background. "He came round about ten minutes ago. All his signs are good."

Jade, Carolyn. Home, I'm going home. I am so overcome with emotion that I am sure I'm crying because the man's face looking down at me from the opposite side of my

bed looks like it is separated from me by a pool of water. He
has short auburn hair, gray eyes, and he is wearing glasses.

"Hello, Jack," he says, bending over me. "Good to see
you. Remember me, Howard Metzler. I took that bullet out
of your head." Then, turning to my wife and daughter, "I'll
need a couple of minutes alone with him. After that, he's all
yours."

I remember Dr. Metzler, his voice his gray eyes, his high-
polished shoes. I remember him in his green scrubs and
surgical mask, poised above me like a matador.

He places both his hands gently to either side of my jaw.
"I'm going to remove the respirator from your throat. Then
you'll be able to speak."

After that it feels like a long, rough-scaled snake is
crawling up my windpipe, scraping the sides, but, finally, my
mouth is clear, and I'm breathing, tasting the air. I meet his
eyes and sense a deep understanding. We've been through a
lot together.

"How's your shoulder?" I ask. My words are
spontaneous, and my voice startles me. It sounds gruff and
strained. It feels like my throat is chafed and raw, and it hurts
to speak. Everything hurts.

There is a look of utter surprise behind the thick lenses
of his glasses. He leans closer to me. Maybe he doesn't want
the nurse to know. His voice is hushed.

"Do you remember that?"

I lower my voice till it's not much more than a rasp.
"Did the biopsy go okay?"

He looks suddenly vulnerable, as if I have pierced the
armor of his expensive suit and professional manner.

Now it's me who feels confused. "The last time I saw
you, we talked—" I stop, feeling awkward. Maybe I shouldn't
be bringing this up, reminding him.

Reflexively, he reaches with his left hand and rubs the
back of his shoulder.

Answering quickly. "It went fine." Pulling back, away
from me. "Just like you said it would."

I smile. "Good, I'm glad."

After that, his manner changes. Metzler is suddenly wary, defensive. "Are you still seeing things?" He studies me with a peculiar look in his eyes like he's a little frightened of me.

At first I don't know what he's talking about.

"Are you still seeing colors around people?" he adds.

Then I remember, auras, that's what Simon Barr called the colors.

My gaze turns into a stare as I search for Metzler's. I can't find it. In fact, things look generally dull compared to the way they were before, with less definition and color.

"No, I'm not," I reply.

He looks relieved. "It was touch-and-go there for a while, but the surgery went well. You should make a full recovery."

"That's good," I answer. "Doctor, could you do me one favor?"

"Certainly, if I'm able to," he answers.

"Could you make that sound go away, that bleep, bleep, bleep?"

Metzler turns and looks at the monitor that graphs my heart.

"Sure, I can do that," he answers, switching off the alarm.

At last, the room is quiet.

"Thanks."

He promises to visit me later and leaves the room.

I am alone, looking around, trying to reorient myself. Beside me, on the table, is the picture I gave Lou Collins. In it, Carolyn is holding Jade in her arms, silhouetted by blue sky, and Jade has the gold St. Christopher's medal around her neck. The picture inspires another rush of emotion and memory. I remember my brother Robert, at the beach. I remember Carolyn, holding Jade in her arms, calling me back from the water. It seems a lifetime ago.

It feels as if I am waking up a little at a time, coming back from a long journey, reentering an old, familiar world. A world in which Jade is safe, and Charlie Wolf does not exist. Ray Sasso kept his word. It was a fair trade.

I push myself up against the pillow, enough to see a newspaper lying on the chair closest to my bed. It's the *East*

Hampton Star and has a picture of exploding fireworks over Boy's Harbor on the front page. I read the date on the top of the paper, July 6, 2002, and get a strange feeling, a lightness in my head. It must be an old newspaper, I tell myself, but something feels wrong, out of place. I feel a chill, then the hair on my arms and on the nape of my neck stands straight up, as if I received a charge of static electricity. I lie still another few seconds as my body responds to this new rush of energy. Beginning to feel my hands and my feet, as if they are awakening from their own sleep as I become physically aware once again. Toes and fingers, my left hand below the sheet, bunched into a fist. Holding something, really gripping it. I lift it up and see the gold chain, which hangs from the underside, below my little finger. As I open my hand I recall the last moments of my last life, because that's how it feels, with all my fears, my regrets, and finally my resolve ... then, the letting go. St. Christopher looks up at me from the flat of my palm.

"Jack?"

I see Carolyn, with Jade by her side, coming through the door, walking toward my bed.

"Hello," I answer.

"How would you like to come home tomorrow?"

Tomorrow? The concept of tomorrow strikes me as strangely foreign, as if I'm emerging from a place beyond the framework of yesterdays and tomorrows.

"What day is tomorrow?" I ask.

"Tuesday," she replies.

"What date?" I ask, remembering the newspaper and wanting to put my mind at ease.

"July 9th," she answers.

I feel my stomach rise and fall, like I've just taken the giant dip on a roller-coaster ride.

"That's impossible," I whisper.

I see compassion in her eyes. "Jack, you've been unconscious, you've lost some time. It's going to take a little while to get used to that."

Now I'm confused again, struggling for clarity. "Who brought Jade home?" I ask.

Carolyn tilts her head, her eyes questioning. "What do you mean?"

"Was it Morgan?"

"Home from where?" Carolyn asks softly.

I hold up the St. Christopher's medal. "From wherever Ray Sasso took her."

"Daddy!" Jade shouts. "You found it!"

Now I'm really troubled. Carolyn steps forward and looks down at the medal, touching it cautiously, without lifting it from my hand, turning it over, staring at the initials on the back. She looks shaken.

"Where did you get this?"

I want to say from Ray Sasso, but I hold my tongue, waiting for my mind to click everything into some rational order, but nothing happens.

Finally, Carolyn speaks. "Jade lost this on the day you went ... " She hesitates. "On the fifth of July, the day you went into the coma."

There's got to be some mistake here, some misunderstanding.

"Where did she lose it?" I ask.

The atmosphere of the room is tense as Jade pulls tight to Carolyn's thigh, holding on as if she's afraid.

"She went to bed at Morgan's house with it on and woke up without it. We looked everywhere, in the bed, under the bed, everywhere. Jack, where did you get it?"

My memory of Ray Sasso and the warehouse seems suddenly out of phase, like a dream that I am trying to recall; it's coming back to me in broken pieces, without continuity. I see another man in my mind, blond and pudgy. I remember his name, Axle Barfoot. I recall the panic in his eyes. He's standing in front of me, his gun raised; it's a small nickel-plated gun, the same gun I used to shoot myself. It's like two dreams, crisscrossing in my mind, neither making complete sense.

"I'm not sure," I reply. "I was holding it when I woke up."

I'm collapsing inside. Every thought is in conflict with the next. I feel completely disoriented, struggling against a feeling of total devastation.

"Didn't Sasso take Jade and—" I falter, gripping the medal tight in my hand.

My daughter is staring at me. She's frightened, and I want to stop, but I need to know.

"And what?" Carolyn asks.

"Was there a kidnapping?"

Carolyn is very still her eyes anchored to mine. "No, nothing like that ever happened," she answers, getting my drift, her voice soothing. "We've been here every day with you." She lays her right hand gently on my forehead, below the line of my bandages. I feel a warmth flowing from her, into me. "You've been asleep, Jack," she says softly. "We didn't know if you'd ever wake up."

I recall sitting in a chair beneath an amber light, with a gun in my hand. Raising it to my head. Pulling the trigger.

"Am I awake now?"

Her eyes fill with tears, and she draws Jade close to her side.

"Yes," she replies. "You are."

I reach up and grip her arm, pulling her close, so that I can whisper in her ear.

"What happened to me?"

She pulls back, wiping the tears from her cheeks with her hand.

"You were shot in the head," she answers, hesitating. "You were pronounced dead, but you came back to us—" She stops and regains her composure. "An abscess developed around the bullet. The abscess ruptured, and you died again. The doctor resuscitated you, but you went into a coma." She glances at Jade. "We did all we could to bring you out of it. Jade's been singing her songs for you, and Morgan James brought in some of your favorite CDs. Tracy Chapman, Jimi Hendrix—"

"How about Simon Barr?" I ask.

The name seems to stun her.

"How did you know that Simon was here?"

"I remember him," I answer.

Her face turns pale behind the tan. Her voice wavers. "But you were unconscious—" Her body seems rigid for a moment, then she exhales and relaxes her shoulders, as if she's practiced the movement. "Simon was here a couple of days ago. I asked him to come. He's had a lot of experience with this sort of thing. He sat by your bed and talked to you for a long time."

I remember his voice. "Death is like taking a walk inside your mind."

There is silence in the room, broken by Jade.

"Mama, I want to go home."

Carolyn holds her closer to her. "Shhh, it's okay, honey. Quiet now, it's okay." Then Carolyn looks at me. Her eyes seem to focus for a second time, losing their fear, replaced by love. "As soon as your condition stabilized, which was yesterday at around three o'clock in the afternoon, Dr. Metzler took you down to surgery, drained the abscess, and removed the bullet."

"So I've been here, in this hospital, since the third of July?"

"Yes," Carolyn answers.

Another silence, before Carolyn speaks again, looking down at Jade. "Maybe I should take her for something to eat. This is all very confusing. For all of us. Jane Carroll is outside, Morgan's with her, they're both waiting to see you. What should I say?"

All at once, I'm clear. There is no more fear, no voices, no doubt. I know who I am and what I must do.

"Say it's okay," I answer.

Carolyn kisses me once more and Jade gives me a careful hug, like I'm breakable, or maybe it's because she's just getting to know me again. They are on their way to the door when I remember the St. Christopher's medal. I hold it out.

"Don't forget this."

They turn around.

"You keep it for now, Daddy," Jade says. "St. Christopher will take care of you."

~ 45 ~

THE DOOR OPENS AGAIN A few minutes later and Jane Carroll enters, carrying a bunch of roses. Her heels smack sharply against the floor, jarring my sense of déjà vu. I believe I know what is about to take place. I recall her silver-gray suit with its pleated jacket and note the hard set of her jaw. She flicks on the overhead light as she passes by it.

Morgan James is limping behind her, looking worried and beat. He clears his throat. "Nice to have you back."

"I'm only here because of you," I answer. Remembering him bending over me, willing me back to life. I also remember following his car to the warehouse—

Jane Carroll places the flowers down on the seat of the chair.

"For you," she says. "A dozen, long-stemmed."

I remember their smell, sickly sweet.

Her voice goes cold. "Officer Lamb, we need to talk."

About what, I wonder.

"Very seriously," she adds, as if I am not paying adequate attention.

There she goes, eyeballing Morgan, crossing her arms against her pleated chest, reciting her lines.

"Your doctor has explained that our visit has to be brief. Look, bottom line. There's a problem with the affidavit that you signed on the fourth."

I acknowledge this with a nod, and she smiles, as if she's got me.

"I'm sure it was due to the trauma at the time of your injury," she adds, speaking through the clenched teeth of her artificial smile. "You must have been very confused."

I nod again.

"I understand the extent of your injury and the effect that the injury may have had on your mind."

Morgan looks like he's dying.

She goes on with barely a pause. "But you were there, and you did witness the exchange between Mr. Sipriani and Mr. Sasso on the third of July."

"No, I did not," I answer.

She straightens up, and the shoulder pads in her suit appear stiff and wide, adding to my perception that her head is shrinking.

"Don't play games with me, sir. You're looking at a felony conviction and jail time."

This is hardball and she's pitching.

"Seven to fourteen years without your wife and little girl."

The old fear returns. I feel the perspiration on my brow, and my hands are sweating. I know the consequences of my actions. I've lived them. I have a moment of regression in which I fear I'm caving in, then I feel the warmth of the St. Christopher's medal in my palm, and hear Jade's voice telling me that he'll take care of me.

"I did not see any exchange," I repeat.

She turns on Morgan. "Will you give us a minute alone, please."

"No," I say. "I want Morgan James here as my witness."

"Fine, stay then," she shoots back, glaring from Morgan to me. "The pair of you are so deep in shit it would take a dredge to pull you out." Then she reels in her tone and makes an attempt at reason. "Raymond Sasso is a hoodlum who heads a conspiracy of organized crime."

I don't argue.

"I want him locked up."

"Good luck," I say without sarcasm.

"I need you to help me do that," she continues.

I shake my head, and answer, "I can't."

"Either Raymond Sasso goes to Sing Sing or you do. It's your choice," she warns.

Morgan's mouth is now clenched tight, and his eyes are aimed directly at me, pleading.

"I've suffered a severe head injury," I answer. "My short-term memory is gone. I don't even remember the third of July. It's like it never happened. Ask my doctor, Howard Metzler. He'll testify to that in a court of law."

Now it's Jane Carroll who is flustered. She places her briefcase on the side of my bed, opens it, and takes out the affidavit.

"But you signed this."

She hands me the document.

"Did I?"

I look down the page, noting the reference to two kilos of methamphetamine exchanged for ninety thousand dollars. There is a signature at the bottom of the page, but the scrawl is so wobbly that I can barely make out the name. When I do, I begin to laugh.

"This is not a laughing matter," Jane Carroll says, her voice close to a hiss.

My laugh is contagious, and Morgan smiles. It's a tentative smile, but it's there, lifting his face.

"Ms. Carroll, you've already got a witness," I answer.

"God damn it, don't play games with me," she threatens.

"There's a name on this document."

Her voice is hot with anger. "Yes, there is. You signed it."

"It's not my name," I reply.

"No, it says Charlie Wolf," she retorts.

"Who's he?" I ask.

If I could still see colors, I know I'd be looking at a display of fireworks, mostly in red and purple.

"I'm warning you!"

"Oh yes, now I am beginning to remember," I say, closing my eyes. "It's all coming back."

When I open them Jane Carroll is standing with her hands on her hips, waiting.

"Charlie Wolf. I used to know him," I continue. "He was a long-haired guy, good with his hands, but a compulsive liar. I could never trust him."

"Damn you," she growls.

I meet her eyes.

"It's like I said, I don't remember the third of July, or the fourth, or the fifth, or the sixth ... " I hesitate, until I'm sure she's got the message.

I continue. "But there is one thing I am certain of, one thing I will swear to. Charlie Wolf is dead."

She glares at me.

"This will be your last assignment for my office," she splutters. And there will be no future recommendations. Your career as an investigator is over. Think about that."

"I will," I answer gravely.

She turns to Morgan. "Let's go."

Morgan winks at me as he turns to leave.

"Ms. Carroll?" I say before she makes it to the door.

She turns, and I can see a glimmer in her eyes.

"I've been thinking."

I see that victor's smile beginning to mold her lips.

"Yes, Officer Lamb?"

I meet her eyes, and ask softly. "Would you mind taking those roses with you?"

Her nostrils flare and her mouth becomes a thin red line.

"I'm very sensitive to smell, and they make me sick."

EPILOGUE

B Y ALL THE DEFINITIONS of modern medicine, I died twice between the dates of July 3 and July 9, 2002.

It is also a fact that something happened to me during the events of my physical deaths and also during the time I was in a level-three coma. It seems I took a long and sometimes confusing trip inside my own mind. I believe the catalysts for my journey during that coma were the voices, prayers, and feelings of those closest to me, intertwined with my own feelings and desires. During that time I experienced a sequence of events that formed a parallel reality, serving to warn me of the possible consequences had I chosen a path other than the truth.

I don't have any hard-and-fast conclusions about where I went and what proof my experience offers as to the existence of heaven, hell, or life after death. I know only that it changed me irrevocably.

Now, when I'm reading a story to my daughter Jade, or sitting by the fire with my wife Carolyn, or riding the old Shovelhead down Route 27, I understand something that I didn't before any of this happened. Human lives are like flowers unfolding. Every moment dictates the next, so I try to live mine well and honestly. Time is precious, and relationships are all that matter in the end, who you've loved, and who has loved you back.

Raymond Sasso's case was dismissed for lack of evidence.

On October 3, less than three months after he walked
free from Valhalla, he was dead—shot through the heart in
broad daylight on the sidewalk of Gramatan Avenue,
executed by the same punk he had tossed out of the butcher's
shop. The kid was seventeen years old, tripped out on crystal
meth, and looking to build a reputation; he disappeared a day
later. Last seen being escorted by a large man with a severely
scarred face to a black Lincoln sedan.

What goes around does come around.

I still see Morgan James; he'll always be a friend,
although I'll never work for the DA's Office again. Jane
Carroll and I came to a mutually satisfactory parting of the
ways. In fact, I quit the force entirely, with a big enough
pension to open a bike shop, the pedal variety, on the main
strip in Montauk. It's mainly seasonal business, but that's fine.
I want time with my family, all I can get.

Simon Barr continues to be a close friend of the family. I
see him at yoga class and enjoy our discussions regarding the
nature of reality and the interconnectedness of all things. His
gold ring, the gift from Sai Baba, is a constant source of
speculation between us, as is how I came to be in possession
of Jade's St. Christopher's medal. Is Sai Baba a consummate
deceiver, did Jade lose the medal in my bed at the hospital, or
are both occurrences proof that mind creates material reality,
and that reality is an objectivized dream.

Carolyn's pregnant. The scan says it's going to be a boy.
Maybe, after all this, Jack Edward Lamb will die peacefully
and fulfilled, as an old man in his own bed, surrounded by his
family.

Hopefully that won't be for a very long time, but then
again, what's time anyway?

It's always now.

R ichard La Plante began his working life as a special
education teacher in Bucks County, Pennsylvania,
where he spent a great deal of time playing the guitar
and working on songs to the amusement of his students.
Following his dismissal, he formed the rock band Revenge
and toured and recorded till egos clashed and noses were
broken.

His first book, *Tegné: Soul Warrior*, a fantasy-fiction novel,
combined his longtime study of Japanese martial arts with his
interest in metaphysics and love of adventure tales.

He wrote a sequel to *Tegné*, entitled *The Killing Blow*, then
switched from fantasy-fiction to hardcore thrillers with a
popular series featuring the characters Josef Tanaka, a
Japanese-American medical examiner and shotokan karate
master, and Bill Fogarty, an Irish-American police Lieutenant.
Mantis was the first novel in the series, followed by *Leopard,
Steroid Blues,* and *Mind Kill.*

A great deal of the money earned from his books ended
up in the chrome and steel accessories that adorned his
custom Harley-Davidson, a 1989 Springer, an obsession
which became the inspiration for his motorcycle memoir,

Hog Fever. Detours, written in 2002, continues the motorcycle theme and traces a solo cross-country journey ending in Sturgis, the famous motorcycle rally in the black hills of South Dakota.

Richard and his second wife, Betina, an accomplished photographer and mother of his two sons, built their first home from the ground up on a bluff overlooking Gardiner's Bay in East Hampton, New York.

In 2004, the family moved to Ojai, a small town in the high desert of Southern California, where they built their dream home on a mountaintop, inspiring his latest memoir, *Never Again.*

Richard's other interests include anything paranormal, western boxing, and competitive swimming

More from RICHARD LA PLANTE *and Escargot Books and Music*

FICTION

First Born

Fogarty-Tanaka Series

    Book 1 - *Mantis*

    Book 2 – *Leopard*

    Book 3 – *Steroid Blues*

    Book 4 – *Mind Kill*

Tegné: Soul Warrior

Tegné: The Killing Blow

MEMOIRS

Hog Fever

Detours: Life, Death and Divorce on the Road to Sturgis

Never Again: Building the Dream House

EAR MOVIE

Hog Fever